THEY KILLED MY WIFE

IVY GLASS

HIROSHI YAMAMOTO

TENYU STUDIOS-BOOKS

COPYRIGHT

CONTENTS

THE INTRODUCTION

Life can be a cruel bastard. Take it from me—I'm the guy lying dead in a cheap motel bathroom, a halo of brains and blood splattered on the cracked tiles, some sick Jackson Pollock masterpiece. You can picture it, can't you? A grimy bathtub, and a half-empty bottle of Jamerson tipped over on the floor, and me, slack-jawed with a semi-automatic in my fucking mouth, fresh smoke wafting up from the still-warm barrel. Charming, right? I know what you're thinking… Jesus Christ!!! What a fuckin' drama queen! You're probably muttering about how life's never so bad that you can't claw your way back.

Yeah, well, let me stop you right there, pal. My mother warned me that there were gonna be days like this, but this day? This wasn't just another bad day. No-no-no-no-no-no! This wasn't just the straw that broke the camel's back. This was something else entirely. See, there's a story here. A real dark, twisted son of a bitch. And it starts with the people who ripped my life apart, who turned me into this shriveled-up, pathetic mess you're reading about now. They were powerful. Untouchable. And they're the ones who killed the only person in the world I ever loved… My Natalie… My wife!

I could start from the beginning and give you the whole play-by-play, but who has time for that? Attention spans these days barely last through a TikTok. So here's the deal: I'm not here to waste your time. This isn't polished, pretty, or polite. If you're still with me, good. If not, no hard feelings—this ride isn't for everyone.

For those sticking around, let me walk you through the madness. This isn't just a story about death; it's about revenge, blood, and the kind of rage that can turn a man into a ticking time bomb. Welcome to the last day of my miserable life.

PROLOGUE

'm a midlevel investor—a good-looking guy, a college graduate, a bit of a jock, and, admittedly, a bit of a dick. But hey, I'm a damn good dick! Happily married to my college sweetheart—the best woman any man could ask for.

We loved each other without question. A life without her? Less than nothing. The crisp and intoxicating scent of success hung in the air, and the clear skies mirrored my mood.

Neighbors waved as they walked their dogs, their smiles brightening the neighborhood. It was the American dream in 4K, and I was living it. Everyone knew my name—star quarterback turned city hero. I'd led my college team to a championship win, a glory still etched in local lore.

And today? Your guy had just leveled up—promotion secured, six-figure salary achieved. "Who's the big man on campus now?" I said, grinning at my reflection in the rearview mirror. Sliding on my sunglasses, I cranked the stereo and let the bass rattle my car windows.

The whole drive home felt like one long victory lap. When I pulled into the driveway of our half-million-dollar home, the feeling was undeniable: life was perfect. The sky was the limit. What more could a man ask for?

"Maybe kids?" I mused aloud, tapping my chin theatrically as a smirk tugged at my lips. The idea flickered briefly before I laughed it off. Not now. I had too much to accomplish first. But as I sat there, soaking in the glow of my success, I couldn't shake the thought: what could go wrong on a perfect day? Turns out…everything.

Chapter ONE

WARNING SIGNS

The unlocked front door was the first red flag of the day. Now, if you knew Natalie, you'd know she wouldn't leave the house unlocked unless she was running from a serial killer or had a gun to her head. Neither seemed likely.

I stepped inside, instantly on edge. "Natalie?" My voice echoed through the house. Nothing. Weird! "Natalie!" I called again, this time louder—still nothing. And then—ohhhhhh-a soft, breathy moan drifted from upstairs.

Oh, fuck no!

I felt it—how my stomach plummeted. My jaw tightened, nostrils flaring. Every muscle in my body went taut, primed to end whatever bastard was currently balls-deep in my wife. I stormed up the stairs, fists clenched at my sides—ready to make somebody's obituary a reality.

Clothes—her clothes—were scattered across the hallway. Lacy panties led to the bedroom door. My gaze snapped over to a bra dangling from the doorknob like a goddamn victory flag. The room door was slightly ajar as I stepped in front of it. And that's when I saw her.

My Natalie…

Straddling some faceless asshole, her bare back arched, moving in a rhythm that left no doubt. A damn tango of sexual body parts. My brain short-circuited. She lifted her head.

Our eyes locked. A voice snapped beside me—sharp, close. Then— bam—a jab to the gut snapped me out of it.

"What the hell are you doing, Lorenzo?"

I blinked. My wife. Natalie. Right there beside me.

Wait. What?

I turned back to the bed. It wasn't Natalie. But her sister, Kelly. Natalie and Kelly were sisters who looked nearly identical—except Natalie had a heart tattoo on her left arm with our names inked inside, and Kelly was half a shade lighter and apparently a full shade sluttier.

"Are you freaking kidding me?" I hissed.

She chuckled, steering me toward the stairs like a kid who had just walked in on Santa.

"Relax, babe. They're leaving soon. We all are."

I blinked, confusion etching across my face. She gave me the look— the look women give when they're about to carve you a new ass. Yeah. One of those.

"Lorenzo," she snapped. "The trip. The one you planned."

I stared at her, my brain fog at full density. "What trip?" I muttered, trying to buy some time and figure out just what the hell we were talking about here.

"Lorenzo, you didn't forget about our trip today, did you? Really?"

Like a bat out of hell, my soul, damn near left my body. I panicked and darted my eyes around the room, like the answers were some- where hidden in the drywall. "Wha—pfft—me? Forget? Babe, come on." I forced a chuckle. "Ah, maybe."

Her expression turned to steel. "Say it, Lorenzo."

"Say what?" I swallowed hard.

"Just say you forgot."

I exhaled through my nose, dragging a hand over my face. "I have a good memory, but it is short."

Natalie didn't flinch. Just drew in a slow breath, eyes flat, lips tight. "Wow," she said—like a loaded gun.

"—Look, it's been a long week and work's been kicking my ass, and I meant to check my calendar, but then—"

"Uh-huh, sure," she dismissed my feeble defense. "—And the bags..?"

"... Bags?" I muttered.

"The luggage," she said flatly. "You were supposed to pack."

Oh. Oh, I didn't like this ride; it's scary…

"… I can handle that."

Natalie's stare was colder than an ex's heart. "You got two minutes."

My hands flew up. "Two minutes? Done." I said, hauling ass upstairs to pack whatever the hell I could find, knowing full well this trip was already a disaster, especially with her annoying lil sister. Who, I just watched exchange bodily fluids with Thor!

My lungs burned as I charged down the stairs, shirt glued to my back. I'd packed half the damn house in under ninety seconds, the suitcase wheezing behind me, zippers ready to explode.

At the bottom step, I froze. My eyes traced across the living room—quick, instinctive. No Natalie. "Natalie?" *Not this shit again.*

I stepped off the stairs and into the open kitchen, leaning past the island. Nothing. Then Natalie's voice drifted up through the floor, casual as ever: "Grabbing some laundry from the basement before we leave."

Of course, she was.

Air hissed out of me as I made my way back into the living room and flopped on the couch. Sunlight poured through the picture window like the universe hadn't just kicked me in the nuts.

Outside, the neighborhood was quiet—just a breeze lifting the trees, a dog barking somewhere in the distance. Inside, it was still. And I knew—my wife wasn't coming back up anytime soon. Natalie took her time with everything—everything except swiping my credit cards.

Next came the sound. Off to my right, through the doorway separating the living room from the stairwell, high heels clattered—hard-soled chaos pounded closer—a rhythmic disaster, like a bad Cha-Cha Slide remix. I didn't even have to look to know who it was.

Kelly! Stumbling down the stairs, tangled with her latest boyfriend, locked in a sloppy kiss. Yet as they moved together, her eyes never left mine—saying more than words ever could. She smeared cheap lipstick across the guy's mouth, then wiped it off with the back of her hand—casual as routine. Messy affection, poor decisions echoing off the Moretti's walls.

She stopped at the front door, twisting toward me with a grin after she had already committed a cosmetic crime in my bedroom. "Tell Natalie we'll be right back. We're about to go grab some snacks."

I didn't even turn my head. Caught her in my peripheral and gave a silent nod, keeping my gaze locked on nothing in particular. It was easier that way. Kept the flicker of irritation from crawling up my ass.

Her latest fuck-toy stood beside her—tall, plus-sized, trying too hard to look polite. He mumbled an apology, like that could erase what I'd just seen—on my Egyptian cotton sheets.

Second thought: burn the whole goddamn bedroom set and send this prick the invoice.

A beat later, he stuck out his hand—some awkward intro move—but I didn't bother shaking it. I didn't catch his name either.

What was the point? She would drop him in a few weeks, tops. Like all the other poor bastards who thought they could weather Hurricane Kelly. *Funny how women always "find themselves" by losing their panties. They throw that line around, thinking it makes the train of discarded bodies behind them disappear.*

I was still chewing on that thought when the door slammed behind them. My eyes flicked up. Speak of the devil, Natalie waltzed in nonchalantly—laundry basket in hand, fresh clothes stacked up in scary ADA fashion. Her favorite anime outfits—the ones she slipped into before sex.

Cosplay *wasn't my thing, but if playing Catwoman got her freaky? Who was I to complain?* Maybe that was her version of a peace offering. Besides… that kitty was dangerous—hell, it should've come with a warning label: *"Enter at your own risk."*

I couldn't stop myself. Threw Natalie a warm, knowing look—the kind that said yeah… You got me, and we both knew exactly why.

"—And what exactly are you grinning about, Mr. Moretti?" she teased, one brow cocked, a mischievous glint in her eyes—and I swear she was purring.

I couldn't help it. Goddamn, my wife looked good. That little smirk, that spark—she knew exactly what she was doing. And I knew exactly what I wanted to do about it.

"I was thinking about how blessed I am to be with my soul mate," I ran a hand through my sandy brown hair, meaning every damn word.

"Awww, babe, you are sweet when you aren't acting so cocky!"

I chuckled. "Yeah, whatever." But then my tone shifted, turning more serious. "On a different note, babe—how your sister looks at me is a little unsettling. I'm thinking she might have a thing for me."

She walked over and sank onto the couch beside me, folding her legs beneath her in a lotus position. "Lorenzo," she said, her voice soft but particular. "Of course, my sister has a crush on you…" Her hazel eyes fixed on mine, pulling me in like they always do. "I mean, look at you. Handsome, fit, smart, emotionally available—hell, you even fold laundry. And you were the college quarterback who brought this city a championship. You're like... the definition of a trophy husband."

I grinned, flattered, and leaned in. Our lips collided in a hungry kiss, my teeth catching her bottom lip before everything spilled into the X-rated lip smack that left us tangled for hours—sheets twisted, pillows everywhere, limbs locked, balls slapping, her laughter echoing off the walls.

The afternoon had slipped past us when we were done and halfway human again. We lay there for a while, bodies cooling, the silence stretching. Eventually, the waiting kicked in after we showered. Natalie called her sister a few times and left voicemails. Nothing.

"We can't miss that flight," I reminded her while I was tossing on a clean shirt. Those tickets weren't refundable, and the driver was already en route.

I barely finished the sentence when I heard—a low engine hum slicing through the still evening air, followed by the crunch of tires on gravel outside just below our bedroom. I peered out the curtain and noticed a clean black four-door sedan with bright headlights pulling into our driveway.

"Natalie! Our ride's here!" I shouted, hauling ass as I hurried downstairs to grab our suitcases before heading out the front door. But the second I stepped outside, bags in hand… I stopped cold.

Guess who I saw? You probably guessed it… Kelly. Curled up in the backseat; sniffling, whimpering, resulting in a tear-streaked face. Classic helpless act.

God, I hated her irritating ass. All I wanted was one good day—just me and the wife. But nope. Kelly had to show up and ruin everything —like she always had. I swear, that drama queen made my ass itch, and not in a good way.

I stood there, suitcase still in hand, debating whether to chuck it at the car or walk back inside. My grip tightened. That's when another ride pulled up—sleeker, newer—our actual ride. And before I could even move, a blur flew past me.

Natalie—bolted out the front door, glassy-eyed, rushing straight to Kelly like she was the damn Red Cross.

Pity party? Checked.

Geez, Louise! The level of attention that woman craved was boundless— and above all, she'd mastered the art of playing the sympathy card, especially when it came to Natalie. Lucky me—I still had to go back inside to grab Kelly's luggage.

As I walked back in to grab a few things from the coat closet, I saw Natalie's laptop on the kitchen counter. Just sitting there. Open. Lit up. Begging to be noticed.

A photo. Handsome. Shredded. A scar slashed across his scalp. And just like that, my stomach dropped. No reason to feel insecure, not after the sex circus I'd survived today. I wasn't about to spiral. Not again. Not today, Satan. You can kiss my white—heavily seasoned Italian—ass.

I closed the laptop, brushing off the twitch that lingered in my gut.

But here was the kicker—*Satan?* That sneaky bastard already had my balls in a vise.

That guy in the photo?

Yeah, Scarface wasn't just some random pretty face. He was the man who killed my wife.

Chapter *TWO*

MILE-HIGH DYSFUNCTION

O n the way to the airport, Natalie and her annoying little sister sat in the backseat whining about men, drowning in the same tired sob stories while tossing back mini-shots of XXXL like cough syrup.

Sometimes, I half-joked to myself that life would've been easier if I were gay—no complaining, had sex, drank a beer, and watched football together. Of course, I was kidding—but if I had to keep listening to all this complaining; I swear the police might one day find me in a motel room with my brains blown out. The longer they went on, the more I questioned Kelly's sanity. She was a fascinating little case study.

Kelly friend-zoned the good guys—the ones who wanted to marry her and build a life—only to chase the same no-good losers every damn time; classic insanity: repeating the same cycle and expecting different results.

Let me be frank—the only way I ever see Kelly's annoying ass being pleased is if she married someone just as broken as she is—a narcissistic psychopath to match her energy.

I usually tuned people out—but after thirty minutes of nonstop whining, even I couldn't ignore it. So, for your sake, let's indulge that curiosity.

The girls were gossiping about Kelly's new boyfriend—allegedly, he was getting a divorce. *The catch?* He was still living with his wife and kid. *And the cherry on top?* He told Kelly she was moving too fast, which ultimately led to the breakup.

Whew. That man didn't just dodge a bullet—he sidestepped a

whole theme park of crazy. It's common sense that most men would not leave their wives and kids for some random woman, most anyway.

But hey, maybe she'd beaten the odds. Perhaps she was the exception to the rule—maybe, if a bear took a shit in the woods, it wiped its ass with a fluffy white rabbit. Either way, I was tired of hearing it and slipped in my earbuds—I wasn't about to invite another headache and ruin the rest of my day.

The ride lasted about half an hour. We pulled up to the departure curb at *Chicago O'Hare* — warm air thick with exhaust drifting between idling taxis and impatient travelers—but with all the nonstop whining; it felt like an eternity.

Desperate for a moment of peace, I stretched my legs, grabbed the luggage, tipped the driver, and stepped onto the sidewalk for a quick smoke. I told Natalie I'd catch up after finishing my cigarette, watching as they disappeared through the airport doors. I really needed this cigarette because my fried brain needed it.

A few minutes passed as I took the last drag, letting my gaze linger for a moment over the beautiful architecture of the city—just a moment of calm amidst the chaos. A deep sigh escaped my lips as I flicked my cigarette to the ground, trying to savor a quick moment of peace. But the moment didn't last long. I turned and bumped into a tough-looking guy in a black trench coat, wearing a Kangol angled just right.

Before I could apologize, he scowled, his eyes glowering as they raked me up and down. He kind of put me in the mind of *Jason Statham*.

"Watch where you're going, mate," he hissed in a low, raspy voice before brushing past me and striding into the airport.

I wanted to say something, but I'm not the confrontational type—and my day had already gone from sugar to shit. I needed no more problems. After years of martial arts training, we learned to de-escalate situations.

As the Aussie asshole walked off, I caught a quick glimpse of his face. Chills crept up my spine, but the sinking feeling in my gut stuck with me. He looked eerily familiar, but I couldn't place where I'd seen him before. "Fuck it. I need no more drama," I muttered, heading into the airport.

After we cleared the security checkpoints, we settled at our gate, cuddled up together, and finally talked while waiting for our flight. I kissed Natalie's forehead and leaned back in my chair, savoring a rare moment of peace.

Ohhh yes, peace—at least I thought so, until I spotted Mr. What's-His-Name headed toward our gate, carry-on bag in tow—making his way downtown, walking fast, passing faces… and now he's fucking homebound.

Suddenly, my moment of tranquility fizzled out faster than a cheap sparkler. Tension simmered. This was about to be a full-blown shit-show. I told Natalie I needed to use the restroom and made my way past the "married boyfriend," briefly locking eyes with him as we headed in opposite directions.

What was this idiot doing? I thought, shaking my head. Did this fool realize he'd dodged a bullet by distancing himself from Kelly? But no —some people just enjoyed learning the hard way. And there he was, back for more abuse, ready to ride the emotional rollercoaster with a busted brake lever.

I noticed Kelly glancing over at Natalie, then back at Mr. Shitface, lifting her chin—nose higher than the moon—as she remained stoic and unmoved by his pleas for forgiveness.

After all, she and Natalie had spent the entire goddamn ride to the airport trash-talking this guy. There was no way he could win her back… right?

He tried everything, pulling out all the stops, while she remained steadfast, consistently rejecting his advances. There was nothing this guy could say or do to change her mind—she was relentless!

Until… he played his last card, dropped to one of his pudgy knees, and proposed to her… I just couldn't make this shit up even if I tried.

Both sisters gasped, covering their mouths in shock. Kelly stood frozen, her eyes wide and softening with love. After a moment of hesitation, she yelled, "Yes!" and began jumping up and down. What the hell, the only lottery she had won was the douchebag fiancé-to-be lottery. Even the bystanders joined in, clapping in bliss, cheering, and smiling, damn rom-com finale.

I was Jedi mind-fucked and stranded in emotional purgatory— frozen in the washroom doorway. And of course, I'd forgotten the Tylenol.

As I made my way to the urinal, the newly minted fiancé walked in —phone pressed to his ear. I couldn't help but overhear his conversation.

"I love you," he said to the person on the other end. "I'm on a business trip," he continued. "And I'll be home after the weekend."

It was apparent that he was talking to his wife.

I hate to say it, ladies, but I told you so... and dammit, I was right. If I'm being completely honest, let's just face it—asshole is in our genes. And yet, those are the ones women like Kelly seem to fall for every damn time. What was the country song? 'Ladies Love Outlaws.'

The clatter of wet footsteps drew closer, piss splashing off the floor as he slid up to the urinal next to me, a smug grin tugging at the corner of his lips.

"You ain't no snitch, huh? Didn't hear nothin', didn't see nothin'... we good?" he asked, one eyebrow cocked just enough to make a threat look casual.

"Nope. Ears don't work so well in bathrooms," I muttered quickly.

"—Hell yeah! Bro code!" he barked, laughing way too loud for a bathroom. Then he slapped a hand on my shoulder—meant to be friendly, but it felt off. Something about the grime under his nails as he walked off whistling made me think I was in a Snow White Elf movie. Life was perfect... yeah, nah! One thought stuck with me—he never washed his hands.

What an asshole. And now the asshole's piss was on my shoulder. Awesome!

I trudged back to the gate and dropped into the seat next to my wife. She gave me one of those long, sideways looks—trying to read my mind — but didn't like what she found.

"What's wrong?" she asked. Her voice was sharp enough to slice bread.

What was right would've been the better question. My head shook, teetering on the edge of spilling the truth, when her sister's brand-new fiancé caught my eye from across the room.

He leaned into the fountain, one arm up like he owned the wall, body cocked half my way. Water slid off his chin. Even drinking, he wouldn't let me go—watching me out of the corner of his eye, dissecting me.

I turned my head, locking eyes with Natalie, wearing a smile that didn't quite reach my eyes. "Nothing's wrong, honey," I muttered, my voice just a little too cheerful. "Just ready to hit the slopes and, you know… and not die on the bunny hill."

Then I leaned back, letting my head fall against the stiff airport lounge chair. The vinyl cushion thudded dully beneath my skull. The air reeked of stale coffee and cheap cologne—thick enough to choke on.

Just across from us, near the corner where the lounge chairs curved, the newly engaged couple sat—wide-eyed and nauseated, damn near choking on each other's tongues. Public decency was a myth they didn't believe in. Tony's phone snapped photo after photo, reminding me of paparazzi at a red-carpet event.

I tried not to watch. I swear I did. But there's something about people in love— a car crash in slow motion. Hypnotic. Gross. But impressive. *I just wondered how long before the honeymoon glow faded into arguments about toothpaste caps and whose turn it was to take out the trash? And of course, how are your wife and your kids doing?* I shook my head and stared ahead, letting the questions hang in the stale airport air. Then came the voice—

A crackle over the intercom. Our flight to Aspen was boarding. Time to go. Time to pretend everything was excellent. Which was not part of my social skill set.

Sleep was a luxury I couldn't afford on that flight—not with the lovebirds beside me going at it, tongues working overtime, slapping and splashing. Each smack was louder than the last, a grotesque soundtrack of wet chaos. Relentless. Torturous.

And if that wasn't enough, Natalie conked out on my shoulder, snoring away—blissfully unaware, lost in some peaceful dream while I sat there, wide awake and miserable. I envied the hell out of her—able to sleep through the turbulence—while I shifted in my seat, trying to ignore the numbness creeping down my leg, when the overhead speakers crackled to life.

"We have arrived at our final destination," a metallic voice declared, slicing through the engine hum. The way it spoke made my skin crawl.

Damn, did I doze off? Hard to believe, considering Kelly and Loverboy over there couldn't stop slobbering all over each other with love spit. I glanced over. Out cold—snoring, slouched, and stuck together like two sweaty slices of ham left out too long in the sun. Christ, I could've hurled. My eyes were still locked on them, caught between disgust and disbelief, when something warm brushed against my skin.

Natalie stirred beside me, her eyelashes fluttering, maybe from some bad dream? Before I could react, she leaned in and kissed my neck.

"Hey, honey… why didn't you wake me up?" she murmured sleepily, her voice soft but uneven, feeling more like a warning than affection.

My face scrunched up before I could stop it—so much for keeping a straight face. Her XXXL wine breath hit. Still, I powered through—leaned in and planted a soft, warm kiss right in the middle of her forehead. No way in hell I was aiming for her lips.

I had to think fast. "Because you looked overwhelmed, and I figured you needed rest, honey," I said, flashing her a smile. *Honestly, after sitting through Kelly's drama, I'm shocked she didn't slip into a coma.*

Natalie's eyes snapped open. "Why did you make that face?"

Fuckkkk. It's like she had some sixth sense for when I was full of it. Maybe women were onto something with all that Ms. Cleo nonsense back in the 90s.

"Lorenzo!" she barked, her voice sharp enough to cut glass.

"—I'm sorry, babe!" My hands flew up defensively.

"Sometimes you're right here—and then suddenly, you're off somewhere else, lost in your head, just staring into the distance!"

"I was just thinking—"

"Thinking of what?" she snapped, eyes narrowing. "Some sugar-coated, Hallmark bullshit to cover up whatever you're thinking—so that you don't hurt my poor and fragile feelings?"

Fuck. Women like her didn't need husbands—they needed CIA badges. Give her a trench coat and a lie detector, she'd have confessions by lunch.

And of course, she just had to keep going. "If my breath stinks, just say it! I'm a big girl—you don't have to sugarcoat everything. Now spit it out!" she said, digging through the bag for breath mints.

Meanwhile, I just sat there, watching her go full FBI mode on a pack of mints—wondering how the hell I always end up in these inter-rogations. I had to figure a way out of this. "It's nothing, babe," I answered hastily, forcing a smile.

"—Wow. Still lying, huh, Lorenzo?"

I let out a nervous chuckle—it slipped out before I could stop it. "I'm not, honey—"

"If you lie to me again, this is going to become a much bigger issue than it needs to be." She rose to her feet—five-foot-four of fury, leggings and all, her glare hot enough to burn a hole through me.

"Okay, fine! Yeah! Your breath was a little tart and smelled like booze. It made things a little uncomfortable when I kissed you—that's all! We can get past this… there, I said it. It's not a big deal!"

Her foot tapped a war beat against the floor as she planted her hands on her hips, eyes locked on a death stare. "Thanks for being an asshole, Lorenzo!" she said, her upper lip drawn tight.

Before my brain could send the Bat-Signal to shut the fuck up, my lips betrayed me. "What!?" I blurted. *What in the entire fuck is happening right now? I didn't remember buying a ticket for this nightmare.* "Wait—why am I the asshole here? I did exactly what you asked me to do." Surely I thought logic had been on my side.

"—You lied about something so simple! And that you didn't see an issue with that tells me you can be a narcissistic dick! Don't sugarcoat it; tell me what you think."

Muffled laughs erupted behind me. I looked over my shoulder, then back at her, my smile tight, not touching my eyes. I whispered,

"Natalie, don't you think you're blowing things… maybe just a little out of proportion?" I edged each word carefully, like maybe tone alone could talk her down.

Sweat beaded down my brow under the weight of the passengers' eyes, every one of them locked on me.

Her lips moved faster than her brain. "Fuck you, Lorenzo," erupted as she shoved her way down the sluggish aisle, aiming for the exit.

The laughter grew louder, scoffs turning into open chuckles—and I'm pretty sure someone even whistled as she stormed off.

Assholes!

I called out her name, but she was hell-bent on getting as far away from me as possible. Silence pressed in as I sank into my seat, wishing I could disappear. Across the aisle, my future brother-in-law stared back—smirking.

I pushed up from the armrest and sighed, trailing after her, dragging behind like a kicked dog. By the time we hit baggage claim, the silence between us was louder than the conveyor's groan. Natalie still hadn't said a word. Every time our eyes met, her jaw tightened—and she rolled her eyes so far back, it was almost graceful like rage ballet.

A few minutes later, our luggage finally showed up, and before long, it was time to catch the shuttle and pick up the rental car. But as we moved along, a creeping unease settled in my gut. Natalie's outburst. Kelly's degenerate fiancé. If I'd had even the slightest clue what was coming next, we wouldn't be here—we'd be halfway to anywhere else by now.

Too bad hindsight's 20/20. Foresight? Blind as a bat on bath salts. I just wanted to add something quickly. I knew Colorado would be cold, but Jesus Christ—did we take a wrong turn into a snow globe from hell? Anyway, let me throw on my big boy coat while you blink, breathe—maybe even close your eyes for a second because the trip was just getting started.

Chapter THREE

LUXURY, LIES, AND BLUE-BALLS

By the time we finally arrived at the car rental place, my fingers had gone full corpse mode, and my nose was flirting with frostbite.

"Sir? Sir! Excuse me—your ID and debit card for the car rental? The pudgy clerk behind the counter squinted at me, her voice flat and impatient, and brought me back from my daydream.

I blinked, nodded, and reached for my wallet. "Um, sure. Sorry about that," I muttered as I handed over the credentials.

Then—like a glass shattering across the lobby—came Kelly's voice. "What the hell are you talking about? There's money on this card— rerun it!" Kelly's shrill voice echoed through the lobby, drawing more attention than she probably realized.

At the far end of the rental counter, she was already mid-argument —standing beside Whatever-His-Name-Is, giving the poor agent hell. *Here we go again. Miss attention-whore had clearly gone too long without her regularly scheduled outburst. Even God and the Postal Service took Sundays off, but not Kelly. No, she treated drama like a competitive sport. And lucky me—I had front-row seats to the shitshow.*

"—Thank you, sir! You're all set to go," the heavy-makeup-wearing desk clerk said, flashing her crooked smile.

My ear angled back toward Kelly. *And what was this I was hearing?* Oh, the new fiancé didn't bring any cards. Just cash? How convenient. Must not have wanted his actual wife tracking his whereabouts, hotel stays, gifts, or whatever kinky shit he and Kelly had brewing. Nope.

Not my business. I'd just stand over here, sip my soda through this straw, and enjoy the show. That was the plan... until he noticed me watching. *And what the actual fuck were you looking at, "new fiancé?"* I thought as his gaze intercepted mine. We locked eyes. I gave the slightest nod, took a slow sip from my straw, and added a subtle lift of one cheek.

Boom. Shaka. Laka. Right back at you, asshole. That was payback for smirking at me on the plane while Natalie ripped my balls off and handed them to me like a souvenir. I wanted to laugh so badly—the way his face twisted with each new horrifying realization that washed over him. I'd be savoring this moment for a long, long time.

Then the energy shifted—the light, the mood. A sudden shadow fell across me. "What's up with that silly grin on your face?" Natalie's voice startled me—appearing at my side, ninja-assassin style.

How ironic—she hadn't said a word to me since we got off the plane, and now, just when I was finally enjoying the peace, she broke the silence. Was I asking too much to keep it going a little longer? Just ten more minutes of shut-the-fuck-up. Please. I wanted to say it out loud... but all that came out was—

"Hey, you!" I said and chuckled—like a damn schoolgirl. Fuck! That was lame.

"What are you doing, silly?" She asked, mouth slightly open, eyebrows raised.

"Umm... nothing much. Just enjoying this soda and taking in the fact that we're about to go skiing for the first time... and how freaking cold it is out here. Geez. Brrrrr!"

She chuckled, leaning into my personal space and twirling her fingers through her hair.

I didn't even know I was that funny.

She glanced away, lips pressing into a pout before she looked up at me with those sad puppy eyes. "Babe... I shouldn't have snapped at you on the plane," she said, quieter now. "That wasn't fair—and I'm sorry." — *What the actual fuck was I hearing? My wife... apologizing and taking accountability? She just shattered the status quo. This woman—my woman—was one in a million; the love of my life. Unlike the ones so many guys complained about. I didn't need to be a Passport–Bro to find love—because I found my queen right here in the good ol' U.S. of A.*

A smile flashed across my face—one that finally reached my eyes. "No worries, honey. I should've just told you. From now on, I'll be more open," I said, as she gave me a quick peck on the cheek and looked into my eyes. *And that's when I knew—nothing could ruin this moment…* until the drums clashed in an unsynchronized mess, shattering my bliss when she said.

"Babe… my sister's card isn't going through, and her fiancé didn't bring any cards—just cash." She gave me that innocent look. "Would you mind letting them use yours? Just for tonight. Kelly will straighten it out with the bank first thing in the morning."

I just knew it was too good to be true. I was an easy mark—that's why I don't play poker. She buttered me up, blew smoke up my ass, and played me—just when I thought I was in the clear. And yet, deep down, I'd been expecting it. Maybe the passport bros had a point after all. I wanted to say no. Every fiber of my being screamed it. But how the hell was I supposed to refuse my beautiful bride?

My head shook no—*but my mouth?* That traitorous bastard lit up with a big, dumb, sucker-worthy smile. "Sure! I'll do it." Before I could even process my stupidity, she jumped into my arms, pressing her warm, succulent lips against mine. Butterflies erupted in my stomach as her tongue teased with every kiss. This woman knew my weaknesses—and she knew exactly how to play on them, the same way her sister knew how to play on hers. *But hey, happy wife, happy life, right?*

On another note, Natalie thought it was an excellent idea for all of us to ride in one car—to save money, since apparently, society decided cash isn't king anymore. I could've sworn cash reigned supreme. At least, that's how it was when I was a kid. Life felt less artificial back then. People seemed more genuine before the social media era turned everything into a highlight reel.

While driving from the airport, we spent the last thirty minutes tuning out Kelly and her fiancé's endless bickering. I needed a cigarette. Thank Christ I paid the extra fifty bucks for a smoke-friendly rental. Otherwise, Kelly and her mouth would've driven me to wrap this car around a telephone pole intentionally—just to escape.

Don't get me wrong—I was grateful for the massive raise. How else was I going to afford this trip? But the price I hadn't known about—the one I didn't see coming until it was too late—was steeper than anything I could've imagined. Because of Natalie. My beloved. My wife. She'd end up being the cost of this deranged transaction.

I popped a cigarette into my mouth and eased the driver's side window down. Freshly fallen snow caught the fading sunlight, casting a warm glow over the hills—a picture-perfect winter wonderland as the last colors of sunset bled into the sky.

Pulling out my cheap gas station lighter, I flicked it twice—nothing. Third time was the charm. *I fucking earned this.* Two deep drags, savoring the bliss—until Natalie leaned over and yanked me back out.

"Um, Lorenzo? What do you think you're doing?" Her eyes went wide as she stared at me from the passenger seat.

I glanced toward the passenger seat, careful not to meet her eyes. "Umm... smoking?"

Her eyebrows stitched together. "My sister's in the back seat with a baby in her stomach, and we don't want my niece or nephew breathing secondhand smoke." She shot a glance over her shoulder at Kelly, then snapped her eyes back to me.

A new baby—really? Shouldn't she have a frequent flyer card at Planned Parenthood by now? I mean, come on. It was Kelly. I thought it, but didn't say it out loud. Barely. "She's only, like... a few weeks in, right?" I said, taking another slow drag. "Pretty sure secondhand smoke isn't doing damage yet—"

"—Lorenzo!" Natalie snapped, whipping out her phone like she had Google on speed dial. "The first trimester is the most important! It's the baby's developmental stage, and children don't need to be around secondhand smoke or—" She paused, letting the words soak into the tension. "Negativity."

I nearly choked on my cigarette laughing at Natalie's rebuttal. "Like... seriously? You said negativity?" I hissed, then kept going.

"Kelly and what's-his-face back there have been arguing before we landed in Colorado—and that doesn't affect the baby? But me blowing smoke out the window does?

She sat stiffly, eyes locked on mine in a hostile glare. At that moment, I knew a confrontation was inevitable. So... I did what any smart man would have done. Yeah, you guessed it—I flicked that goddamn cigarette out the window like it had offended me—because at that point, I just wanted peace. Besides, the Aspens looked beautiful... and I wasn't trying to get murdered before we even hit the slopes.

"Alright, babe!" I murmured, rolling the window back up.

"Thank you," she said flatly.

I reached for her hand slowly and sentimentally—but she snatched it away without pause. *Cool... Guess we're still doing the passive-aggressive Olympics.*

A scoffed laugh came from the backseat, pulling my attention to the rearview mirror.

It was he—my soon-to-be nemesis, brother-in-law, and a permanent thorn in my ass.

"—You know those things are a slow suicide, right?" the smug prick of a fiancé said through a mouthful of pepperoni pizza—his shit-eating grin practically glued to his face.

Yeah, bud—and so does diabetes, high blood pressure, and cholesterol. But hey, what the hell did I know? I guess I was just raw-dogging life one cigarette at a time. I wanted to punch his chubby, grease-smeared face so hard my eye twitched.

"Sure thing," I shot back, layering on enough sarcasm to choke a horse. I bit my bottom lip and jaw, fighting to say what I thought.

Fucking prick!

The minutes crawled, silence thick and sour in the car—just tense breathing in the backseat. Then we pulled up—and something in me, despite everything, a half-smile crept in against my will.

The Miracle Hotel!

Tucked beneath a snow-drenched mountain, it looked like a Christmas card... if the card had a drinking problem. Red brick, sharp spire, glowing like it knew it was better than me. My jaw went slack. "Honey… are you seeing this?' I muttered."

Natalie didn't move. Didn't blink. Just sat there—stewing in silence. It didn't matter—I couldn't tear my eyes off it. The place oozed class—old money dressed to kill. The kind of hotel that didn't just pour your scotch—it knew your demons and kept the bottle warm.

I glanced over. Didn't need her to speak. She took it all in, a kid window-shopping on Fifth Avenue. However, she kept her lips sealed, still holding that grudge as if she had glued it on. She was impressed, sure—but hell would freeze before she gave me the satisfaction.

My eyes settled back on the perimeter of the hotel. The pines stood tall, decked in golden lights, trying too hard to be charming, while a narrow road curled past the front and wound up toward the ski slopes —where rich folks paid to snap their spines. Across the way, a brick bridge linked the main lodge to its twin—same red brick, same smug attitude, like a mirror flexing for the camera.

Doors slammed in unison as we stepped out of the ride. Tony and I went to the trunk to grab the luggage. I saw Natalie and Kelly up ahead, holding hands and laughing. They behaved as though nothing was broken, and the world behind them had not yet stopped burning.

I followed, dragging along the luggage through the towering double doors—and I'll admit it hit me. Inside, it looked like royalty threw up all over the place. Polished floors, chandeliers the size of egos, gold trim on everything. It didn't whisper of wealth. It screamed it.

I side-eyed Natalie—real casual—just long enough to catch the wrinkle running from her nose to the corners of her mouth. That little crease she got when she tried not to smile. Her eyes were damn near glowing. I could tell she wanted to jump out of her skin with joy, but after our little blowup, she was playing it cool. Nice try, babe. I saw it. I smirked and turned toward the counter.

"Mr. Moretti," the clerk called from behind the desk—swimsuit model vibes, but polished into something the rich could stomach. She waved me over, all polite smiles and practiced grace.

"Yeah, right here," I said, strolling up to the front desk. You can just call me Lorenzo." I smiled at her—one of the good ones—while reaching into my back pocket for my ID. "Hey!" I uttered, my brows raised. How did you know it was me?" I asked, looking at the clerk. Our eyes met. Her lips tightened for a moment—then slowly curled into a smile.

"You look familiar," she said, her tone light but curious.

A smug grin crept across my face. "We must have met in a past life or something." I chuckled.

"The guy I'm thinking of had bad blond hair, blue eyes with some woman on his side… and had a real bad attitude."

—I'm Italian—we're all inbreds with bad attitudes," I said with a chuckle. "Part of the charm. But no, most of us don't fit the stereotype. As you can see, my hair's brown."

Then came that look—steady, unreadable; she was sizing me up for the kill. And just as quickly, she dropped it. "I just wish my doppelgänger owned this dang hotel," she said sweetly. "Thank you for choosing the Miracle Hotel. The rate is $4,500 a night, but with the weekend package, it's $8,000 total. Check-out is at eleven am on Monday. Will you be paying today with a debit or credit card?"

Fuck! Those numbers died in the back of my throat.

Suddenly, I felt it—that tight smile and slow blink tell—the universe's way of handing you the win. The cards in my hand felt like they were burning holes through my fingers, *and the clerk?* She knew it. Dark and beautifully wicked. And way too damn calm about taking my money. This was a fucking Nightmare on Elm Street—and I couldn't wake up from it.

Not until Natalie's voice cut through my financial horror and her hand gripped mine, pulling me aside.

"This hotel is way too expensive! We can stay somewhere else— maybe there's a motel nearby that's cheaper," she suggested, her gaze locking onto mine as snowflakes slid down her cheeks and caught in the fur of her trapper hat.

That was just like Natalie. No matter how many petty arguments we had, she's always been by my side—never swayed by society's bullshit, never chasing illusions—my ride-or-die since day one.

If I'd known this trip would end in blood, I would've turned the fucking car around and booked the first flight home. In that moment, nothing else mattered—just her.

She didn't even have time to react. I leaned in, brushed past the fur of her hat, and pressed a gentle kiss against her lips.

"Babe, don't worry. What's eight grand and taxes weighed against your beautiful smile?" I flashed a confident smile and kept the words flowing. "Plus, you mean the world to me. I want my beautiful bride to have a lavish lifestyle—whatever you desire!"

I took a step back and did my little two-step shuffle dance. "Besides," I added with a smirk. "I did get a raise today."

Her cheeks lifted, eyes squinting as she damn near squeezed the life out of me—hugging me like a python crushing a mouse.

"Okay, babe, don't hurt me now," I chuckled, looking down at the love of my life.

She pulled back just enough to jab me in the gut. "Lorenzo! You got a raise today and didn't tell me?" Her eyes narrowed—sharp, playful, and expectant all at once.

"Because there were a lot of things going on—like your sister having sex in our bed with whatever-his-name-is—"

Natalie tilted her head, lips tightening as she leaned in and cut me off. "His name is Tony, babe."

"Tonyyyy?" I blurted. "Who—the fucking Tigerrr?" I drawled, eyes rolling so hard they nearly scraped the ceiling.

"—Shhh! Be quiet, he might hear us," she whispered, pressing a finger to her lips to stifle a laugh.

"So what? What's he gonna do—give me health advice when he's one cheeseburger away from a heart attack?"

She scoffed, laughing. "Babe! Quit being mean—"

"What'd I do?" I chuckled.

"—Ahem," the clerk fake-coughed, yanking our attention back toward the clerk. "Excuse me! Mr. and Mrs. Moretti."

We strutted back to the hotel clerk like runway models, confidence in every step. I handed Natalie the card, watching as she swiped it with zero hesitation—it was pure purpose in her hands. And damn, the way she moved. Fluid. Effortless. Every motion radiated self-assurance. That woman looked fierce. Watching her reminded me of something my grandmother used to say: *'When the essence of a real woman comes around, boys pull their pants up and men straighten their backs.' And Natalie?* She had that presence—that elegance, which commanded respect.

I stood there, caught in the web of her glow and femininity—lost in it—when a deep, raspy voice behind me cut through the moment like a dull blade.

"Yo, Lorenzo—mind swiping your card again? I got the cash on me right now," Tony said, his tall, rounded frame hovering close. His eyes tracked my every move, voice low with just a hint of concern.

Fuck no! I would not give this clown eight grand of my hard-earned working money. And honestly? That he existed in the same space as me diminished my will to live—just a little more—and I've only known him for a few hours. Not to mention, cheating on his wife with my sister-in-law in plain fucking sight. And on top of that—got her pregnant, then had the nerve to touch me in the washroom without washing his fucking hands! How dare you, swine. Filth, absolute degenerate. How. Fucking. Dare… You!

"No!" I barked, squaring my shoulders. "I'm not giving you eight grand—are you insane?" My voice was flat, final. "Maybe try a motel… hopefully a few miles away." My face stayed dry, unreadable—*but inside?* Pure fucking joy. Shutting down this titanic fuck-up of a man was easily the highlight of my day.

Kelly looked Tony over, a frown etching across her face. "Yeah, eight grand is kinda steep." She shrugged. "Maybe we should stay somewhere cheaper. I need to contact my bank and get my cards straightened out, anyway. Besides…" She paused, making that pity face she does when she wants to get her way. "We don't want to burden anyone." She cast a pitiful glance at Natalie's way.

Damn! This was my shot to plan an attack. I smelled blood in the water—like a shark circling in. And hell no, I was letting Natalie slip back into her master manipulator routine.

I chimed in fast. "Great idea!" I said, already pulling out my phone before the moment could slip through my fingers. I started nudging

Tony toward the door by clapping a hand on his shoulder. "I can drive you guys to a cheap motel. There's one two miles out—decent rates, no frills." I flipped the screen around to show Google Maps. My lips curled into a wide, mischievous smile.

Natalie turned to Tony. "You said that you got the cash, right?"

He turned around and jumped in a beat too soon. "—Sure, sister-in-law," he replied—too quick. Too cheery. His voice was all sunshine and syrup.

That son of a bitch!

All three of them looked at me. I turned tail, attempting to walk away—but I already knew what was coming next. I didn't trust this clown. He was a snake, rotten to the core, another manipulator like Kelly. I didn't want this bastard anywhere near me—let alone staying in the same hotel as me.

I sauntered toward the front doors, tossing a wad of bills at the bell-boys. "Handle it," I muttered, not even breaking stride. Then I doubled back—slow and smooth—drifting through the marble haze of the lobby before sinking into one of those overpriced, under-cushioned designer sofas. My body slumped under the weight of today's past bad decisions, trying to pull myself together before the next round of chaos struck.

To no one's surprise—least of all mine—I wound up ringside for another round of the lovebirds' quarrel… *Perfect!* Over by the drama couple, I caught Natalie locking her sights on me from across the lobby.

Damn… Just what I needed!

I glanced down at my phone, pretending like I didn't see her heading my way—those damn sad puppy eyes dialed up to eleven. *You know the half-guilt trip, half-soap opera audition?*

She plopped down beside me, all soft limbs and silent drama, folding her legs like we were about to meditate our way out of this mess.

I could go over the details, but even I was running low on the attention span meter. Long story short—she convinced me just to take the cash, find an ATM, and put the money back on the card. Oh, and she threw in the promise of that thing she does with her tongue that I love so much. Yeah. That sealed the deal. Alright, back to the hotel clerk where we were now standing—

"Thank you. That comes to $16,234. Receipt or email?"

"Email, please," I muttered, my tone heavy with dread.

"Here you go, bro."

Tony slapped a suspiciously small wad of cash into my hands, a shit-eating grin plastered across his face. I counted it. Once. Twice and one more time, just to be sure... Before I could even process it, the words slipped out. "Hold on, this isn't enough. You're short. Almost five grand—"

"—Oh, sorry, my guy," he said with a lazy—shrug. "Don't worry—I got you."

"...Unfucking-believable," I muttered, jaw so tight my molars were filing for divorce. My head twitched. I already knew this conman's game—slick talk, empty promises, and a tab with my name on it. I bit the bullet—salty, bitter, coated in betrayal. *And God, that smooth-ass Barry White voice of his?* Made my fist clenched even tighter. All I wanted to do was choke the living shit out of him.

"Thanks," he said, full of himself, clamping a hand on my shoulder like we were besties.

Took everything I had not to puke on his shoes. If this were Uno, the bastard just slapped down a Reverse card and grinned while doing it. "Absolutely," I answered, my voice dry as sandpaper. I watched him strut off like he was Tony Montana, Kelly clinging to his side—wide-eyed and swooning.

I stood still, shaking my head slowly. *I was in the same club as every poor soul who'd ever crossed paths with Tony, or a knockoff just like him. The difference was, this one had all the charm of a mosquito. You know the type who only remembers your number when he needs something.* But whatever—my stomach was louder than my thoughts, and I needed food in my system—fast!

The lobby hummed quietly for a second, then—footsteps behind me. Light. Intentional. Just as I could turn, a hand grabbed my arm and pulled me away from the front desk. It was Natalie...

"Are you ready to see our room, Lorenzo?" Big eyes. Curly hair.

Full lips and those damn freckles. She could melt my heart in half a second—and she knew it.

I smiled. "You bet your ass." I slipped my arm around hers and we headed for the elevators, where the dramatic couple was standing. With all the chaos, I didn't know which room to go to. "Hey, babe," I muttered. "Which floor are we on?"

She glanced at the little envelope holding our keycard. "Fifth!"

"Seriously?" Kelly chimed in, standing across from us. "We're on the fifth floor, too?" She gasped, lighting up as she looked at Tony like he'd just handed her the keys to a penthouse. She latched onto his arm, practically bouncing.

"What's your room number?" Natalie asked Kelly.

"5017—"

"Ours is 5018," Natalie answered, grabbing my arm just as jubilantly. "Tell me this isn't perfect, babe."

I forced a smile. "Positively." My fingers curled into my hands, nails biting deep—to keep from clawing my face off. But then I noticed something—Tony's reflection angled in the elevator's side panel, just behind me, staring back clear as day. His lips pressed tight, then stretched into a strained smile.

Oh, shit... He didn't want to be around me any more than I wanted to be around him... Hilarious!

I laughed so hard on the inside that my heart fluttered. *Was the King of Trolls and Grief upset? Didn't matter—I didn't give a flying fuck. But one thing was sure: the smirk on my face. Priceless. Watching him glare at me for that entire sixty-second elevator ride? Core memory. Locked and cherished 'til the day I die.I loved small victories!*

The sisters glided out when the elevator doors parted—moving in perfect sync, a choreographed sister act. While Mr. Shithead shuffled behind them in awkward silence, the tension hung thick enough to slice with a room key.

"All right, this is it," Natalie beamed, giving her sister one last squeeze before looping her arm through mine and dragging me toward our eight-thousand-dollar palace. We were barely at the threshold, and I was already questioning my life choices.

The drama couple stood off to the side, mid-bicker. I threw them a peace sign over my shoulder, smirking as Natalie pulled me through the door. Click. It shut behind us—sealing us in.

Then I stopped cold. Eyes wide. Jaw slack. Had I just stepped into a Disney palace? Massive windows framed a postcard-perfect view of the Aspens, snow-dusted trees stretching into the clouds. A king-size canopy bed dominated the room, its carved rails damn near kissing the ceiling.

"—Lorenzo! Are you seeing this!?" Natalie's voice trembled with excitement as she bit her finger, trying to contain herself while flitting from room to room.

"How could I not?" I said dryly, watching her dart around.

Then came the screams — "Babe… We have a *jacuzziiii!*"

I stepped into the bathroom—and that was it—the coup de grâce, the cherry on top… the final, glorious blow of mercy. I stood there, letting it all sink in. "Holy hell, this place is beautiful," I muttered, my voice barely above a whisper, full of awe as I took in the coliseum of marble and gold.

Before I could even fully process it, she leapt into my arms and kissed me—deep, passionate, breath-stealing. Her tongue danced with mine, slow at first, then hungry.

Clothes vanished. Time blurred.

We found ourselves on the bed, my head tucked under the blankets, swallowed by the fantasy of our palace. I spread her legs and lowered my face to where heaven resided. I was ready—ready to follow her rhythm, to worship her body with unshakable focus.

Nothing could ruin this moment. Absolutely nothing. And then— through the hotel walls—a loud, wet one ripped from Tony's ass.

Brrrumpppppp—brap-brap-brap-pit… pit!

I froze. *Jesus Christ—did Tony just shit himself? It sounded like it broke the sound barrier on all continents. It wasn't just gas… it was nuclear.*

Natalie jerked back. Her head rose from under the blanket—lip curled, nose wrinkling, like she'd just smelled death itself. "I'm totally grossed out and turned off," she muttered. Any moisture down there was now a desert.

I groaned, dragging the blanket down just enough to free my head—still nestled between her thighs. "Seriously? You want me to stop?" I asked, glancing up at her.

I hoped—prayed—she'd let me keep going. I needed this… needed to release some tension. But the damage was already done. That's just been my luck ever since he crashed into my life.

And honestly? I didn't know how much more I could take before I completely lost my shit.

"I'm going to freshen up—and take a cold shower," she said, tossing the rest of the blanket off her legs as she stormed out of bed.

I raised up slightly on my hands and knees, trying to salvage the vibe. "Want some company or—?"

"Nah, I'm good," she said flatly, putting her panties on. "And from the sound of it, your stomach wants dinner more than I do."

There I was—naked… face down, pale ass up. She had a point. I was starving—and I'd just tried to feast before Super Gas-Man carpet-bombed the entire vibe. And now I was starving, and I had a raging case of blue balls to go with it. *But hey… isn't that the rule? 'Happy wife, happy life, right?'*

"Sure, why not?" I forced a smile. "I'm famished—could use some calories to restore my energy." My cheeks lifted as I thought about a juicy cheeseburger melting in my mouth.

"Uh, babe…" Natalie's tone tilted upward as her thumb swiped across her phone screen at lightning speed.

"Yeah!" I answered, sitting up in bed with my arm wrapped around the big-ass teddy bear I forgot to mention—probably because I was too busy trying to get laid.

"Kelly's hungry too, and she wanted to know if it's okay if Tony rides along with you to the store." Natalie glanced up from her phone, locking onto me like a sniper sighting its target.

Crap!

I felt like scaling the nearest mountain to scream at the top of my lungs. This dance… was exhausting. And I can only imagine how sick of this guy you are, dear reader. But just imagine—if you had to look at him.

If my life were a book, it'd never hit the New York Times bestseller list—

and it was all his fault. Calling him the Antagonist of my story? Too gener-ous. Even villains had depth. Tony? He was the fucking Antichrist—and I didn't have a drop of holy water to exorcise him. Just a first-class seat to hell… wearing gasoline-soaked underwear. And the worst part?

I didn't even know it was only the beginning of his bullshit. And before the trip was over, I'd have blood on my hands.

Chapter FOUR

PEACE, DORITOS, AND DEATH

No need to explain—Tony had been riding shotgun for the past hour while we drove in hopeless circles. Between the shit GPS, Aspen's sorry excuse for cell reception, and the joint we split, it was like the universe had conspired to make me homicidal.

Funny thing, though—this asshole bitched nonstop about my cigarettes, yet here he was puffing my joint and singing Willie Nelson, which annoyed the hell out of me. Hypocrite of the year? Check ✔. Peace and relaxation—for how long? My question did not wait long for an answer.

"I think we're going in circles, genius." His voice cut through my bliss, eyes still glued to the window.

Shit. We were doing so well with the silence. "Yeah, I figured that much," I muttered, gripping the wheel a little tighter.

"Hey, pull over right here—I'm picking up a signal," he said, nodding toward the shoulder. Just beyond the roadside, a narrow strip of icy gravel gave way to a snow-blanketed hill, sloping gently into a quiet field edged by skeletal trees.

"You sure?" I asked, stalling.

"—Yeah, man, do it."

I sighed, flicked on the hazard lights, and pulled over. Tony popped the door and stepped out without a word, wandering into the cold. I lit up the last of the dobie, kept the heat running, and cracked the window to clear the smoke. "Anything yet?" I called out, watching him wave his phone around like a lunatic.

"Shut up!" he snapped. "I can't hear myself think—"

"Can you actually do that?" I shouted back.

"—What?"

"I said, keep up the good work!" I yelled, taking the last drag off my roach as he waved me off dismissively.

A few minutes passed. He was still out there—high, stiff, and cold. I almost felt bad for the poor bastard.

Almost…

I cranked the stereo. The Allman Brothers—Midnight Rider, I Gotta Run—started to play. I didn't know which hit me first—the bass-line or the weed—but damn; I was in the Zone. Windows cracked, smoke swirling, head nodding. I was vibing hard, mouthing the lyrics.

That's when I saw them. Rabbits. In the snow. Just… hopping around. Then one of them stood up—no joke—and locked eyes with me. Swear to God, he raised a paw in military salute fashion. Then he started signing. *Sign language?* Like, I was supposed to understand *rabbit ASL.* I stroked my chin, gaze locked.

Was I high?

Were those rabbits trying to communicate… possibly? I blinked. Behind them, a rainbow emerged out of thin air—a literal rainbow, in the snow. But there was no rain. Okay… I was definitely high as a kite. No question.

And—just past the rabbit rave—a family of elk wandered into view. Massive things. Regal. Graceful. One of them even looked back at me, and his lips moved. "Hey, man. Beautiful day to vibe, huh?"

It was almost peaceful. Almost…

And just like that is when everything changed. The elk froze—ears up. Noses twitching. Then they ran. Full sprint—cutting across the slope, just ahead of Tony. It wasn't a casual jog either. I'm talking panic-in-the-eyes, hooves pounding, 'every elk for themselves' kind of sprint.

What were they running from?

My eyes lingered for a beat or two before I mashed down on the horn.

Honk! Honk! Honk!

"Tony! Get the hell in the car!" I yelled, but the idiot just waved me off again. By this time, the elk were gone. The area had gone deathly still. That's when I saw it—a shadow, quick and low to the ground, weaving between the trees. The snow crunched—deliberately. Two yellow eyes gleamed in the fading evening glow.

A mountain lion stepped into view. And not just any mountain lion. Muscles rippled beneath its fur—tail swaying. Eyes locked. Ready. Scar from The Lion King's long-lost cousin. It crouched.

Oh, hell no!

"Shitttttttt!!!!!!" Tony screeched—voice cracking. His body finally caught up to the level of danger his dumbass brain had been ignoring. He froze. Turned slowly. Real slow facing the big cat. The moment his eyes locked with those glowing death-orbs, he stiffened.

"Staaay calm!" I yelled from the car, dragging it out, warning Tony not to make any sudden movements.

Spoiler alert… he did the opposite!

Panic downloaded in real time. Arms flailed, legs went rogue—he took off in this jerky, off-balance sprinting like a pregnant yak. It'd have been comedy gold if it weren't for the snarling murder-cat behind him. A panic even I shared.

The stiff, lumbering movements from standing in the cold too long weren't doing him any favors. He tried to sprint, but his legs weren't cooperating—stumbling once, twice—then completely wiping out. He rolled, scrambled, and hauled ass toward the car. He reached the door and yanked at the handle, desperate. Nothing. A dull THUD shook the frame as he slammed into it face-first.

Thwack!

His eyes snapped up to mine, vast and wild, pure fear. "OPEN THE FUCKING DOOR!" he screamed.

Shit. I'd forgotten to unlock it.

I fumbled for the button, hit it just as he lunged again. The car jerked forward, dragging him through the snow—one leg still caught outside as the lion sank its teeth into his shoe.

"Get in!" I shouted, but I wasn't slowing down.

Tony scrambled inside, boots kicking up slush, nearly decapitating himself on the doorframe before collapsing into the seat, panting.

Silence.

A few beats passed.

I looked over. "You good?"

His head whipped toward me. "WHAT THE FUCK DO YOU MEAN, AM I GOOD!? I ALMOST GOT MAULED TO DEATH AND YOU WOULDN'T LET ME IN THE CAR!" He clutched his chest, gasping for breath, eyes still wide with panic.

I shrugged. "Dude, I blew the horn and yelled out the window. What else did you expect me to do?"

"THE WINDOW WAS BARELY DOWN!" he shrieked, jabbing a finger at me.

I snorted. "Look, I honked. Be thankful."

He just stared at me, sucking in air. "Motherfucker…"

And just like that… silence fell over us again.

Eventually we found our way back to the hotel, gripping plastic bags of snacks. *The rest of the ride?* Not one word exchanged. *In the elevator?* He had one shoe—pun absolutely intended. I guess the lion kept the other as a souvenir. *Did I mind?* Hell no. I thrived in the silence, it gave me time to contemplate.

Our doors slammed in unison as we split off to our separate rooms. As soon as I stepped inside mine, I dropped my bags, flopped onto the love seat, and tore open a bag of chips—pure bliss.

The 85-inch TV hummed to life on the wall, filling the room with a cool blue glow. Natalie strolled in, didn't say a word—just reached straight into my bag. She didn't even blink.

I side-eyed her, watching her tear through my chips, manic like.

"Babe, these are really good," she said, mid-crunch—mouth full, no shame. Then, right on cue: "You do know everything you brought back is unhealthy, right?" Her gaze flicked my way for half a second—just long enough to acknowledge my existence—then snapped back to the TV, utterly oblivious to me.

"Yep!" I responded loud and proud, savoring the glorious taste of the Dorito.

Her eyes narrowed. "Why are you acting like that—"

"Acting like what?" I countered, popping another chip into my mouth.

Head tilted, eyes narrowing just slightly. "That thing you do," she said, studying me. "All nonchalant and chill—like you're not upset, but are."

"—I am not," I said flat as drywall—then followed it up with the loudest crunch I could manage.

Just as she was about to call me out again, her phone rang. It was Kelly. That ringtone should come with a warning label: *'Incoming Drama Detected.'*

Here we go. I already knew shit was brewing—probably bubbling over. But honestly? I didn't give a single damn. I just wanted to sit here, eat my chips, and be left the hell alone. But the longer Natalie talked, the more her gaze shifted—eyes still pretty, sure, but now they had that "somebody's about to die" gleam. Drilling straight through my skull.

And—she snapped… "HE DID WHAT TO TONY!?"

I didn't get the chance to blink. She snatched the bag of chips straight out of my hand—my chili-and-cheese-coated, gloriously seasoned Doritos. The elite flavor. The chosen bag. A goddamn masterpiece.

A crime had just been committed. You don't mess with a man's Doritos. She had no idea what she'd just started. Blood feuds have erupted over less. And she had officially crossed the line. This was war!

My eyes widened in horror. I was frozen, mid-chew, and then it hit me. "Natalie!" I snapped, my voice was dead serious. "Give me back my chips, honey—"

"—Not until you tell me what happened between you and Tony first," her voice was calm, but that I-will-hunt-the-truth-down-myself edge was creeping in fast.

I leaned forward just a little, resting my elbows on my knees, face flat and unbothered. "Nothing major happened," I uttered, holding her gaze. "The prick's still alive, isn't he?"

Her brows furrowed. Mouth dropped. "Kelly, I'll call you back."

She ended the call without breaking eye contact—those bulging eyes and death glare locked onto mine.

At the moment, I knew that *this was bad...*

"Lorenzo. Anglo. Moretti!"

Fuckkkkk... worse than I thought. Full government name? Yeah—I was five seconds away from getting verbally shanked in the throat.

"What now?" I asked, my voice already riding that thin line between confused and full-blown fed up. "What's the problem this time?" My eyes trailed her as she paced the room.

Oh no... this was even worse, the pace of death.. I didn't like this ride; it's scary.

Arms crossed. Chin up. Stance locked, hands firm on her hips. "Tony said you tried to kill him," she snapped.

Pause.

One beat.

Two.

"But twice!" she snarled.

I blinked. "Whatttt!?" My voice cracked, curiosity spiking through the confusion. **You, reading this—don't look at me. I was just as blind-sided as you. Straight-up Jedi mind fuck—no lightsaber required.**

"I didn't try to kill anyone—not even once, let alone twice!" I fired back quickly.

What the hell was she even talking about? It didn't take a genius to figure out that Tony had exaggerated, twisted, and straight-up fabricated the whole damn story. But seriously? He couldn't wait to throw his little pity party after I had a chance to break in this stupidly expensive hotel room with Natalie?

Selfish bastard!

My eyes flicked up as she stepped in front of me—looming. Dangerous.

"He said you let a mountain lion attack him," she barked, voice climbing. "And then you dragged him with the car!"

A laugh slipped out—half scoff, half disbelief. Couldn't even stop it.

She stared.

I straightened up.

She glanced down.

I looked up.

Yeah. This was going downhill fast.

"...There's nothing funny about this, Lorenzo—" her voice cut sharp, no warmth, no wiggle room.

"—Honey," I sighed dramatically, pinching the bridge of my nose. "It's funny because he's lying."

She didn't budge. I could practically feel my teeth grinding together. I told the entire truth, well... left out the smoking pot part. But... somehow she still made me feel guilty.

"Then why didn't you say anything when I first asked you what was wrong?"

"I just didn't want to talk about it, that's all," I muttered. "...And I hadn't eaten—"

"This little rivalry needs to stop between you two."

My thumb stroked my chin methodically. "What little rivalry? I don't have an issue with anyone," I replied, then glanced away for a split second.

Damn. Did she catch that?

Her eyes narrowed. "You're lying to me again, Lorenzo!"

Damn! She read my body language. I'm totally convinced that all women work for the CIA's profiler division.

"Yeah, you're right," I threw my hands up in defeat, my voice dripping with reluctant surrender. "I can't stand the son of a bitch, but I promise you—I didn't try to kill him!" I pleaded my case, hoping desperation might earn me a pass. It didn't.

"Lorenzo, you need to be the bigger man and apologize to him— right now! Before we all go out to my birthday dinner!"

And that's when I knew she had completely lost her mind. If she thought I was about to apologize to that narcissistic fuckboy, she had me—and the entire game—fucked up.

No way.

No how.

And over my dead body. Would I apologize to Lucifer's tall, plus-sized minion, she would have to pry it from my cold dead lips—

. . .

Deadpan cut.

"I'm sorry, Tony!" Those words tasted like shit on a shish kabob stick—charred, bitter, and somehow still undercooked coming out of my mouth. Yet there I was, standing in the hallway, choking on pride while apologizing to Tony, Natalie, and Kelly right there, grinning, or should I say smirking,

The air was thick with bullshit and injustice. And there he was—posted behind the doorway, wearing a neck brace and all.

I wanted to puke. Right onto his smug, self-satisfied face as the girls were beaming. Tony's grin just kept growing. And I wanted to slap it clean off.

"Well… we're sorry, Tony," Natalie said with a sigh, standing beside me. She offered him one last smile before we stepped back into our room—directly adjacent.

My hands dragged across my face as I watched Natalie disappear into the bathroom, the door clicking shut behind her. That's when the thoughts started.

You better believe this meant war. His ass was grass—unwashed grass. I was ready to return the favor tenfold. In hindsight? I should've left him out there in the wilderness and let nature take its course. Play stupid games, win stupid prizes. That prick deserved whatever karma he had coming.

Natalie's voice rang out from the bathroom as I scrubbed the day's shame and grit off my face—

"Get dressed!" she called out from the bathroom, voice bright and bossy in the best way. "We're taking that new underground Metra to an *East Indian* spot I've been dying to try—and there's a bunch of cool shops along the way. Oh! And we're going to the *Foxxhole nightclub* after. So hurry up—I want tonight to be perfect!"

Indian food? My stomach was already filing a formal complaint. She knew it upset my stomach. But so did Doritos, and I still ate those. Let's get to the point. I loved women who knew what they wanted. That could take control.

That kind of confidence? A turn-on. All women aren't created equal, but this one? The hands made this one of the divine.

"Sure!" I called out and headed to the bathroom. I took a quick shower, dried off, and grabbed a towel. "Let me freshen up. This will be a night I'll be telling stories about for years!"

She opened her mouth to reply—

I snapped the towel at her ass. Crack! (Pun intended.) A sharp pop cut through the air.

"Lorenzo!" she shrieked, laughing as she dodged.

I lunged after her, grinning like a damn fool—chasing her barefoot through this overpriced luxury suite I secretly wouldn't admit I liked.

Tonight? Oh yeah. This night had potential. Major potential. One for the books. Time passed, and we were finally in the car—Natalie looking flawless, me feeling like a dad in an indie film.

And then we waited.

And waited.

Then, finally, there they were. Bobby and Whitney 2.0. On their imaginary red carpet. Probably just finished rehearsing tonight's big argument or a synchronized side-eye routine for the ride.

They slid into the backseat without so much as a sorry. Tony adjusted his snug jacket and then leaned into his seat. Kelly hugged Natalie, fake and puke city.

Meanwhile, we were on the clock.

Natalie had already set the whole night in motion—reservations, train times, the works.

Now? We had exactly ten minutes to make it to the Metra station, or we'd be stuck freezing our asses off for an hour waiting on the next train to Carbondale.

And missing that train? Yeah, that was not an option—not if I valued my life... or my sex life.

The restaurant was a 45-minute ride from the station, and if we missed this train, we'd be eating cold-gas station leftovers instead of whatever fancy, spice-sprinkled masterpiece Natalie had in mind.

I flicked my eyes down at my phone—GPS, time, all of it. Seven minutes 'til the train left. Fantastic. Just enough time to have a panic attack and pretend I had it all under control. Had to haul ass.

Now, I know you're dying to hear the glorious details of the ride there…

But let's be real, time was tight.

Couldn't "write" and drive. That's dangerous. So buckle up. I can barely focus on one thing at a time as it is. And yeah, I had a few sips. Don't judge me. A little drinking and driving never hurt anyone—unless you count the statistics, the guilt, and the occasional fiery wreck.

But me? I had somewhere to be. Priorities.

Time ticked faster than it had any damn right to as we screeched into the Metra station—two minutes to spare. Not that I'm about to admit I spent the whole ride twenty miles over the speed limit. But hey… like I said—priorities.

Natalie had pieced together this itinerary, and the last thing I needed was to screw it up. We snatched our tickets and made it to the platform, panting like idiots—but we made it. Feet planted. The train pulled in, and we climbed aboard—slightly crowded, slightly chaotic —and found our section.

We floated into our seats like war survivors. I tried to stay awake, I did.

But if you've been paying attention, you know I haven't slept since we landed.

This power nap? Yeah… it was long overdue. My body hit the kill switch before I could protest.

Forty-five minutes felt like forty-five seconds. Next thing I knew, Natalie was shaking me. "We're here," she said.

I sat up, my back cracking like bubble wrap, my neck was stiff, and my brain was foggy.

People were already shuffling off the train.

The restaurant was just a few blocks away, but Natalie? She wanted to walk—take in the scenery. Of course she did. No big deal… just ignore the part where my legs were still halfway asleep and my soul hadn't caught up yet.

There had been one thing, though—

The cold. The Colorado night hit me as I stepped outside—sharp, rude, and fully committed. Still… I had to admit, the place had that quiet, postcard kind of majesty. The small buildings, the snow-dusted rooftops, the mountain peaks looming in the distance—it had the kind of quiet beauty you'd expect from an old Western movie set. Only cleaner.

And with a lot more glowing storefronts and tourist traps. It wasn't the urban chaos I was used to, but hey… even I had to admit—it had its charm.

"Babe, look!" Natalie lit up, tugging my hand like a kid and pointing ahead at a small clothing store with wide front windows.

"What?" I glanced over, already half-smiling just from her excitement.

"They've got that sweater you wouldn't shut up about a few months ago—the one you said made you look like a 'sexy lumberjack.'"

I scoffed. "Please. I'm over it."

"You sure? We can grab it."

"Nah, I'm good. But hey… thanks for remembering." I squeezed her hand. Out of the corner of my eye, I saw Kelly glance over—probably checking out our rings.

"I can't wait to get married," Kelly sighed, looking up at Tony with puppy eyes.

"Yeah… sure," his voice was tight, the kind that didn't match the script, as he squeezed her hand—a little too hard.

"Ouch!" Kelly winced, pulling back.

"—Oh uhh… sorry," he muttered, bending down to kiss her forehead like that would erase it.

I let out a dry chuckle, clapped him on the shoulder, and gave him a slow blink.

"That's quite the *Cinemax* grip you got there, pal."

Tony's eyes narrowed, just as he opened his mouth to fire back—when Natalie chimed in, effortlessly diffusing the moment. "Oh look, we're here," she said, pointing toward a cozy Indian restaurant with warm lighting, gold-trimmed windows, and the faint scent of spice wafting through the air.

We crossed the threshold, and the whole world changed just like that. The scent hit stronger—warm spices, charred meats, a hint of jasmine rice, and something sweet I couldn't place hit me. Whatever it was, it wrapped around me.

The place was packed—buzzing with laughter, the clink of silverware, and the low hum of music that sounded expensive. Yeah. This wasn't just dinner. It was a whole damn experience.

Then came the waiter. Said his name was Raghid. Cool. Real cool. Tall, muscular, mid-twenties, Indian, with a perfectly groomed beard and a head full of long, silky hair. Strong jawline, dark complexion—a guy who probably never heard the word no, especially from the ladies.

And Kelly? Already throwing out the bait. He welcomed it—his tongue tracing his lips as he fixed his gaze on her. "My name means 'pleasant' in my language," he said smoothly. I caught Tony stiffen. Goddamn, this was gold.

I liked Raghid; he was pissing Tony off.

And it felt—GRRRRRREAT! (*Ha. No pun intended. Promise.*)

He led us to a low table surrounded by floor cushions. We had to cross our legs on the floor, surrounded by bright, plush pillows that looked straight out of a high-end interior design catalog. The setup was luxurious, and despite the restaurant's crowded atmosphere, the energy inside felt warm and alive—everyone appeared to be having a great time. Everyone—except for Tony, that was.

I glanced around, then leaned toward Natalie. "Wait, so we're really eating everything with our hands?" I asked, straight up, culture shock.

Natalie chuckled. "Of course, silly. It's a traditional restaurant. A lot of Asian cultures do this."

"Oh... okay, I didn't know that—" but I didn't even get to finish. Tony's voice bulldozed through the conversation.

"—Yeah, man! That's because the Chinese were samurai. In the past, they conquered several other Asian countries. And one guy—uh, some Asian dude—almost took over the entire world! What's his name again..?"

Jesus. I rubbed my temple, already seeing the trainwreck unfolding in slow motion. "Genghis Khan. And he wasn't—" I answered. Then Natalie cut in, voice crisp and unwavering.

"Genghis Khan was Mongolian, Tony. Not Chinese. He led the Mongol Empire. And samurai? They came from Japan."

Boom!

The air around us shifted. The entire table froze for half a second. Even the restaurant noise seemed to dip long enough for the impact to land.

Damn, my wife was on fire. I told you—one in a million. No—scratch that. One in a billion. Brains. Beauty. Cultured. Fluent in five languages. And she worked as an accountant for an international bank. I had it all. And the tragic part? This was the last night I'd ever have it. Because this was the night my wife was murdered.

Chapter FIVE

CURRY, CHAOS, AND CATASTROPHE

raised my glass toward her, swallowing down the weight of that thought. "Here's to you, babe," I murmured. Natalie winked, that soft, knowing smile curling at the edges of her lips. Just as I went to savor the moment, a sharp prickle crept up my spine.

I looked over—instinct pulling me before logic could catch up. And that's when I saw it. Kelly. Staring at Natalie with pure, unfiltered disdain. The expression was quick, subtle, but sharp enough to make my stomach twist. *Sibling rivalry? Maybe.* Wouldn't know—only child. But why the hell glare at her own sister like that, when Natalie had been nothing but kind, understanding, and patient?

Kelly shifted in her seat, just enough to catch my attention. Her lip curled. Then her nose wrinkled, like she'd caught a whiff of something rotten. "Natalie's a know-it-all. She always has been. Ever since we were kids."

Natalie's eyes narrowed, caught off guard. "Sorry—what in the hell did you just say?" Her tone stayed level, but the chill behind it was unmistakable. Controlled. Precise. "I'm a know-it-all now?" A small, dangerous smile tugged at the corner of her mouth. "This isn't about showing off, Kelly. It's called knowing basic history."

I jumped in, half-assing some damage control. "Hey, hey—common sense these days, right?" I threw Natalie a quick glance across the table, hoping to convey the message to calm down.

But both sisters turned on me at once, eyes locked and loaded like a shotgun. "Stay out of this, Lorenzo!" Natalie snapped.

"Yeah, stay the hell out of this," Kelly echoed, her tone even sharper.

Tony's forehead scrunched. He laced those sausage fingers together and parked 'em on the ledge of his gut. "So what—you saying I ain't got common sense now, Lorenzo?" The man looked genuinely offended.

Jesus… take the wheel.

"Relax, man—I wasn't aiming it at you," I said, throwing my hands up. "Just stating the obvious. If it stings, that's on you." I glanced at Natalie—she wasn't having it.

She leaned forward slightly, voice calm, sharp. "A know-it-all?" she said and took a sip of wine, eyes pinned to Kelly. "Didn't realize being the smartest in the room was something I had to apologize for."

Facts. Because let's be honest—these two jackasses weren't exactly the sharpest tools in the tactical box.

I smirked and took a sip.

Then Tony's finger jabbed toward me. "So you're calling me a dumbass—"

PFFFFT!

He must have been reading my mind. Wine nearly shot out of my nose—I damn near choked, spit, and had a mini-stroke all at once. "What the hell are you even talking about?" I coughed, my hands suddenly moving in Italian New York style. *I thought that should've been the end of it. Nope.*

Kelly turned on Natalie, eyes blazing. "You think you're so fucking smart. Like you've got all the answers—but you can't even figure out your shit with Lorenzo!"

Damn. What the hell did I do?

Natalie didn't flinch. Took it like a champ. Her resting bitch face was locked in, cold and unbothered. "I don't have the answers to my own life?" Her voice was calm—too calm. "That's rich coming from someone still hung up on her ex. Remind me—which one are we pretending never happened?"

Show time! This was getting too good.

Natalie kept going, deadly cool. "Are you seriously talking out of your ass about my husband right now?"

Kelly scoffed, but Natalie leaned in, just a hair.

"If you keep smiling, Kelly," she said, voice dropping to a warning growl, "I swear to God—I'll slap that smug little grin right off your face."

I barely had time to react as Tony stumbled to his feet, the soles of his bare feet slapping against the floor, shaking the entire floor table.

Nearby guests turned, wide-eyed. That was when Raghid came sprinting out from the back.

"Is everything okay here?" his voice was tight, professional—but his eyes darted around the room, scanning for witnesses, making sure things didn't spiral. All four of us whipped toward him, barking out at the same time— "YES!!!"

Silence. A bead of sweat rolled down Raghid's perfectly sculpted face. He forced a chuckle. "Okay—hey, it's alright. Let's all just take a breath, yeah? No need to get worked up. Your food's here now, fresh and hot. Made with love, I promise. You'll feel better once you eat."

Love? I could already taste the poison. Ten minutes. That's how long we sat in complete, deafening silence, shoveling down food with our hands. The awkwardness was so thick you could cut it with a dull butter knife. We dipped pieces of chapati into the bubbling, lava-hot curry, the rich, reddish-brown sauce steaming like a volcano on the verge of eruption. And damn, was it good. So good that for a fleeting moment, I completely forgot we were all at each other's throats minutes ago.

That was… until Tony's pudgy, unwashed hand swooped in like a seagull on a French fry, snatching the very piece of chicken I'd been reaching for.

My stomach lurched. Has this motherfucker even washed his hands since the airport? I hesitated. Stared at my fingers. Yeah, I suddenly didn't want any more of this.

Setting down my chapati, I muttered "Excuse me," and swiftly bailed from the table, heading for the washroom. The second I stepped inside, my stomach twisted into knots. Oh, no. I darted into one of the two stalls and—Unleashed. The. Magic. Dragon. Jesus Christ.

The heat of the curry was nothing compared to the inferno

currently raging inside me. My soul left my body at least twice. By the time I was washing my hands, exploding my anal track, and gargling with the fire extinguisher, I realized people in the washroom had begun taking shallow breaths, side-eyeing me.

One guy broke out into a sprint. Another one looked like he wanted to call the authorities. The door swung open and slammed shut repeatedly as more people fled in horror. Yup. Time to get the hell out of here.

I made my way back to the table and immediately caught a couple of guys from the bathroom cutting their eyes at me—followed by a few deeply disturbed faces.

Damn. Was it that bad?

I cleared my throat and sank into my seat, trying to ignore the lingering looks of disgust aimed in my direction.

"So, did we really all yell at Raghid at the same time?" Kelly asked, turning to Natalie.

Natalie frowned, guilt settling in. "Yeah… we have to leave him a huge tip," Kelly snickered. Natalie giggled. Tony chuckled. I raised my brows and grinned.

And bada bing, bada boom. Problem solved—right?" And just like that, we were all friends again. Except for me and Tony, of course.

The laughter flowed. The food was incredible. The night was finally falling into place. I felt at peace for the first time since we landed in Colorado. And just as I let my guard down… My stomach twisted into knots. Again. Oh, no. Not this shit again. I barely got the words out before excusing myself—once more. This time, I could feel the irritation radiating off Natalie. Eyebrows lifted. Eyes narrowed. Lips pursed. Yeah. I'd be hearing about this later.

I hustled back to the bathroom, doing the poop scoop bogey, barely making it inside before the inferno reignited. By some miracle, I snagged the last open stall—right next to an old man patiently waiting in line. God, just end this suffering.

Just as I was about to contemplate the meaning of life, a soft knock tapped against my stall door. I froze.

What. The. Hell?

Then the old man's voice drifted in—low, raspy, almost... sympathetic. "Son, you sound like you're fighting demons in there. I've got some extra medicine in my bag. It'll settle your stomach."

A bottle slid under the stall. I eyed it like it was either a gift from the heavens or a trap from the devil himself. "Uh... I'm good, no thanks—"

"Suit yourself," he uttered, with the kind of knowing chuckle that made me second-guess my entire existence.

Another cramp hit. Fuck it—I downed the bottle like a tequila shot. He told me it would take about an hour to kick in. But I was willing to believe in miracles. Twenty minutes later. I checked my phone. Shit. (pun intended.) I'd been here way too long. But I felt like a brand-new man. Lighter. Free. Reborn. Maybe that old guy was onto something after all.

I strolled out of the bathroom as if I almost didn't die. As I made my way back to the table, Natalie locked onto me instantly. "Are you feeling okay, Lorenzo?" she asked, suspicion flickering behind her eyes.

"Sure, honey. I'm fine," I said, forcing a smile. That's when my eyes landed on it—a cocktail—sitting right beside my plate. I frowned. "What... is this?"

Natalie grinned, tilting her head. "Just try it, silly."

I narrowed my eyes at the evil drink like it had personally offended me. Not after everything I just went through.

"A *Chai Martini*. Have a drink for my birthday!"

Oh, hell to the no!

Natalie had impeccable timing—because my stomach had just survived a ritual holocaust, and I wanted nothing more than to crawl into a grave and sleep off the trauma.

But hey, I'd taken mystery medicine from a stranger in a bathroom, so what's the worst that could happen?

"Sure. Why not..." I grumbled, taking a sip. *Holy shit!"* My hand flew to my mouth. I took another sip. *What the hell is this? Liquid heaven? Angel tears?* "Wowww," I muttered, still trying to process the mind-altering goodness swirling on my tongue.

Natalie grinned, leaning in. "Told you! Best food and drinks in town."

I turned toward the mystical beverage wizard himself—Raghid, standing a couple of tables away. "What's in this?"

He winked. "A secret family recipe. Passed down for generations," he threw a quick glance at the bartender. A subtle thumbs-up was exchanged.

These guys definitely had my vote!

For the first time on the entire trip, I felt invincible. Almost like Wolverine—impervious to pain, spicy food, and lactose intolerance alike. Nothing—absolutely nothing—could ruin this moment. Until... My stomach clenched.

A deep, sickening rumble.

Not again. I couldn't afford to have Natalie more pissed at me for running back and forth to the bathroom. I needed a plan. Fast. Another emergency trip? Industrial-strength Depends? Risk another public demolition of plumbing infrastructure? Or... a controlled release. A silent, ninja-like, stealth fart. Just a little one—to let the gas escape without raising alarms.

I lifted my ass slightly off my floor seat, angling just right to let one out. But at the last second of detonation, something felt wrong... A warm liquid trickled down my leg. *Oh shit...* **Literally.** *God, was this happening???*

My body went cold. Brain shut down. Muscles froze. I had maybe two minutes before the smell from my anal sludge hit the olfactory of everyone within a one-square-mile radius. *Escape plan. Now!* A voice echoed in my head.

I turned to Natalie, voice unnaturally casual. "Hey, babe... um... I think we should head back. You know, gotta get ready for later—"

Natalie frowned, taking another sip. "Babe, we were just starting to have fun—"

"Yeah! Yeah, I know! But we really should—"

And right on cue, Tony chimed in.

"Heyyy," he slurred, wearing that classic shit-faced grin. "We still have time for another round. Why are you being a buzzkill?"

NOOOOOOOOO! I internally screamed into the abyss as my veins pulsed with raw, unfiltered rage. All I wanted was to get out of here before my pants turned into a crime scene.

"One more drink, babe, pleeeease!?" Natalie pouted.

Damn it, woman! I clenched my jaw. Trapped. My only hope was to speed up the drinking process and flee before the biological fallout commenced. "Yeah! Why not? Just one drink," my voice sounded like someone had a gun to my head.

Natalie beamed. "I love you, Lorenzo Moretti!"

"Love you too!" I threw my hand in the air, a hostage negotiating his own ransom, then turned to my savior—Raghid.

"Tequila shots. NOW. And bring the check,"I said.

Tony's moist-ass voice cut through. "Since he's paying, make that a double for me!"

I just wanted him dead. I didn't argue.

Time was bleeding out, and disaster was seconds away. I scanned the room—where the hell did Raghid go?

A few agonizing beats passed... and finally, there he was, sauntering back with a tray of glasses like I wasn't on the verge of imploding. Glory be.

"Shots for everyone!" Raghid said, placing them on our floor table. We threw them back. I slammed my glass down, feeling the burn—but freedom was near.

I motioned to Raghid for the check, hoping to wrap this up before disaster struck. But with every passing second, the tension climbed.

And then—out of nowhere—Natalie sniffed the air.

Paused.

Sniffed again.

No, no, no… this was bad.

Her brows arched. "Do you smell that?"

My soul flatlined. This was it—the moment of reckoning. I panicked. "Whoops! Emergency work call—gotta take this. Outside!" I slapped my card on the table like it was part of the plan and slipped out the door just as the others were starting to rise—perfect timing with the check hitting the table. They trickled out a few beats behind me while my brain scrambled for a lifeline.

I needed a Hail Mary. Quick. I shoved my phone into my pocket, eyes cutting across the storefronts—heartbeat thumping, light snow flurries brushing against my face, like they were trying to rush me. The trio was already pushing out the door—voices getting louder, closer. And then—bam. Right there, my prayers were answered.

Just a little further down the block, half-sunk in shadow, stood the same clothing store Natalie mentioned earlier—the one with the sweater I'd been eyeing for months. Still open. Just barely. The lights flickered like they were about to hit the kill switch.

Natalie and the gang stepped out. I shoved my phone into my pocket before she could say a word, then I pointed, casual but desperate. "Hey, babe, real quick—I need that sweater. I've been thinking, I've been wanting to get it, so why not—"

"You mean the one you made a big fuss about? The one you said you didn't want anymore because it was old—"

"Yeah, that one. I changed my mind."

She crossed her arms. "Lorenzo, what has gotten into you!?"

More like… what's gotten out of me would be a more accurate assessment.

We headed into the clothing store while Tony and Kelly waited outside. I had to find a way to ditch Natalie… My eyes scanned the store—no changing rooms. Bathrooms closed. Why did God hate me today of all days?

I spotted them—new khaki pants, the same exact color as the ones I had on—folded neatly on the shelf directly across from the counter.

Behind the clerk, a mannequin stood slightly offset, modeling the sweater I'd been eyeing. Jackpot. "Hey, Babe," I said, pointing toward the nearest aisle lined with Hello Kitty panties. "Don't you like those? They're cute."

Her gaze followed my hand, landing on the shelf of cartoon-covered underwear. "They are cute," she smiled. "Let me go check them out," she muttered, already drifting toward the wooden pile of panties at the end of the first aisle—just a few feet from the counter.

She took the bait.

Not my finest work—and time definitely wasn't on my side—but I had maybe thirty seconds to pull this off.

I grabbed the pants from the shelf, stepped to the counter, and casually placed them down like it was all part of some normal errand. Gave the clerk a quick "hey," then glanced over my shoulder—I glanced over my shoulder—Natalie was still lingering by the aisle but starting to head back. Shit.

Panic.

I shoved the pants toward the clerk. "Give me the sweater too," I whispered. But the universe wasn't done screwing with me.

"Lorenzo?" Natalie's voice materialized out of thin air.

Smooth. I slipped the sweater over the pants and turned towards Natalie, leaning my back against the counter. "Hey, you," I said too cheerfully, turning to face her while casually leaning with my back over the counter—praying the situation in my underwear wasn't screaming louder than I was.

She wore her signature pout. "These are all teen sizes. Nothing fits my hips."

"—Are you sure, honey? I think they've got women's sizes right across from it," I said, pointing.

She turned to look. Perfect—her back to me again. I kept my face toward Natalie, leaned back further toward the clerk like a man disarming a bomb, and whispered, "Scratch the sweater—just give me the pants."

Natalie glanced back. "Nah, I checked. They only have kids sizes."

"Ohh, babe, that sucks," I muttered, hearing the beep of the register. The clerk bagged the item fast. I needed to disappear. Quickly. I tossed a wad of cash on the counter, grabbed the bag without looking, and headed for the exit.

"Sir!" the clerk called out just as we reached the door. "Do you want your change?"

Didn't even look back. "Keep it—it's a tip," I muttered as the door shut behind us.

We caught the last train back to the station lot. I had the bag in one hand as the car vibrated beneath us, metal wheels screaming through the tunnels. We crammed in with the late-night stragglers—most seats taken, a few of us left standing. The whole car pulsed with fluorescent buzz and body heat.

I stayed upwind from Natalie and Kelly, posted at the far end of the train car, one hand gripping the corner pole—my asshole in full pucker mode. They were seated in the middle row, side by side, heads tilted together in low conversation. Tony stood near them, leaning against the door by the exit, arms crossed, eyes fixed anywhere but on me.

Meanwhile, I was dying.

My eyes scanned the car—no clear path. The bathroom was all the way at the opposite end, past a dozen tired strangers swaying under flickering lights. I kept watch like a hawk, waiting for a shift in the crowd, a sliver of space—anything that'd let me slip away unnoticed.

Finally, the bathroom door opened. This was my chance. I moved backward, keeping my soiled side away from Natalie's view. But then. Natalie's eyes locked onto me.

"Where are you going, Lorenzo?"

"Just need to use the restroom. Be right back!" I said, already moving—slipping between bodies with barely a brush. I slammed the door shut behind me and ripped my pants off like they were on fire.

I was overwhelmed by the stench. Oh, dear God. I turned on the hot water and scrubbed my legs as if I were erasing a crime scene. Then I realized—no tissue. I grunted. I had no choice. I wiped myself with the clean side of my pants.

Dignity?

Dead.

Self-respect? Buried.

But survival? Still kicking.

Trash can? No where in sight.

And I needed to dispose of the evidence.

I wrapped my underwear inside the pants like a burrito and crammed it through the train's tiny bathroom window and let them fly onto the tracks.

Gone. Forever. I felt reborn. Small victories.

Then came the knock...

POUND—POUND—POUND!

"Hey, hurry up! There's a line out here!"

"—Okay, okay!" I shouted, grabbing my shopping bag off the cramped metal ledge by the sink and frantically tearing through it. And then, my heart stopped.

What was wrong with this picture? No pants. Only the sweater that I didn't want.

…

FFFUUUCCCCCKKKKKKKKK!

I wanted to scream, wanted to rip every goddamn strand of hair from my scalp. Another nightmare—inescapable, diabolical in every sense. *How the hell did the clerk mess that up? I clearly told her: pants only. No sweater. But she rang up the wrong thing anyway—and I had the nerve to leave a tip.*

Fuck me!

What the hell was I going to do? A few beats passed as I bit into the web of my hand—a weird little gesture we Italians did when our world went to shit.

My brain spiraled. *My options? Slim to none*

BAM. BAM. BAM!

Hard knocks rattled the door, snapping me out of it.

Perfect—more trouble!

There I was—bare ass on the cold tile, back jammed against the door like it was my last line of defense—

"Come on, man, hurry up! People are gonna piss themselves, and the line's growing—geez!" a gruff voice barked, loud enough to turn heads across the train.

Great. Just great.

For a fleeting moment, I actually considered squeezing through the tiny bathroom window. But yeah—if shoving my pants through it was a struggle, there was no way my shit coated and full-grown disaster of a body was going through it.

My phone buzzed. Natalie's face lit up the screen. I didn't answer. I just slumped onto the cold tile floor, bare skin pressed against the chill, sitting on top of that cursed sweater. I leaned back against the door, blocking it, tuning out the pounding fists, the buzzing phone, and the chaos inside my head. There was no easy way out. No backdoor escape. No do-over button. So I did what any rational, desperate man would do...

Deadpan

The train erupted in laughter the second I emerged—loud, contagious, merciless laughter. Even the babies were smiling. There I was—parading through the crowd like a low-budget Spartan, the too-small sweater wrapped around my waist, barely covering what needed to be covered. The hemline clung to my thighs as if it were fighting for its life. Phones came out. Someone yelled Worldstar. People smirked, giggled, shook their heads, quietly recording the spectacle. It was a viral moment waiting to happen.

But that wasn't the part that cut me. It was her. The moment my eyes found Natalie's, everything slowed. The noise faded. Time stretched out like an old film reel stuttering in a dusty projector. Her expression stopped me cold. The soft crease formed between her brows. Her lashes lowered like she couldn't bear to see me like this. The slight downturn of her lips—quiet, but loaded.

That look... that look wrecked me. Because it wasn't just embarrassment I saw. It was a look of disappointment. Hurt. Sadness. In that instant, I knew I'd done more than just ruin a night and a pair of perfectly good pants. I ruined *her* night. Her birthday trip. *And for what? Ego? Pride?* A pissing match with Tony? I lost sight of what mattered. *Her.*

Every step toward her felt heavier than the last. Her eyes stayed on me, distant now, like she was looking through a stranger. That frown didn't lift. Not once. I had good intentions. I swear I did. I've been trying to be the man she deserves—the one who puts her first. But right now? I was just the guy who embarrassed her. Hurt her. And no apology in the world felt big enough to fix that. I didn't feel like a man. I felt like less than shit. And I had no one to blame but myself.

Chapter SIX

THE BATHROOM STALL FROM HELL

As I stepped closer to Natalie and extended my hand, she swiftly slapped it away without hesitation. "Natalie, wait, I can explain," I pleaded, watching helplessly as she stormed off toward another cart, with Kelly hurriedly following behind her.

I sat in Natalie's seat because I couldn't afford to go chasing after her with a sweater tied around my pelvis. I looked down at my phone, but from the corner of my eye I caught Tony snickering by the train doors, phone aimed at me. I didn't have the energy to deal with his nonsense anymore. My mind was elsewhere, focused on how I would make things right with Natalie and explain everything to her.

Leaning back against the train seat, I avoided eye contact with anyone. I stared out at nothing—until a baby locked eyes with me. Instinctively, I waved and offered a faint smile. The moment was short-lived, though, as the mother caught sight of my gesture, quickly covering the baby's eyes and turning him away from me. Yep. Just kept getting better and better. I shut my eyes and sighed.

Eventually, Tony and I made it back to the hotel. But the second we stepped into the lobby, the stares started—piercing, relentless. Humiliation didn't even cover it. Multiply that by ten and we were getting warmer.

Kelly had texted us earlier—she and Natalie had arrived at the hotel about twenty-five minutes before us. And me? I'd forgotten I'd handed Natalie the car keys before we even made it to the restaurant. Meanwhile, Tony and I had been struggling to find a cab—unsurprisingly, no one was willing to pick up a half-naked man dressed like an ancient Roman. The ancestors would've disowned me on the spot.

To make matters worse, we were delayed even more when the police stopped us while we were trying to flag down a cab. They threatened to arrest me for indecent exposure, then laughed, handed me a warning, and even offered us a ride back to the hotel.

Although Natalie didn't want to leave the room after all the chaos, Kelly convinced her the night was still young. Against her better judgment, she agreed to go out for drinks at the Foxxhole, a club that stayed open until 4 a.m. I didn't care. Didn't want to go. All I wanted was to lie down and forget this night ever happened.

As we made our way to the elevator, I couldn't ignore the stares. Eyes met mine—some amused, some confused. Then came the cherry on top: three senior citizen women stepped in, all smiles. One of them even whistled at me, asked for my number, and invited me up for a "private chat." I forced a polite smile, declined, and silently begged the universe to let me erase this entire day.

After sliding the room keycard through the door, I kicked off my shoes, rushed into the shower, slipped into my pajamas, and collapsed onto the bed, staring up at the ceiling. I had maybe thirty seconds of peace before it ended.

"What are you doing, Lorenzo? Get dressed," she urged.

"I'm not going," my voice was steady. I didn't flinch—not even an inch.

Her arms hung by her sides, tense, as she loomed beside the bed. "First, you're going to tell me what happened to your pants and why you came out of the bathroom dressed like Julius Caesar."

I sighed, dragging a hand down my face. "Look, I made a mess of myself earlier at the Indian restaurant. I didn't want to upset you, so I tried to make light of it. Then, at the store, I told the clerk to ring me up for the pants, not the sweater. But she did the opposite."

Natalie stifled a chuckle, but a shit-eating grin still tugged at her lips.

"When I finally reached the train's bathroom, I tossed my pants out the window. And when I opened the bag, there it was—the sweater I didn't even ask for. And no pants."

That was it. She couldn't hold back anymore. Natalie erupted into laughter—loud, full, and unrestrained.

"—Oh, so you think this is funny, huh?" I asked, though a grin was already creeping onto my face.

"Yes! It's hilarious," she managed between laughs, wiping a tear from her eye.

"I… I thought you were upset with me—"

"I was at first. But now that I know what happened, it's epic," she said, still chuckling. "Lorenzo, you should've just told me. You always make things more complicated than they need to be."

She sat down on the bed, her laughter softening into a warm, affectionate smile. Reaching out, she gently touched my face. "I'm your wife. I'm with you every step of the way."

That hit me harder than I expected.

She had this way of reaching into places I didn't even know existed —pulling out the parts I'd buried, forgotten. With her, I didn't just feel whole. I felt seen. And this moment? I'd carry it forever—the kind that reminds you you're alive. And in love. Our eyes locked, steady and unguarded. No hesitation. No walls. Before I could stop myself, I blurted, "I love you, Mrs. Moretti."

She didn't say a word. Just leaned in, heart in her eyes. Our lips met—slow at first, then hungry. Heat curled in my chest, wrapping tight around the moment.

It wasn't just want. It was her. The only one who ever saw me come undone—and stayed. Her breath lingered on my skin. Sweet. Warm. Close enough to make me forget everything else.

She leaned back, a playful smile tugging at her lips as teeth grazed her bottom lip—teasing, almost impossible to resist. The moment hung between us, delicate and electric.

"Sure," I murmured, my voice low and strained. Each word chipped away at a piece of my very soul, leaving behind an ache too deep for expression. My eyes narrowed, not in defiance but in the quiet surrender of someone who had just lost something they didn't know they were holding.

Natalie rested her hand softly on my lap, her gaze piercing my existence. In that silent, charged moment, her voice cut through the stillness, filled with gravity and meaning: "Get dressed."

So, of course, I got dressed—watching as Natalie slipped out of the room and headed next door to finalize the pregame plans with Kelly. She left her phone behind, face up—lying on the bed, unlocked. I couldn't help but notice a few new followers on her social media account.

I told myself not to snoop. Especially after already seeing that handsome foreign guy with the scar across his forehead. But let's be honest—almost everyone, at some point, feels that pull. That curiosity about what their partner's up to when they're not around.

I'll admit, it was tempting. So maybe—accidentally—I picked up her phone. Just to flip it over. That's it. And what do you know? There he was. The same guy from her emails. Same smug face. A scar slicing across his forehead like a Bond villain. And now his screen name lit up the screen: "MarkTwain_Now_U_cum201."

What. A. Fucking. Creep!

Were people that desperate for attention on social media platforms? Had he been stalking my wife? Did she know him personally?

My thoughts were spinning when I suddenly heard the door creak open.

Panic.

Shit! I tossed her phone onto the bed like it bit me and scrambled to look casual—too casual. The harder I tried to act natural, the more stiff and suspicious I probably looked.

"Are you okay?" she asked, a subtle look of concern crossing her face. Before I could answer, Kelly and Tony stepped into view behind her—hovering just outside the doorway.

"Absolutely!" I stressed my words.

You guys know damn well that I wasn't fine. I had concerns, but I realize now that looking at her phone wasn't the right thing to do. Besides, he was just a follower on social media, not even a friend. I had plenty of followers myself that I didn't know, so maybe I was overreacting. After what happened today, I think it was best if I just stayed calm and didn't let this get to me. You know, play it cool.

"Hey there, Spartan," Tony said from the doorway, that smug grin stretched wide across his face. He took a step into the room—just enough to make his presence annoying—when Kelly elbowed him hard in the ribs. Her voice followed, low but sharp.

"Cut it out," she muttered, but I heard the bite anyway.

Tony winced, stifling a laugh as he turned away. Then, back at full volume, he grinned. "So… we are turning up tonight, or are we just standing around being awkward?"

I shrugged, grinning. "Hell yeah, let's do it. Tonight's all about bad choices and good liquor."

We had a game plan—just had to make a couple of stops first.

First stop? A drive-through liquor store. We grabbed a few drinks to kick things off.

Second stop? A tattoo parlor offering $70 flash tats—guaranteed to be done in under thirty minutes, or they were free. The girls decided they wanted tattoos, and naturally, us guys followed suit. I was buzzed and feeling adventurous.

Natalie? She went full fangirl. Got a small, precise tattoo on the back of her hand—Akira Nakamura, the anime character she loved from SPK. Pretty sure it was one of those deep-cut manga titles from Tenyu Studios or whatever. She was obsessed.

The others got tattoos of different main characters from the series, while Kelly—freshly inked a couple of weeks ago—was now getting a name cover-up in hers. I didn't see it, and I didn't care to. But me—I kept it basic: the Roman god Janus, two faces looking opposite directions, inked on my right forearm.

Funny thing—Tony chose two demon characters, inked right over his heart and neck. Fitting, honestly. A little too fitting. But yeah… I think I need a break from talking—or even thinking—about that guy for a while. He was an unnecessary pain in the ass. But just then, something else caught my attention.

Kelly got a phone call and immediately started acting weird. She stood up and stepped out of the tattoo parlor, glued to her phone, pacing back and forth outside the window.

It was probably another one of her "flings"—who knew? Kelly was always on the prowl, drawn to any unstable joker who showed the slightest interest. But that didn't concern me. I had her sister—the smart one, and that was all that mattered.

A few moments later, Kelly walked back in and sat down, a hint of disgust etched across her face.

"Who was that, sis?" Natalie asked as the tattoo artist carefully finished the small face on her hand.

"Chad's trifling ass," Kelly replied with a sharp edge in her voice.

Natalie paused, frowning, and momentarily stopped the artist to take a sip from her styrofoam cup filled with a potent mix of alcohol. "Girl, fuck him."

"—Exactly," Kelly agreed, slapping her sister's hand in a quick high-five.

Now, before anybody gets their panties in a twist—I know you're not supposed to drink or be pregnant while getting a tattoo. But these folks? Yeah, they had serious ex-felon energy, the kind that said rules were more like suggestions. No one cared. We were vibing and living our best, questionably legal lives.

And if you don't mind, I'd like to take this moment to snap some selfies with the ladies shamelessly.

"Photobomb!" I yelled, throwing my arms around their shoulders. My eyes were already starting to gloss over. Tony, of course, refused to be in any photo that wasn't on his phone—big surprise from a guy cheating on his wife with his pregnant fiancée.

But Kelly? She was quick on the trigger. Angled the shot just right and caught his guilty ass in the corner anyway. Also worth noting— Kelly had been our designated driver. And by "designated," I meant she had the aux plugged in and blasted music at skull-fracturing levels the entire way to the club.

Pretty sure my eardrums were still recovering. But none of that mattered. We'd all been caught up in the moment, having a great time.

And for a while, I almost forgot about the train incident... well, not quite but you catch my drift.

By the time we hit the block, the night had shifted gears. The club swallowed all of it the second we pulled up—Club Foxxhole. Looked like the entire damn state decided this was the only place on earth. Full-on Vegas Strip energy.

Neon lights lit up the street, bass shaking the pavement, and a crowd was already in full-blown party mode. Gorgeous women dressed to kill. Laughter was spilling out from the line. Drunk dudes trying to charm their way past the bouncers. Sleek luxury cars lined the curb; the entire block looked like a red carpet premiere.

We hopped out, dropped fifty on the valet, and headed into the scene. Up ahead, near the velvet rope, Tony stepped forward. Slipped the bouncer a thick wad of cash—finally paying for something—and just like that, we were in.

As soon as our shoes passed the threshold, the bass hit like a brick wall. Lights pulsed, blinding and nonstop. Heat radiating from every sweaty body packed on the dance floor. People grinding, groping, lips locked in a triangle, and three floors of madness—each one bumping a different beat.

The ceilings were ridiculously high, giving it cathedral-like dimensions. Speakers rattled the walls. Flat screens flashed footage from the camera drones overhead—couples losing themselves in rhythm, bodies tangled in pure, sweaty sin. It was two floors of mayhem, the upper level wrapped around in a square balcony so everyone below could look up and see the madness above—in the best way.

But upstairs? That's where the real circus was. VIP was a full-blown jungle—dudes popping magnum bottles, surrounded by women in outfits that might as well have been drawn on. Eyes hungry. Tables packed. Champagne was raining like it was payday for everyone.

Then came the waitresses—two of them, strutting toward us like sin on heels. Black leather clung to every curve, chokers tight at their throats, leashes hanging loose. Tony's eyes damn near fell out of his skull. I couldn't even be mad. They were stupid hot. *And me?* I had eyes for only one woman—

Natalie!

My wife. My fire. My calm. My chaos. The only woman in the room who could've killed me with a look and brought me back to life with a kiss.

We grabbed a table and ordered drinks, but Kelly shot Tony a sharp look. No words—just tension. He was smiling a little too long at one of the waitresses, and Kelly wasn't having it. Her mouth moved, tight-lipped, furious, but I couldn't hear anything over the blaring music. And honestly, I didn't care because Natalie had just grabbed my wrist and pulled me onto the dance floor.

Her hips moved to their own rhythm, and my hands kept the beat. Every sway, every grind, every spin—she owned it, and I was just lucky to orbit in her gravity. The heat. The bass. The alcohol was still working its magic from earlier. Everything else disappeared. It was just me, her, and the beat, lost in the moment, wild and free.

While we tore up the dance floor, a waitress slid over, eyes twinkling, and handed us our drinks with a knowing smirk. Natalie was all over me—twerking that curvy ass, hypnotising me.

I bet a lot of you didn't know some of us White boys had rhythm, huh? But let's be honest—you guys could hear my thoughts.

My hand gripped her hip as the bass pounded harder, the heat rising with every move. The crowd blurred and lights melted and in that moment, it was just her and me—flames licking at our skin, burning down the room one beat at a time.

After a few minutes of showing out, Mrs. Moretti and I stepped aside to catch our breath, greeted by high-fives, whistles, and cheers. The club's cameras had seen the whole thing, throwing our performance onto the big screens as we made our way back to our seats. The DJ gave us a shoutout. Spotlights hit.

And for a second, it felt damn good being back in the limelight. I was used to it—from my days as a star quarterback. Natalie… She used to be a cheerleader in college, though she said that phase was rough. Lots of parties. Too many bad influences. Some drugs.

But—who *didn't* experiment in high school or college? If you didn't, that's great. But let's be real—no one was writing your name in the yearbook margins.

The atmosphere was electric. Eyes followed us from every corner of the club, even up in VIP. The same waitress reappeared and led us to a prime booth near the corner—sleek leather couches, a modern fireplace embedded in an abstract glass table, and a few others already posted up, sipping and vibing.

We exchanged polite nods and casual greetings. No drama. Just good energy. Natalie and I melted into the circular sectional like royalty. She leaned into me, that playful smirk dancing on her lips. I wrapped my arm around her, pressed a soft kiss to her mouth, and just looked at her. Everything about the moment was perfect.

The vibe? Untouchable. Music thumping at just the right tempo, neon lights swirling overhead like we were floating inside a dream. Picture that, get the image stuck in your head real nice. And look at me now. For a second, it felt perfect. But the magic was fleeting.

Out of the corner of my eye, I spotted Kelly walking up, carrying two drinks pressed to her chest with her forearm. I froze as I saw her drop something—a pill—into both drinks.

Kelly tried to enter our section but was stopped by a bouncer. I glanced around, realizing Tony wasn't with her. I briefly wondered where he could be, but then reminded myself of his character and decided it wasn't worth dwelling on. I was moving on.

"She's with us," Natalie shouted, striding over to the bouncer and grabbing the drink from Kelly.

The second I saw that, I was on my feet. I stormed over, pulled Kelly aside—low, controlled, but burning. "What the hell do you think you're doing?" I hissed. "I saw you slip something in her drink. What the hell was that?"

Natalie slapped my hand away from Kelly's arm. "Hey! Don't grab my little sister—and don't talk to her like that!"

My eyebrows shot up faster than a speeding bullet. "Wait! Huh!?" I said with my hand halfway raised, as if I were unsure what to do next.

"We do this all the time," Kelly shouted over the music, her eyes narrowing as if I were clueless, for only now realizing that my wife had been using drugs right under my nose.

And of course I was an idiot.

The news hit me like a punch from Mike Tyson, knocking the wind out of me. I staggered back a step, though maybe the alcohol amplified the impact. Still, I felt betrayed. We never kept secrets from each other —at least, that's what I believed.

I leaned in, close enough to feel her hair against my cheek, and murmured near her ear, "Be straight with me... do you and your sister pop pills?" I pulled back slightly, locking eyes with her, waiting for her to meet my gaze before she answered.

"Relax, Lorenzo. It's just birthday fun. Not like I do this every weekend," Natalie's voice carried a sharp edge of annoyance.

Kelly sneered. "Bro, why don't you chill out? We're grown ass women—"

"—Why don't you mind your goddamn damn business, Kelly!" I snapped, struggling to keep my voice steady.

"Lorenzo. You need to back the hell off," Natalie responded sharply, grabbing my arm firmly.

"Natalie, seriously? You gave me a hard time about smoking a cigarette in the car, but you're not worried about your sister popping pills while she's pregnant? And who knows what's even in those things?"

"I'm only a few weeks—my body, my choice," Kelly said, venom laced in every word.

I was stunned. Not because I was surprised—they'd been reckless all night—but because Natalie knew, and said nothing. And Kelly? She was treating this baby like a minor inconvenience.

My eyes studied Natalie one last time. Then she chugged the drink. Right in my face. Disbelief. Disgust. Betrayal. I turned away, lips tight. "I'm going to the washroom," I muttered and stormed off before I said something I couldn't take back.

The moment I stepped outside, I realized I didn't even need to pee —I just needed air and a damn cigarette. Patted my pockets. No lighter.

Across the street, two women leaned against a graffiti-tagged brick wall beneath a buzzing neon sign. Smoke curled from their lips, heels swinging from their fingers, laughter drifting between drags. I crossed over, hands in my pockets, shoulders tense.

"Hey, mind if I borrow a light?'" One of them handed it over without missing a beat. I lit up, took a long drag, let the burn settle the chaos in my chest. Exhaled slowly. Time slipped by. I checked my phone—almost midnight. I had to head back inside. For Natalie's birthday. Whether I liked it or not.

And Tony? He had a right to know what his girl was doing to that unborn baby. *Snitches get stitches?* Screw that. This wasn't about drama —this was about the kid. And I wasn't keeping my mouth shut.

I headed back inside. The club was still rocking, so I made a beeline for the restroom before I exploded. Luckily for me, the people milling around weren't actually in line. Just as I reached the door, it swung open and some guy shot out, damn near running.

What the hell was his problem?

I found a urinal, unzipped, and had just started to relieve myself when I heard it—moaning. Rhythmic, loud, flesh slapping. Jesus! At the far end of the washroom, the last stall in the corner rattled— someone was going to pound-town. At first, I smirked. But something was off. The sounds—grunts, snorts, sniffing—started to shift. Wrong tempo. Wrong energy. Curiosity prickled.

I zipped up and crept toward the stall, leaning in to peer through the thin slit between the door and frame. My breath caught.

It was Tony!

Bent over. Getting his ass cheeks clapped by a short Asian guy with a mohawk. A thin white line smeared across the back of his hand. Nostrils flaring. I froze. Brain locked.

"What the fuckkkkkk?" I whispered.

The guy paused. "What was that noise?"

Shit!

I scrambled back—too late. The stall door slammed open, cracking me in the face and sending me sprawling across the floor. "Owwww!" I winced, tasting blood. Pain screamed behind my eyes.

That moment? Marked the beginning of the absolute worst night of my life.

The little treasure troll of a man narrowed his gaze as he approached, yanking up his underwear. "Do you know this fucking pervert?"

Tony exploded. "What the hell, Lorenzo? Why are you spying on me?"

I rubbed my face. "I wasn't spying on you—"

The troll's voice cut in, high-pitched and full of mischief. "Umm, seriously? What do you call someone creeping through the stall while two people are fucking?"

"Good point," I muttered, rising from the floor, cradling my aching head, vision still spinning.

"'Why are you even here?' Tony snapped, his voice carrying the slightest tremor."

"—In what? A public restroom?" I said, grabbing some paper towels from the dispenser next to the sink.

Tony's voice dropped low. "You better not say anything about this to Kelly, or else—"

"Or else *what?*" I shot back, stepping toward his doughy, half-naked body—his shriveled pink sausage dangling like regret.

The wiry man slid between us with the grace of a panther, his eyes flicking over me as his slender fingers brushed my chest—subtle, calculated. "Now, now, boys. There's enough of me to go around. No need to fight."

"Pass," I deadpanned. "I don't swing that way."

"Well… you did just watch two gay men go at it," he said, flashing a devilish smile.

"That was an accident—I thought it was a straight couple—"

"I'm not gay," Tony blurted, fumbling with his pants—avoiding eye contact.

The man's gaze snapped to him, sharp as a whip. He crossed his arms, one brow raised like a silent challenge. Then he turned to me again, smirking like he'd just won something we didn't know we were playing.

"I'm done with this," I growled, flinging my hands up. The bathroom door slammed behind me, loud enough to rattle the damn walls.

"Come back now, y'hear," the Mohawk gremlin called out. Tony's voice echoed behind me. "I'm not gay!"

"Of course you're not," the man teased, grinning as he pulled Tony back into the stall by the wrist. The door clicked shut behind them. "Let's finish what we started."

Round one wasn't over.

Chapter SEVEN

RED LIGHT, GREEN RAGE

shoved my way through the crowded club, the pulsing lights and sweaty bodies pressing in from every direction. But something was off—Natalie and Kelly were nowhere in sight. I scanned the room, checked the bar, the booths, and even the dance floor. Nothing. I asked a few people in our private section, but they blew me off.

The plan was to pull Tony aside, confront him about Kelly, and give him a heads-up—but the washroom scene had erased every coherent thought from my brain. But at this point, I just wanted to return to the hotel with Natalie and pretend this day had never happened. It hadn't even been 24 hours since we landed, and already I'd been mistaken for a Roman stripper, assaulted by a stall door, and caught in a gay porno plot twist.

Now, as if the universe hadn't had its fill, I stood just outside the crush of bodies swarming the packed bar, my shoulder brushing a sticky column, and called out Natalie's name—but the music throbbed so loudly, I doubted she'd hear it. So I pulled out my phone and fired off a few texts. No response. Not even a read receipt.

The bartender leaned across the bar again—second time now—and shouted something I couldn't quite make out. Probably asking if I wanted a drink. I shook my head.

Perception was a funny thing. When you were drunk, everything felt electric. You were part of the noise. But when you were sober and surrounded by idiots slurring their words and dry-humping couches? You just wanted to punch someone in the throat.

"Fuck it," I muttered. Then leaned into the bartender. "Double shot of Patrón—"

"Coming right up!" the bartender chirped, shaking those bottles. Shirt snug. Leather pants tighter. He moved like a hawk dancing into a chicken coop, swiping my card with the finesse of a man who's stolen hearts and wallets.

I took the shot in one clean pull. It burned—sweet, sharp, perfect. For a moment, I felt it—the buzz, the fire in my veins, the silence in my head. Then the spell broke. Because up on the VIP balcony, in a flash of blue and red light, I saw her. Natalie. *And right next to her?* Some fit guy with a hat on. Couldn't make out his face from this distance.

My heart raced as I watched them together, a mix of disbelief and fury bubbling inside me. The same gut-deep feeling I'd had right before loading Kelly's bags settled over me again

What the hell was Natalie doing with that guy?

I moved on instinct, legs cutting through the crowd while my knuckles clenched so tight they ached. Weaving between bodies, I started climbing the stairs to the VIP section—where a lineup of questionable characters loomed, each one stamped with jailhouse ink and the kind of energy that said they'd done time and didn't regret it.

My eyes snapped to two bouncers—tall, jacked, dreadlocks swinging—posted near the upstairs bar. As I pushed through the narrow stairwell, they broke off and shifted toward the entrance. Pure intimidation. Old-school. Straight-up WWE.

I burst out of the stairwell onto the VIP floor, barely a few steps in before they blocked my path. My shoulders squared, eyes locking with both of them. "My fucking wife's in there," I snapped. "I need to see her. Now."

Both bouncers let out low chuckles, trading a look before turning back to me, grins spreading wide. "If your girl is in there, that's 'cause she wanna be," the shorter one said, flashing a gold tooth. "Ain't nobody makin' her stay, you feel me?"

"—Look, I don't want any trouble. I just need to get my wife so we can leave, that's all."

The bouncer swaggered my way, carrying enough menace to start a bar fight without even opening his mouth. Just as the tension reached its peak, his partner—a towering figure with a thick Caribbean accent—intervened.

"Hold up, bredren," he commanded, exuding authority that was impossible to ignore. "Yo mon! Wha did yuh say your wife's name is?"

I cleared my throat. "Natalie. Her name's Natalie." I eased up a little.

These guys weren't just big—they were built from brawls: scars and cauliflower ears told the story. You don't get that in a gym. I was just glad one of them had the sense not to escalate—for both our sakes.

"Wait here," he said, disappearing into a shadowed corner on the far left—half-concealed behind smoked glass and a faint strip of LED glow crawling along the floor.

I nodded, but the shorter bouncer's gaze stayed locked on me—sharp, restless, like he was itching for an excuse. Around us, a few people in the section had started to notice.

After a few moments, he walked back over to me and said, "There's no Natalie in there. I'm sorry, mon—but you gotta leave."

Rage simmered just beneath my skin. I locked eyes with the bouncer, jaw tight. "I'm not going anywhere until my wife's with me. I saw her inside," I snapped, teeth grinding. I was ready.

Before I could move, the shorter bouncer grabbed my collar and slammed me back, pinning me against the velvet-paneled wall near the corridor entrance—just outside the roped-off lounge. Bottles rattled on the nearby table, and a hookah tipped sideways as startled guests snapped their heads toward us.

With sharp precision, I struck the pressure points in his forearms—quick hits that broke his grip clean. No hesitation. I followed with a cupped-hand clap to both ears—a thunderous crack that knocked him off balance.

He dropped to one knee, yelping loud enough to turn every head in the room. Phones flew up. Eyes locked in. The crowd was hooked.

Then came the taller bouncer—eyes blazing, muscles twitching, fury in every step. He was fast. Too fast for his size. Built like a heavyweight, but moved like a jaguar. I could feel it radiating off him—he wanted blood.

As he lunged, I snapped a vicious kick into his chest, sending him reeling backward—right into his partner's path. That brief collision was all I needed.

The shorter bouncer recovered quickly and charged. His punch crashed through the space where my head had been a second ago. I parried, twisted, and threw him off balance.

He stumbled. I struck a knife-edge chop to the back of his neck. He buckled. I caught his arm, twisted it forward, and slammed my palm down on his elbow, quick and hard.

The snap didn't come—but I felt the strain. A sick bend, right at the edge. He dropped. I didn't want to hurt him. At least, that's what I kept telling myself. But something inside me had cracked open—something I couldn't seal back up. A deep, molten rage long buried beneath fake smiles and swallowed words was bubbling to the surface.

Maybe all the shit I never said to people—everything I'd ever held back—was coming out now, not in words, but in bone and blood and violence. There was something sinister waking inside me. Something primal. Something old. And I wasn't sure I could stop it anymore.

Through the madness, I heard my name—splitting the noise like a blade.

"Lorenzo, stop it! What do you think you're doing!?" Natalie shoved through the crowd, fists clenched, eyes blazing. Fear and fury in one look.

I wanted to stay calm—God, I tried. Told myself again and again not to lose it. Not to yell. However, after everything that happened today, I was hanging on by a thread. A single, fraying thread soaked in gasoline—and lit on both ends.

My patience? Gone. My dignity? Burned alive hours ago. And now she was standing there, screaming at me like I was the villain? I paid for over half of her sister and Tony's hotel room—no thanks. Covered the dinner bill—no acknowledgment. Every damn minute of this trip had drained my wallet and my pride.

But the cherry on this steaming shit sundae? She made me apologize to

Tony. And for what? For warning his dumb-ass about a mountain lion? For saving him while he flailed like a Walmart mannequin in a windstorm? And I'm the bad guy?

Nah. I was done. Done being the peacemaker. Done catering to her bratty moods and her entitled sister. I've had enough of biting my tongue just to keep the peace. She had pushed me to the edge—and now? I wasn't stepping back.

"Get your things, we're leaving. Now." I growled, holding his elbow to the edge, tendons straining under my grip. His eyes went wide, sweat breaking as he winced.

"Let him go! What's gotten into you!?" she yelled, storming toward me, heels snapping against the floor as she shoved my hands off the bouncer's arm.

—What's gotten into me? That's what she wanted to know—seriously?

In one swift motion, I delivered a well-placed, gentle knee to the bouncer's face. His body crumpled to the ground in an almost graceful collapse, as if I had laid him to rest.

"Stay down," I snapped—more to the chaos inside me than to him. I grabbed her wrist, turned, and pulled. "Let's go, Natalie."

Those three words tore from my lips, sharp with frustration—as cameras flashed and phones clicked, catching the moment in bursts of blinding light. I nearly flinched like a vampire caught in daylight. The glare was threatening to drive me back into the shadows.

Kelly came charging out from the back, eyes blazing, with the same guy I'd seen at the airport right behind her—the same guy from Natalie's emails. "Let go of my sister, you bastard!" she shouted, stepping between us. "You're hurting her. Let her go, now. Lorenzo."

I sent her a withering glare. I'd had more than enough of her irritating ass for one day. I was about to fire back, but a voice cut in smoothly.

"Oi, mate," the man said, stepping forward. Australian accent. Dressed head to toe in black. Kangol tilted just right. "That's no way to treat a lady."

Something in his tone—something behind those eyes—made my hand drop from Natalie's arm. I didn't mean to. It was like instinct took over. But then I stepped forward. Closed the gap between us. Invaded his space. Dared him.

The air around us tightened, every second stretching like a taut wire. We stood eye to eye—both around 5'11"—but that's where the similarities ended. I was 170, lean but scrappy. *Him?* Built like a weapon. Compact muscle, smooth posture, the kind of presence that said: I've done worse than fight.

A chill crept down my spine. Something about this guy... wasn't right. Perhaps he'd carved someone open before. But none of it mattered—not when the blood was boiling in my ears.

My hand knotted into a fist, and I surged forward. I shoved him. Hard. He staggered back just a couple of steps. Just enough. His kangol went flying, smacking the floor beside him with a slap that echoed louder than it should've. Time slowed as he bent to retrieve it. And that's when I saw it—a scar. Thick. Jagged. Snaking down his scalp.

My breath caught.

That was him. The guy from Natalie's DMs. The face from the email on the laptop. That scar. *Who was this guy? Better yet—what was he? Ex–special ops? A hitman? Mobbed-up muscle? A walking nightmare with a passport?*

My thoughts collided. Alarms screamed through me. Then—he did it. Drew out a long suck-your-teeth, that Caribbean hiss of disdain, sharp as a curse. History in the sound. Pain practiced into habit. This wasn't just a stranger. This was a warning—wrapped in human skin.

Natalie and Kelly stood between us, like a bright duo bridging the space with their presence, drawing all attention toward them.

"You'd better get your boy before I put a good whipping on his arse —" he barked.

"—Come do it then, tough guy!" I spat, rising to my full height. My chest puffed out as I spread my arms broad, wings of a pissed-off American eagle.

My stance screamed defiance. Daring him to take the next step. I wasn't backing down. Not anymore. Not from anyone.

In front of me, Natalie's voice cracked through the air.

"Leave... now!" she snapped, voice shaking as her finger stabbed toward the corridor.

Her pitch? Furious—laced with a rage sharp enough to cut through steel. The kind of voice that could silence a room... or command an army.

But me? I stood frozen. Not from fear—but disbelief. Was she really talking to me like this? My wife. My soulmate. My college sweetheart.

That voice—once the sound that made the world fade away—now sliced through me like a blade. Cold. Final.

I used to know how her eyes lit up just for me. The curve of her laugh. The softness in her touch. But now? All I saw were walls—brick by brick, built between us.

How did we get here?

I remembered the way she used to say my name—like it was sacred. Like I was home. Now she couldn't even look at me. This was the same woman who promised me forever. Who held my hand through hell. And now she was slipping through my fingers—piece by piece.

Maybe I'd seen the signs. The quiet pauses. The way her eyes didn't linger. The way she looked through me, not at me. But I never wanted to believe it.

Not her. Not us. I kept replaying it, trying to trace the moment I started losing her. And now—here, in this club, surrounded by strangers—I finally saw it: the woman I loved was an illusion. And maybe... love was, too.

My shoulders caved under the weight of it. "Honey... please," I whispered. "I'm sorry. Let's just go back to the hotel and talk. Please."

There was no anger, no sharpness in my tone. Only desperation—the kind that comes when you know everything could slip away with one more wrong word. But beneath the apology was the quiet, unspoken fear—maybe this time, words wouldn't be enough to pull us back.

She glared at me—eyes sharp, voice cold. "No, I'm not going anywhere with you! Now suddenly you want to talk?" She shook her head. "To talk about what exactly, Lorenzo? Every time I try to get you to open up, you shut down. You never actually say what you're thinking, and I'm always the one asking. You're so wrapped up in your own head, and honestly, something is seriously wrong with you. I can't do this anymore. I can't do you, anymore."

Club drone cameras hovered above, catching our faces—transmitting our wreckage to the screens around us.

I reached out, my hand trembling, but she pulled away. "Please… don't do this," I whispered, voice cracking. "I need you. I don't know what to do without you."

She turned to walk back to the section.

And I couldn't help but wonder—will I ever hear her say I love you again?

Or was this how our story ended? I didn't even care if she was seeing him. I just wanted my wife. I stepped after her, reaching out again—but my words and actions were cut short.

The man's voice cut sharp, seizing the tension. "Don't you bloody touch her!" he snarled, his accent thick with fury. With a slow, deliberate motion, he adjusted his hat, tilting the brim just enough to cast a shadow over his narrowed eyes.

Even the air felt thin, suffocating, as if the room itself was holding its breath while security rushed in from every crack and crevice. I hadn't known how tight the net was here, but I stood my ground, every inch of me coiled and ready.

"Just fucking leave!" Natalie snapped, turning to face me standing by the glass divider. Her voice pierced straight through me.

My teeth dug into my bottom lip as the weight of defeat settled over me. I didn't need to look up to feel Kelly's presence beside her, the smug grin barely hidden on her face.

My hand trembled as I reached into my pocket, pulled out the rental car key, and placed it on the nearby table. No words were left; they'd be wasted. I stepped back, the silence heavy between us. Every part of me wanted to lash out, to hit him, but the cameras were rolling, and I couldn't afford another public scene. Not again. The thought of lawsuits and more humiliation held me back. So, I swallowed the anger, tucked in my pride, turned away, and walked toward the stairs; of course, security trailed close behind me.

Each step felt like a surrender, breaking my spirit a little more the further I walked, as people covered their mouths, looking on as I took the walk of shame.

As I was being escorted from the club, the men's washroom slowly opened up, and a familiar face peered at me. It was Tony.

"Hey, what's going on, little guy—' that smug grin didn't get the chance to land.

My fist did.

WHAM!

Right in the fucking eye. My fist drove into his socket, snapping his head back. That smug look didn't last. One punch, and he was flat on his ass, scrambling like a dropped puppet across the bathroom floor.

That punch? It wasn't just a hit—it was a message. A message written in already-bloodied knuckles: not to fuck with me. I was tired of his shit. And yeah, the cameras caught it. Yeah, I could get sued.

But was it worth it?

You bet your ass it was!

You all know Tony—he had it coming.

Of course, after that, security tossed me out on my ass fast—right through the doors. But still, a small victory for Lorenzo Moretti.

"That's why everyone will remember my name," I whispered, a sly grin curling on my lips as I staggered to my feet.

Beyond the glass, onlookers stared—curious, cautious—as I rose from the cold embrace of concrete.

Chapter *EIGHT*

HOPE

Snowflakes clung to my hair like tiny messengers. The first whispers of snowfall had arrived, but it carried more than cold. The world felt paused. Still, like something irreversible had just happened.

Natalie made her choice. Turned her back on everything we built. Choose him over me. Anger burned through me so fast, I forgot the only question that mattered—*how long had she been hiding this? Sneaking around with that smug Aussie? The betrayal cut deep. And the worst part? I never saw it coming. Or maybe I did… and just didn't want to believe it.*

Denial was a powerful force, especially in relationships. It seeped into everything. Blinded you and made you hold on to the very thing that would break you.

And that guy?

Strutting around like he was God's gift, hat tilted just so— "Don't talk to a woman like that, mate!" I mocked, should've popped him on principle. *But why?*

He wasn't the one who betrayed me. I wasn't married to him. Natalie was the one who made promises. Vows. The kind that were supposed to mean something. We were supposed to be a team—ride or die. I guessed not everyone valued loyalty the same.

And now that I thought about it… they said a drunk mind spoke a sober heart. Yeah, she had been holding onto this for a while.

I thought I was doing everything right—perfect husband material. Yet here I was, out in the snow, gutted. How the hell did I end up the one who got shit on?

Part of me wanted to storm back in, throw it all back in her face. But maybe that was just my pride talking. Perhaps I just needed to call a ride, get the hell out of there, head back to the hotel, clear my head, and warm up my fingers before they snapped off.

My fingers, frozen stiff, fumbled with my phone and booked a ride. No way I was going back inside that club—not after everything. I waited outside a neon-lit coffee shop. Mannequins posed in the window—assless chaps, sailor hats, glitter smeared across plastic abs. Perfect. My night just kept getting better.

The driver pulled up a few minutes later. Didn't matter—I was too checked out to care. The backseat already held a drunk couple, slurring through the same story twice before throwing up over my shoes.

I ended up riding shotgun with a service dog in the front—a massive golden retriever sprawled like royalty, drool glistening on the upholstery. *But you know what?* I didn't mind. Dogs were honest. Loyal. Creatures with eyes too pure to lie. They didn't care about status, money, or who you pretended to be. Their love was simple. Real. And somewhere along the way… I'd lost that kind of trust, especially with my wife.

My eyes kept drifting to my phone, hoping for a message. An apology. A sign she still cared. But it never came. That kind of thing only happened in movies.

Midnight came instead. When I finally reached the hotel, the front doors hissed open, spilling me into a lobby scented with polished marble and floral air freshener. The space was quiet, dimly lit, with just a night clerk at the desk scrolling on his phone behind the counter.

I made my way toward the elevators—head low, shoes echoing softly off the tile. That's when I heard it—jazz. Faint, smooth, drifting in from deeper inside the building. Notes curled through the air. Warm and inviting. Out of place in the cold weight I'd been carrying all night.

My ears caught the sound and pulled me toward a wide-open doorway near the back of the lobby. Low golden light spilled from within, and the soft clink of glasses added to the hush. I paused at the threshold, peering in at the hotel lounge.

Sparse crowd. A few scattered guests at small tables, nodding along to the music. A bartender was cleaning a glass behind the counter. Thick carpets. Velvet chairs. Everything was too plush for how I felt—but for the first time that night, I didn't feel like bolting.

I lingered, listening and letting it wrap around me. For a moment, I almost forgot why I was there in the first place. Eventually, I stepped inside. The light was soft. The air was warm. I made my way to the bar and slid onto a stool, ordered a beer, and chased it with a few shots of tequila, raising it quietly in a toast to Natalie for her birthday.

By the third shot, I was an emotional wreck. Then she walked up—

Bronze skin. Long curls. Eyes that could've lit a cigarette just by staring too hard—a goddess, dropped in the middle of assholes and stale bar talk.

The bar fell silent—at least in my head—as she slid onto the stool beside me.

"What's a handsome guy like you doing in a place like this, all alone?" she asked, running her fingers through her curls, her voice smoother than the tequila I'd been drowning in.

I smiled, but the pain behind it was hard to hide. "Well, I could ask you the same thing."

"Touche," she chuckled softly, reaching into her purse. "What are you drinking?"

"Tequila," I answered, staring into the empty void of the shot glass.

"Not my thing," she said, signaling the bartender with a flick of her hand. She leaned in slightly, her shoulder brushing mine. "What's your name, handsome?"

I hesitated for a second, not ready to spill everything to this stranger.

Think fast.

"Uh… uh… Rick. Yeah, it's Rick."

Why 'Rick'? Probably because I'd been binge-watching The Walking Dead again.

"Rick?" she repeated, raising an eyebrow as she studied me. A grin spread across her face. "Alright, Rick. I'm Esperanza."

She leaned toward the bar, her arm brushing mine as she flagged the bartender. "Two shots of Jameson—for me and my friend here."

Then she turned back, that playful glint still dancing in her eyes. "You've gotta try Jameson. It's better than whatever you've been punishing yourself with."

I chuckled, easing into my seat as the bartender poured our drinks.

We talked for a while, letting the conversation flow easily, trading laughs, taking sips between stories.

When the shots came, I raised mine with her. To my surprise, the Jameson went down smoothly. Maybe it was the company. But for the first time all night... I could get used to this.

A little over an hour had passed, and the hotel bar was starting to close. We were among the last remaining. Maybe we'd lost track of time, caught up in the moment—or perhaps we just didn't care. Either way, the night had been a breath of fresh air I hadn't realized I needed.

We got up and stumbled out of the lounge, still laughing like teenagers. The lobby was quieter now—just a sleepy clerk at the front desk and the soft hum of distant jazz fading behind us. We made our way across the marble floor, arms brushing, steps unsteady.

We stepped into the elevator. I tapped the button for my floor—the elevator was moving—then I turned to her.

"What's your floor?"

To my surprise, she said two floors below mine. I smiled, glancing at my phone—no messages from Natalie. My stomach twisted a little, but I ignored it, focusing on the moment.

The elevator slowed as we neared her floor, but before I could step aside, I realized we'd missed it. "Hey, you missed your floor," I said, turning to her.

She grinned mischievously, her eyes locking onto mine. "No, I didn't," she whispered, and suddenly I felt her hands pushing me against the elevator wall.

Her lips crashed into mine, and then, with a playful squeeze of my ass, I was caught between the thrill of the moment and the guilt brewing beneath the surface.

At that moment, the air between us felt electric, every touch sparking with a dangerous mix of excitement and hesitation.

Was it wrong? Of course it was, but it felt too right to stop.

The elevator chimed. The doors slid open. We stumbled into the hallway, barely breaking stride. She grabbed my jacket, pulled me with her, and her lips crushed against mine again.

By the time we reached my door, I was already breathless. She slammed me against it, hands in my hair, mouth on my neck. It was the kind of moment you'd see in the movies-drenched in heat, reckless, and hungry.

I fumbled for my card key, heart pounding in my ears. My fingers slipped. The phone hit the floor with a dull thud. But Esperanza didn't miss a beat.

With a sly smile, she crouched down to grab the phone—then paused. Her lips brushed my zipper. Slowly, deliberately, she unzipped my pants with her mouth, her eyes never leaving mine—full of intent.

My breath faltered, head tilting back against the door. I was frozen in that heady moment—every nerve in my body screaming for more—until a flash of reality hit. Natalie. My wife!

Still… guilt had a way of hitting you when your pants were down. And your penis was up.

I had to check the room first to make sure she wasn't in there—catching me in the act. *But why in the hell should I even care? She has already made her decision.* I damn near stumbled, darting through the massive hotel suite to make sure that the coast was clear.

Empty.

"Good. She's not in here," I muttered, heading over to the bed as Esperanza made her way toward it.

She scrolled my screen. "Who's Kelly?" she asked, eyes on my phone as she sat down, still holding it in her hand.

One unread message. From Kelly. My thumb hovered before I took the phone from her hand and tossed it onto the bed, face down. Didn't want to deal with her either—not right now.

"Nobody at all," I said, pulling Esperanza close, my hands gripping her waist as our lips met again, harder this time, more urgent.

She stood, turned, and pushed me onto the bed—straddling me. Her underwear clung to one leg, barely hanging on, as she tore at my clothes.

She was classy and slutty at the same time—a combo I could never resist. Horny, fun, and the only damn thing that felt right in the suffocating mess my life had become. Gorgeous didn't even cover it. *So why the hell couldn't I get an erection? Did Natalie hex me? By Voodooing my manhood?"*

A soft sob cut through my spiraling thoughts.

I turned. Esperanza had shifted to the edge of the bed, one hand over her mouth, shoulders trembling. Moonlight rested across her face, catching the glint of tears she didn't want me to see. I blinked, sat up, pulled on my briefs, and slid beside her. "What's the matter, Esperanza?"

She shook her head, her fragile voice cracking with dejection. "You—you don't like me."

Her Paisa accent—God, even now, it turned me on. I know, wrong moment—but come on. Honest emotion and a sexy Colombian accent? Bellissimo. Even if that's Italian.

"What? No, I like you. I do." I reached for her hand as she turned to me, her tear-streaked face defiant.

Her eyes met mine, steady. "Then why don't you fuck me!?"

Well damn… her words were bold, hitting me square in the chest.

I squeezed her hand, fingers lacing with hers. "Oh, trust me—I do wanna fuck you. But right now, my heads, both of them, are all messed up… thinking about her."

She wiped her tears away, her expression softening. "Natalie, right? The one you mentioned back at the lounge?" She asked, wiping the tears from her eyes.

I nodded. "Yep, that's her name. Natalie." I barely whispered, my lips curled in as I placed my hands on my knees, feeling my heart break just a little more as I said her name out loud.

Esperanza looked at me, quiet for a beat, then gave me a small, sad smile.

"You're a good man. She should be celebrating you—not making you feel like shit.

My throat tightened. "Sometimes, we good men finish last." My head felt heavy, and I couldn't lift my gaze from the floor. Her fingers threaded through my hair, gentle but firm.

"Hey," she said, her voice a little steadier now. "If she can't see you for who you are, someone else will. I would. I do. I see you, Rick."

I smiled despite myself, the weight in my chest lifting a little.

"And if she ever hurts you again…" she grinned, a wicked gleam settled over her eyes, "I'll kick her ass."

I chuckled, but I knew she wasn't joking and meant every word of it. Our lips met again, slower this time, a lingering kiss that tasted bittersweet. This was goodbye, and we both knew it. She pressed her lips to my forehead, a gesture so tender it broke me.

Esperanza stood, slipping into her clothes with quiet grace. I followed her to the door, unsure of what to say, yet unwilling to let her leave. I handed her my phone. She handed it back with a smile and a prayer emoji next to her name.

"My name means Hope in English," she said, her smile lighting up her face. Not a mark on those teeth.

"I know," I said softly. "I speak Italian, the Latin language of romance. In Italian, we say *speranza*."

"Wow, almost the same," she mused, tilting her head.

"All from the same Latin-derived family," my voice almost cracked, trying to hold onto the moment for just a little longer.

She stroked my chin; her touch was light but lingered on my skin. "Hope we meet again, Rick," she whispered, then turned toward the elevator—just as I called out behind her.

"I... I should come clean. My real name's Lorenzo."

She paused, half-turning with a smirk. "Figured it wasn't Rick. But hey, everyone's hiding something. Still—good meeting you, Lorenzo."

I watched from the threshold as the elevator doors slid shut in front of her, her shy wave the last thing I saw before she disappeared behind the elevator door.

The door shut behind me. I flopped onto the bed, fluffed the pillows, and just stared at the ceiling—thinking how damn close I came to cheating on the only woman I've ever called the love of my life.

I grabbed my phone. No messages from Natalie. Zelcha. Niente. Nada. Not even a "Fuck you, Lorenzo." Silence was worse. At least hate felt personal. But honestly, yhe fuck you part might've made me feel better. At least it would've meant she still gave a damn.

My stomach growled. I scrolled through missed messages. A cheesesteak burger was practically sexting me. I placed the order with 24-hour room service—

Already on the way up, the message read.

I blinked. *That was quick…*

Whatever. Maybe the cook felt bad for me. Or Hope may have sent it. Either way, someone knew I'd need it.

I let the thought linger a second, then tossed the phone aside and sank into the pillows—stomach growling, eyelids heavy.

Chapter NINE

THE KNOCK

The early morning stillness was shattered with a thunderous knock on my hotel room door—not the polite rap of room service or the hesitant knock of a lost guest. This was heavy. Authoritative. I jolted awake, still tangled in the haze of half-sleep. For a second, I thought it was part of a fading dream—until it came again. Louder. Harder.

Fumbling for the bedside lamp, my hands shook as I flicked it on. The clock glowed beside it—6:29 a.m.—a time when the world should've been quiet, the hallway calm. Instead, the pounding continued—fierce and unyielding—followed by a sharp voice that pierced the stillness:

"Police! Open up!"

I gasped. *What in the hell were the police doing here? Did they have the wrong room —*

"Open up, now," a voice commanded from the other side of the door, firm and impatient.

"What's going on?" I whispered, pulse thudding in my ears. "Just a second!" I shouted, my voice cracking like a guilty man caught mid-confession.

I scrambled into my pajamas, hands fumbling as my heart slammed against my ribs. Dread cinched my chest. I staggered to the door, drew one shallow breath, and opened it.

"Hi, um—is everything okay? What seems to be the problem, officers?" The words felt fragile…

Two cops in plain clothes stood outside the threshold. The first was overweight, his tight button-up strained across a gut that had long given up. Tinted glasses clung to the slope of his nose, and a greasy mullet framed a 70s mustache.

The second was the opposite—shorter, clean-cut, sharp. His prescription glasses glinted beneath the hallway light, shirt tucked crisp beneath a slim tie. Professional. Collected.

But their faces? Blank.

And behind them, a wall of uniformed Colorado police officers. Silent. Still. And undeniably here for something serious.

"We need to come inside. It's urgent—it's about your wife."

"What do you mean? My wife is right here—" I stopped. My eyes flicked to the bed. Empty. Confusion hit like a slap.

Last night rushed back in broken fragments—the fight. The drinks. The bar. The silence.

I ordered room service and… what? Passed out? I must've missed her coming in… right? Or did she never come back? On her birthday? Did she leave with him?

Something was wrong. The cops wouldn't be here if it weren't.

"Um, yeah… sure. Come inside," I said, moving aside, holding the door as the officers filed in, their eyes sweeping the room like they were trained to see what normal people missed. "You said it's about my wife—Natalie?" My voice cracked. "Is she okay? What's going on—"

"Mr. Moretti," the slim officer stepped forward, his expression unreadable. "You may want to take a seat."

My heart lurched, and I dropped into the nearest chair, legs nearly folding beneath me. "Where is she?" I snapped, eyes darting between them. "Where is Natalie? What happened?"

The heavier cop finally spoke, his voice gravelly. "I'm Detective Kowalski. And this is my partner, Detective Hoffpauir. We're with the *Carlson–Scott* Homicide Division."

Homicide???

I didn't move. Didn't blink.

Kowalski inhaled, slow and deliberate. "We have reason to believe your wife may be the victim of a homicide."

I shot out of the chair, heart exploding against my ribs. "Maybe a homicide? What the hell are you talking about!?"

The room tilted. The air thinned. I gripped the edge of the coffee table to keep from blacking out.

Kowalski raised a calming hand. "We received a 911 call from her phone at 4:29 am this morning." He paused. Something dark flickered in his eyes. "We found a severed hand. Fingers were missing… but there was a fresh tattoo—an anime character."

He exhaled through his nose. "There's only one tattoo shop nearby. The artist had your information on file—names, the hotel you were staying at. That's how we found you."

My mouth went dry.

"We believe the call came from your wife's phone—"

I gasped, chest tightening as the air caught in my throat. *Who could do this to her? My Natalie—gentle, beautiful, mine.*

We argued last night, but none of that mattered now. I loved her. I still love her.

My mind clung to a sliver of hope—maybe this wasn't her hand. Perhaps I was still dreaming—a nightmare, vivid and cruel.

But as the detective handed me the photo, that hope slipped away. My lips trembled as I held the photo. My eyes stung. I blinked, slowly, but the tears came anyway. One fell my cheek—hot, silent, final. I didn't need to answer the officer. My face said everything.

Another knock blared like a siren.

I knew it was Kelly—I could hear her shouting from the other side of the door. "What the fuck is going on?"

I wanted to get up, but the pain was too much, pinning me in place.

A couple of beats later, she convinced the officers she was my sister-in-law, and they let her and Tony in.

"Lorenzo, why are you crying? What happened?" Her frantic eyes darted around the room. "Where's Natalie? What the fuck did you do to my sister!?" she shouted, lunging at me, but the cops blocked her.

She paced back and forth, her eyes scanning the room desperately to find any sign of Natalie.

Detective Hoffpauir stepped in between us, his voice low and heavy. "We found a hand. Based on your brother-in-law's reaction... We believe that the hand belongs to her. It's possible that she may already be deceased. If she hadn't bled to death."

Kelly's scream shattered the silence—raw, unfiltered agony that punched through the room. It wasn't just loud. It was the kind of scream that made your skin crawl, your spine tense, something primal inside you recoil. She stumbled into Tony's arms, shaking. He caught her easily, still wearing that black coat—like he'd just come in from a run.

"No—no, this can't be happening! No!" Kelly wailed, her voice splintering as she clung to him.

Tony held her up, unmoving—his face blank, like none of it touched him.

Then—all three of our phones buzzed at once. My eyes snapped wide. Disbelief hit like cold water. "It's Natalie," I uttered, breath catching in my throat as the cops rushed toward my phone. My fingers fumbled at the screen, trembling, barely able to swipe and open the recorded video.

"Mine too," Kelly and Tony echoed in unison. The officers leaned in behind us, trying to get a look.

And then, Natalie filled the screen. "Stop! Stop! Please! Help, Lorenzo—please help me, baby! Please! I love you!" Natalie's voice cracked.

Her eyes were bruised and swollen—wide with terror. Chains clinked at her ankles. She was barely clothed, shivering. Shadows crowded the room; a single flickering light danced across her face. Every word she gasped cut like a blade.

I gripped the phone so tight my knuckles went white. That sound she made—*that sound*—would haunt me for the rest of my life.

The video cut off.

A guttural growl tore from my chest. Rage, grief, horror—everything I'd ever buried erupted at once. *Who were these monsters?*

"I hate to ask this..." Detective Hoffpauir's voice was sharp. "Where were you between 3 a.m. and 5 a.m this morning?"

My head snapped toward him.

"Are you fucking serious?" I spat. "I just watched my wife—beaten, chained, begging for help—and you're interrogating me?" My fingers curled. Jaw clenched.

"You insensitive son of a bitch."

"It's protocol—"

"Fuck your protocol," I blurted. "She's in danger, and you're wasting time with your goddamn checklist." I stepped forward, fists trembling. "I've been here. In this hotel. Asleep. And if you're even hinting that I had anything to do with this—" My voice cracked. "I've been here since I got back from the club. All night."

"Mr. Moretti, were you alone?" Hoffpauir asked.

My gaze flicked to Kelly, then back to him. "Yes. Why in the hell are you even asking me that?" My eyes drifted to Kelly again before dropping to the floor.

His tone cooled. "You sure about that?" A smirk played on his lips —like he knew something I didn't. He stepped in closer, invading my space, eyes hard enough to draw blood. But beneath that edge, I saw it. Urgency. A quiet plea to work with him, not against him.

Hoffpauir's gaze slid to the nightstand, lingering on the lipstick tube before cutting back to me. "You want us to believe you've been here all night, alone? Fine. Then tell me whose lipstick is on your collar —because that tube doesn't match the shade smeared on your shirt on the floor."

That was it—the spark.

I lunged. Grabbed his collar. Slammed him back into the wall—not hard enough to break anything, but hard enough to rattle the room.

Chairs scraped. Officers moved—hands twitching near their belts. But Hoffpauir lifted a hand. Just once. Calm. Controlled. "Stand down," he said. His eyes never left mine. "Talk."

My grip tightened—then faded. The strength left my hands, my heart sinking under its own weight. That's when I lost it. Tears burned their way out as Detective Hoffpauir stepped forward and wrapped his arms around me. My legs gave out. He and two uniformed officers helped me into a chair. I couldn't stop seeing it—her, bound and broken, the terror in her eyes replaying in a loop behind mine.

"It's okay, Mr. Moretti," Hoffpauir said, giving my back a quick pat before resting a hand on my shoulder. "You look like you've got something to say." He paused, eyes steady. "Go ahead. Get it off your chest. We want to help you—but we can't unless you help us first." His gaze didn't flinch. It wasn't cold. Just honest. Searching for the truth.

"Someone else was here with me last night," I glanced up—caught Kelly's eyes narrowing, suspicion darkening the space between us. The room felt smaller. Tighter. Like the walls were closing in.

I swallowed hard. "I was with another woman," I admitted. The words soured in my mouth. "I'd ordered room service—I thought she was out all night with him."

"—You what?" Kelly's voice cracked like a whip. I turned my head toward her slowly, her rage trembling just beneath the surface.

"I was with another woman last night," I said, then quickly added, "but nothing happened." I turned to Hoffpauir, like I needed him to believe me. "Me and Natalie had a fight at the club. She was with some guy—" The rest of the sentence crumbled in my mouth before Kelly cut me off.

"Are you fucking kidding me?" Kelly snarled. "While Natalie was being tortured—begging for help—you were getting your fuckin dick wet?"

"I didn't know!" I shouted. "I didn't know! I thought that she was out with him. You and her, drugs, Tony in the bathroom…"

The cops' eyes shifted—landing on me, Kelly, and Tony all at once.

"You son of a bitch!" she lunged, shrieking.

Officers jumped in, grabbing her arms as she thrashed and cursed and clawed the air toward me like a woman possessed.

Hoffpauir adjusted his collar, coughed, then nodded to the other detective. Detective Kowalski stepped forward, his voice low and level. "Enough."

The room froze.

"We're all going down to the station. There's still a chance she's alive—but if we keep throwing punches, she's as good as gone." He pointed at me. "We'll deal with the assault charge later. Right now, we need to relocate." His eyes cut to Kelly and Tony. "You two, get dressed. We roll."

No one moved. Not at first. But the temperature in the room had shifted. The silence that followed wasn't peace—it was the eye of the storm.

Chapter *TEN*

The Cleanest Scenes are the Dirtiest Lies

At the station, the cops took our phones, saying they needed to trace the source of the video. Ninety minutes earlier, they'd pushed me into a polygraph—I agreed, even after lying about being alone last night. Then came the forensic sweeps, fingerprints, and recorded statements. They split us up, avoiding interrogation rooms, but it was still an interrogation—just dressed up to look friendly.

I was ready to explode; my wife was out there being tortured, and I was stuck in a dingy office frozen in the 1970s. Maybe that's why Detective Kowalski still sported a pornstache. Ren and Stimpy—as I'd started calling them—looked like they hadn't caught anyone since Nixon resigned. I knew I couldn't rely on them to solve this. I'd have to do it myself.

"Coffee?" Detective Kowalski asked, tinkering with the machine in the northeast corner of his cramped station office.

My brows furrowed as my fist struck the table in front of me. "I don't want any coffee. I want answers!"

"About that, Mr. Moretti..." Detective Hoffpauir said smoothly. My eyes snapped toward him as he rose from his chair across the table, adjusted his glasses, opened a folder, and began pacing the room. "I have some questions... How well do you know your wife?"

"What the fuck is that supposed to mean?" I snapped, glaring at him.

"Hey, let the man speak—let us do our jobs!" Kowalski chimed in from across the room. "Ah, there we go," he said under his breath as the coffee finally poured into his cup.

I cast my gaze back to Hoffpauir, who continued, unfazed. "Did you know your wife had offshore accounts tied to the Russian mob?"

"Excuse me?" I uttered, the words tasting bitter. *That didn't sound like Natalie—not the woman I knew. But after last night at the club, how could I be sure?* "What husband and wife sit around talking about accounts?" I shot back. "We don't discuss work at home. My wife wouldn't hide something like that from me."

"Fair enough… and did you know that your wife took out a four million dollar life insurance policy on herself, six months ago–"

"What?" my jaw damn near fell on the floor.

He stopped near the office door, tilted the blinds to dim the light, then glanced up and caught my expression. "Well, it's obvious you didn't. I'll cut to the chase—the guy your wife's been talking to is *Frank Richardson*. He's tied to the Russian mob. And his boss? He's in on that account with your wife's company."

My knuckles went white.

Hoffpauir didn't let up. "And here's the funny thing, Moretti — Mr. Richardson, the same guy your wife was working with, just happens to show up in Aspen the exact same day you, your wife, Kelly, and that tall, heavyset guy who's walking like he just got off a horse."

"Tony…" I muttered.

"Yeah, he's a character."

For once, I was glad to share the same sentiments as Detective Pornstache.

"Thing is," Hoffpauir continued,

Richardson usually arrives at the Aspens a week earlier, according to his usual schedule. Let me be straight with you, Mr. Moretti. Have you ever suspected your wife might have been having an affair?"

"No," I said, the lie slipping out so easily it startled me. *I wasn't a liar, but damn, I felt like one now. A part of me still wanted to protect Natalie, to defend her against these smug detectives. But how could I, when my woman might've been with another man right under my nose—and I'd been too blind, or too fucking scared, to even suspect it. Maybe I'd cared more about appearances than facing the idiot in the mirror.*

"So what can I do?" I asked, trying to keep my voice steady, even as it cracked. Natalie's life had been in danger. Anger and resentment had been luxuries out of my price range."

"Absolutely nothing, for now. Whoever has your wife hasn't made any demands yet, so we need to track her phone and work around the clock to piece everything together—"

"So what—you want me to just sit here while you guys twiddle your thumbs and my wife suffers at the hands of some sick fuck!?"

"No, we're doing everything we can to find her, Mr. Moretti," Kowalski said firmly. "Your phones are tapped, locations monitored—everything comes straight to our computers. We'll find whoever has your wife, and they'll pay for what they've done. That's a promise. The uniforms will run you back to your hotel. And remember—do not engage with Mr. Richardson. He's dangerous, and we don't know yet if he's a suspect."

I shot to my feet. "And I'm dangerous!" I snapped. "Whoever has my wife is gonna pay!" I stormed out, nearly knocking a stack of folders from a female officer's hands entering the office.

Hoffpauir's eyes narrowed toward Kowalski. "What do you think about him?"

"I think he's going to get himself killed," Kowalski answered, lowering into his chair and setting his coffee cup on the desk in the corner of the office, a few feet from his partners.

"I'm with you," Hoffpauir muttered. "Let's stick a couple units on him before he finds a way to screw himself over."

Officer Susan—the short, curvy cop Lorenzo had bumped into, with bleached-blonde hair and green eyes—approached the space between the two detectives' desks. "Howdy, Detectives Kowalski and Hoffpauir."

Detective Kowalski straightened his back, sucked in his gut, and held his gaze a beat longer than usual. Susan glanced away, twirling a lock of her hair. Hoffpauir watched the exchange, raising an eyebrow.

"You don't have to call me that," Kowalski said, his tone softening. "Just call me by my name, Ephraim."

"Sorry," Susan chuckled, setting a file on each desk. "Lie detector results, plus nightclub footage, and last night's hotel feed. It should already be uploading to your phone."

Kowalski placed his hand over the file, his gaze still fixed on her. "Thank you, Susan."

"You're welcome," she said as the door closed gently behind her. Hoffpauir grinned and shook his head.

"What's up with that silly grin on your face?" Kowalski asked, glancing over at him.

"Nothing—nothing at all," Hoffpauir replied, opening the folder and unable to suppress his amusement.

"No—what is it? Now I gotta know."

"Come on, it's obvious you two like each other—it's clear as day," Hoffpauir said.

Kowalski let out a sharp breath. "I'm not entertaining your crap right now, Hoffpauir." He opened a folder, then glanced back at him. "I'm not saying I believe your nonsense, but… You think I've got a shot with Susan?"

"—Oh, sir," Hoffpauir said, giving him a piercing stare. "I'm certain of it."

A sly smile crept across Kowalski's face as his eyes ran over the results. Hoffpauir leaned in, eyes gleaming. "He passed."

"He sure did," Kowalski drawled, eyes never leaving the screen as the video played on his phone. "There's Moretti, heading up to his room with a hottie—it's almost 2 a.m." His eyes flicked to the time stamp on the bottom of the screen. "She leaves a little after that. Then, at 2:31, room service shows up—food on a linen-covered trolley—and leaves. A few hours later, around 4 a.m., they're back to collect the plates." Kowalski pointed at the screen. "What time was the call made when the hand was found?"

"Call came in at 4:29 a.m. Officers were on scene eight minutes later," Hoffpauir tapped the screen to enlarge it. "Hey, look, Kowalski —there's you, gut and all, knocking on the door a couple hours after." He smirked.

"Ha-ha, real funny, wise guy. But in cases like these, we treat everyone as a potential suspect. Nine times outta ten, it's the husband. How long's it take to get from the hotel to the scene?"

"Roughly over an hour. Are we still considering him a suspect even after everything checked out?" Hoffpauir asked.

"We'll check every suspect, cover every detail. But remember this —" he leaned in, voice dropping to a low rumble—"when it all lines up a little too perfect, when it feels gift-wrapped… that's when you dig deeper. The cleanest scenes hide the dirtiest lies."

"Hmmm," Hoffpauir's smile was slow, deliberate—as if he was savoring the danger in the thought. "What do you think about a real plot twist?"

"What do you mean?"

"Suppose the wife cut off her hand, created an elaborate illusion to stage her disappearance, then faked her death to collect the insurance money and run off with her boyfriend to some exotic island?"

Kowalski pointed his index finger upward. "Or girlfriend nowadays."

"—Yeah, that too. Or the simple solution, maybe it's Frank, and his Russian mob goons."

"But why send videos?" Kowalski thumbed the corner of his notepad, eyes narrowing. "He's an enforcer from a mob in her city. If he wanted her gone, he could've had professionals do it without involving himself. Why didn't he do it before coming to the Aspens, when he had the chance? And what did they talk about at the club? Did she have sensitive information he didn't want getting out?" He paused, flipping through his notes. "What did Kelly—the sister-in-law —say when you interviewed her?"

Detective Hoffpauir's gaze sharpened, his tone turning precise, almost clinical. "Here's what Kelly told me," he began, laying out the details as if placing evidence on a table. "She was at the club, waiting for Natalie to finish her drinks so they could all head back to the hotel. Tony was struggling—he had lower back pain, could barely walk, and was completely wasted."

"Kelly said that Mrs. Moretti told her that she'd catch a ride with Frank, which sparked a bit of an argument between the sisters. Kelly didn't want to leave her sister behind with a stranger. But she did say Mrs. Moretti seemed pretty comfortable with Frank, like they'd known each other for a while. The plan was for Mrs. Moretti to join her and Tony back at the hotel later."

Hoffpauir paused, letting the weight of his words linger. "Kelly and Tony made it back to the hotel... but the victim never did. The sister in law mentioned that Mrs. Moretti changes when she drinks—gets stubborn, a little rude, and almost like a different person."

"Well, it sounds like Frank was the last person to see her before this abduction. What do you say we pay him a visit?" Kowalski said.

"Yes, sir. Though you know he's going to lawyer up."

"I wouldn't doubt it. He should be at the *Chariot* Hotel, where he usually stays."

"No," Hoffpauir's voice was low, almost a growl. "Not this time. He's staying at the Miracle Hotel—the same place we just came from." He was already halfway to his coat, eyes locking on Kowalski's. "Coincidence—"

"Fuck no. I don't believe in coincidences," Kowalski snapped.

They traded a quick nod. "Let's ride, partner."

Kowalski's breath came hard, each word a push past his tar-stained lungs. "After that, we hit the club for the security footage. I want every face, every step that hand took before it landed where we found it. Then we start knocking on doors—see if anyone's got a Ring cam in that area. Somebody saw something."

Kowalski shrugged on his jacket, the fabric whispering in the silence. "Let's go drag some shadows into the light." The two of them strode out the station doors.

Chapter ELEVEN

HOPE RIDES SHOTGUN

We dragged ourselves into the hotel like a couple of losers fresh off the world's worst vacation package—anger, fear, and doubt knotted up inside me, ready to snap. The silence pressed in, thick and unyielding. Even the walls seemed to hold their breath, waiting. My wife was out there—abducted—and the police had ground to a halt. Now Kelly, Tony, and I were left under their cold gaze, not as victims, but as suspects.

Time was bleeding out, each second a razor cut, and I wasn't about to rot in some overpriced hotel room, twiddling my thumbs while my wife's life hung in the balance.

I steered us out into the sunlit hush of the lobby. The lobby's tile gave way to a patch of thick carpet that muffled our footsteps as we passed a pair of abandoned laptops on a low table near the wall. Their screens cycled through a slow, looping screensaver while sunlight spilled across the marble floor. We dropped into the chairs around them, the vinyl cushions sighing under our weight.

None of us said a word; we couldn't even bring ourselves to look at each other. Tony's phone buzzed—it might've been his wife, hell, it might've been the president for all he cared. He didn't even glance down, not even a peek, but that's how thick the tension was.

Kelly sat across from me and Tony, chair tipped back just enough to look casual, eyes locked on me like she was lining up a shot. "So you were off with another woman last night… while my sister was out there missing?"

My teeth clenched as her eyes locked on mine. "Look," I said, voice cold. "Natalie was with the guy she wanted to be with last night. Even so, I still tried to bring her back here. So here's the deal, Kelly—either we figure out how to save my wife, your sister… or you back the fuck off."

She gasped, looking at Tony.

"I'm with Lorenzo," he said without hesitation.

"You're just saying that because he gave you a black eye—"

"I'm not. But he's right," Tony insisted, nodding at me. "You love her, both of you, in ways the cops never will. They don't feel it, they don't see her like you do. We can wait for them to move… or we take this into our own hands. For her. Because that's what family does."

In that moment, it was clear he wasn't just some outsider. He cared —not only for Kelly, but for Natalie too. I almost felt bad for punching him in the eye… almost. But let's not ruin a rare moment of kindness. I tipped him a small, sincere nod.

Kelly's voice cut in before I could lean back. "So… what now? Where do we start if we're gonna find my sister?"

I cleared my throat, that prickly unease creeping in. "The fat cop? Yeah… Frank Richard—no, hold up. Richardson. That's it. Frank Richardson."

Kelly didn't miss a beat. Her fingers flew over the laptop keys, the cursor gliding across the screen. "Got him." She slid the laptop toward me and Tony, a hint of grim satisfaction in her eyes.

I didn't need a second glance—the sour taste in my mouth said enough. "That was him, alright." My voice was low, dark, damn near ominous as I pushed the laptop back to her, unable to tear my eyes from that stupid, smug face staring up from the screen.

"Wait," Tony's eyes went wide. "How do we know if he's the right guy?"

Kelly's gaze flicked between me and Tony, slow and sizing us up. "We don't," she said, voice tight. "But he was with my sister last night —before we left the club. You were so hammered, going on and on about your back hurting."

Tony's face went pale, his gaze flicking to mine with unease. A prickle crawled up my spine. Not the time to push it. I cleared my throat. "So… Natalie wanted to stay at the club with this guy?"

Kelly took a breath that sounded like it hurt. Pain was etched into her face, but she wasn't going to break—not in front of me, not for Natalie's sake. She walked us through the night, voice low and quick, until she glanced down and saw her phone about to die. Typical.

She shot us a look. "Cops are monitoring our phones. We need burner phones — cash only, no ID." Her eyes flicked between me and Tony, sharp as glass. "And we keep them off whenever we're near our regular phones or the hotel. If both are on in the same place, GPS and tower pings will link them. We can't afford that."

We didn't waste time. A short drive later, we spotted an old Radio-Shack clinging to life beside a rundown strip mall. I pulled over, and Tony went in to buy three burners for cash. I was more shocked that RadioShack still existed in 2026—once everywhere like weeds, now looking like it was just waiting to be buried.

About an hour later, we stepped back into the hotel. The lobby was quieter now, the morning rush long gone. Kelly was already at a corner table near the window, hair pinned up with loose strands framing her face, coffee at her elbow. Sunlight stretched across her laptop as she worked, her focus that of someone who knew her way around a motherboard.

She looked up, eyes wide, a flash of guilt cutting through before she masked it. "Okaay… why are you two looking at me like that?" Her voice aimed for casualness, but the tremor betrayed her.

"I had no idea you were this good with computers," I said, dropping into the chair across from her.

She arched her brow. "Lorenzo, you've literally seen me on a computer before."

I frowned. "Yeah… don't remember that."

"I majored in computer science. Minored in acting and art. Dropped out to help Natalie," she said, fingers flying over the keys. She glanced up with a smirk. "What, you thought I was some dumb bimbo?"

It was uncanny, the way they could read my mind. First Natalie, and now Kelly—both with that knack. But this time I really looked at her—complicated, restless Kelly. A drama queen, always chasing the spotlight, bouncing from one guy to the next, blind to the burn waiting at the end. But today, there was a glimmer—a hidden edge I'd ignored for too long. Maybe it was intelligence. Perhaps it was something I just never paid attention to.

My heart skipped. "N—No," I said, trying to sound steady, even as I crossed my arms and shook my head.

"S—sure, Lorenzo," she rolled her eyes. "I think Natalie might know him, but I don't know from where—she's never mentioned him." Her gaze dropped back to the screen, fingers tapping a little harder on the keys. "Then again... I guess even sisters keep secrets from each other."

"This isn't the first time I've seen him—"

The keyboard fell silent as Kelly and Tony's eyes snapped to me.

"I'd seen his picture on Natalie's laptop before we even left for the airport—then ran into him outside it," I confessed.

Tony's eyes narrowed. "Wow. Saw his picture, ran into him, and thought... what, nothing? Brilliant move, man."

Heat crawled up my neck. "Look, you two were in my bed. I thought it was Natalie." My voice had that low, flat edge you get when you're swallowing glass. "I'd already made an ass of myself once in front of her. Didn't need an encore. So I shut the laptop and hauled the luggage to the car."

"Perfect," Kelly cut in, voice dry as she tapped at her keyboard. Tony and I turned to her, blank-faced. "Not this mess—the photo in the email. Maybe there are messages between them." She didn't look up. "Do you have my sister's email password?"

I shook my head. "No. How the hell would I know that?"

She sighed, tapping her fingers with a menacing calm. "Then this might take a minute." She opened another window and dug into Frank's information, her fingers gliding over the keys. "Got him!"

Tony and I looked up. "What did you find?" Tony asked, beating me to it by a second.

"Police file on him," she said, turning the screen toward us while flicking through the slides with one hand and working the keys with the other. "They've got him tagged for RICO, extortion, mafia ties… maybe even a couple murders, here and overseas. Nothing proven, of course." She smirked. "Real fucking Boy Scout."

I glanced at Tony, a cold sliver of dread inching up my spine. My gaze stayed on the floor. "Yeah," I said, almost to myself. "Could he be the guy who has Natalie?"

"Maybe," she answered, quick as a snap. "But I'll tell you this much —she was the last one seen with him at the club. And this guy? This guy is the kind you don't look at wrong if you want to see the next day." Suddenly, Kelly's eyes widened as she turned the screen back towards her, covering her mouth.

"What—what do you see?" I stammered, pulling the laptop back toward me. The words felt too big to say. My heart pounded.

He wasn't some pen pal from across the country—this sick bastard lived here, in our city, breathing the same air. Natalie… Jesus Christ. I'd given you everything, and now you were tangled up with a guy who wouldn't think twice about burying us both. Somewhere in the corner of my mind, I clung to the hope that there was a clean explanation. But no matter how hard I looked, all I saw was cold, empty silence.

Kelly's voice yanked me back. "Wait, there's more—"

"More?" My voice was all edge, no curiosity.

"According to these files, he's listed as a guest at this hotel. I did some more digging, and it turns out that the Petrov family owns the club we were at—the same Russian family he's connected to."

I had to sit back down, the weight of it all hitting at once. My head was spinning, trying to make sense of it, but every detail just kept piling on.

Tony stood up and put that same hand—one I'd never seen him wash—on my arm. "You okay?" he asked. It was unusual to hear him sound concerned.

I jerked my arm back like I'd almost lost it to a bear trap. "Do I fucking look okay to you?" I snapped. A few people in ski jackets turned to stare. Skiing—that's what we were supposed to be doing on this trip, not this.

"Hey, buddy, I'm just trying to be nice, alright?"

I let out a low, mocking laugh, my glare locked on him like I could burn a hole through his skull. "Nice? You, trying to be nice?" I leaned in, jaw tight. "You've been an asshole since we got off the plane—mocking me, lying about me, even blaming me for that mountain lion crap. I've covered more than half your hotel bill, and you still owe me money. So yeah, your version of 'nice' doesn't mean shit to me. You can take it and shove it up your ass. You seemed real good at that the other night."

Kelly threw him a quick, questioning look. "What the hell is he talking about?"

Tony turned, his face hardening.

"What are you talking about, Lorenzo?" Kelly repeated, rising from her seat.

He turned his head just enough to meet our eyes, a smug grin tugging at his lips. "He's not talking about anything."

I laughed without warmth. "Sure. Whatever you say."

Tony's brows furrowed. "You want me to kick your ass?"

"—Like you did last night, tough guy?" I shot back, eyes narrowing.

"—You got a lucky shot! Try it again…"

Kelly stepped between us. "Enough! Both of you. My sister needs help, not this crap."

A hotel security guard appeared. "Everything alright here?"

"—Fine," Tony said, eyes still locked on me.

"Just peachy," I didn't blink.

Tony jerked his arm from Kelly's grasp. "I'm going outside." Kelly moved to follow him, catching up just as he reached the lobby doors. "Tony, wait—" He shoved past her, hard enough to make her stumble sideways, then threw the doors open. The hinges rattled as he stepped outside, nearly colliding with an older man.

She stopped short at the threshold, watching him disappear into the cold before her gaze slid back toward me. "Watch your ass out there. Wouldn't want that lower back pain flaring up," I called after him. "—Fuck you!" he yelled, turning heads across the lobby.

The guard gave me a look. "Sir, if this keeps up, we'll have to ask you both to leave permanently."

"Yeah, yeah," I muttered, waving him off. I sank into my seat, eyes still on the doors, a twisted satisfaction curling my mouth.

Kelly crossed the lobby toward me. "I don't care about whatever macho bull you two have going on. My sister's out there, and I'm gonna find her. Got it?"

"Got it," I said as she sighed, fingers moving over the laptop keys in a dull, practiced rhythm. I kept one eye on the hotel clock, its minute hand ticking forward with a painful slowness, as if time were unwinding itself just to keep us stuck in this lobby.

Hours crawled by, yet we were no closer to uncovering anything beyond what Kelly had already pieced together. Tony drifted back and parked himself at a nearby table, coffee in hand. He stared out the window, watching skiers carve down the mountain, oblivious to the storm at our table. Kelly was hunched over our phones, working her own brand of MacGyver magic with a focus that made me wonder what other secrets she kept stashed away.

Tony and I? We avoided each other's eyes like two wolves circling, both too proud to make the first move, too stubborn to let it go. I felt a twinge of satisfaction for standing up for myself at last—something Natalie had hounded me about for years. But then, as the coffee cooled, so did my pride.

Hell, maybe I'd overdone it. Tony had shown a bit of humanity, a shred of compassion, and I'd swatted it away like a mosquito. I wasn't mad at him... or maybe I was. A little. No—more than a little. Still, perhaps I owed him an apology. The tension between us had taken on a life of its own, a ghost of a grudge hovering in the air, waiting for someone to break the spell.

"Hey, guys," Kelly said without looking up from the laptop.

"What's up?" I asked.

"Russian mobs got their claws in everyone in this town—politicians, cops, the whole damn ladder," she said, scrolling. "Explains how this guy's stayed a step ahead."

I shook my head, feeling that old, familiar dread. "Just perfect. Now we can't even trust the people we're supposed to rely on."

She smirked, a little too sharply for comfort. "I just ghosted our GPS. As far as the cops know, we've been in the hotel room all day. They'll still see everything else—just not where we actually are."

"Why mess with the GPS, though?" I asked, trying to keep my voice steady.

"Remember how they said they slapped a tracker on our phones? If any of them are dirty, they'll want eyes on us. Maybe even keep us from getting too close."

I blinked. "You're saying they're watching us right now?"

She gave me a look. "You didn't clock the unmarked gray Mustang outside? Been sitting there since we left the station."

I pushed up from the chair and strolled toward the lobby windows, aiming for casual. Midday sun spilled through the tall panes, throwing reflections across the polished floor. Out in the front lot, rows of cars sat baking in the light, but the gray Mustang in the space facing the hotel stood out. Inside, two guys—cops, no question—stared straight ahead, motionless, their silhouettes framed by the glare on the glass.

I sat back down, the muscles in my neck tightening. "They're following us. And those two in the car? Cops."

At that moment, I was dead sure every woman in my life was on the CIA's payroll. Her awareness was almost supernatural—like she saw the whole damn play before it happened.

Tony sat at the other table, stiff as a corpse. His eyes went wide looking across the room to the window, mouth slack. Slowly, he lifted a trembling finger. "Hey… isn't that our guy over there?"

"Wha—what!" The words tore out of me as I whipped my head toward the lobby window. And there he was—Frank Richardson—pulling into the front lot in a glossy black 2026 Chevrolet Equinox, nose to the hotel.

He sat in the back like royalty, guards fanned around him, eyes scanning. Natalie's life was on the line, and I needed answers. If he wouldn't give them, I'd beat them out of him—and I wouldn't mind that one bit.

My jaw clenched as I shoved the chair back, fists curling. I stormed across the lobby, each step echoing like a warning. Just as I reached the door, Kelly yanked my arm.

"Lorenzo, we don't know if he's involved. Don't blow our cover. Right now, we've got the advantage—"

My nose twitched, a bitter smirk sliding up. "Advantage? If he's got Natalie, he's holding all the cards."

"He doesn't know we're in the same hotel. And you think you can just stroll past his security and the cops to get to him?"

I snorted. "Didn't seem to be a problem last night when I kicked his security's asses."

Her voice dropped, sharp as glass. "Okay, say you do get to him. If he's got her and stays quiet, what then? And what if he's innocent? Now you're in jail—or dead—and we've got one more person to worry about. Congratulations."

I took a deep breath, feeling my eyebrows loosen. "So, what do you suppose we do?"

She didn't hesitate. "We follow him. We get his phone, dig around, see if there's anything—anything at all—leads us to Natalie."

I reached for the door, and it slid open with a quiet whoosh. "He's mine," I spat. The thought of him having her—doing God knows what—twisted something ugly inside me.

Kelly stepped in, voice hard. "You think you want to save her more than me? She's my sister, my blood. I've known her my whole life. You charge out there playing hero, and if he's got her, we might never see her again—alive." There was a haunted look in her eyes, the kind born from late nights and bad dreams. Natalie was my wife, but Kelly was her sister. And that mattered more.

I froze, every instinct screaming to get through that damn door. But Kelly was right—I'd learned the hard way that letting my emotions drive usually ended badly. I forced a breath, dialed it down. Just then, I spotted the detectives—Dumb and Dumbass—strutting toward the front of the hotel, making a beeline for Frank.

Kelly and I pressed against the side wall, slipping into the shade near the front doors, hoping to catch some of the conversation outside.

The clerk's eyes flicked our way. We tried to play it casual, but it probably made us look even more suspicious.

From inside the lobby, Kelly and I watched through the tall, panel-glass window. Frank and the detectives stood out in the lot, close enough to see their faces but too far to hear. Lip-reading was half guesswork, half junk, but whatever they said put a little too much confidence in Frank's step. He laughed, smirked, and I started wondering if those two cops were on the take from the same greasy hands.

My lips pressed into a thin line, fists tightening—until Kelly's eyes flicked to me and she gave a quick shake of her head. Clear warning: don't even think about it.

Was I seeing this right? They let him walk—no cuffs, no shouts, nothing. Either they were dirty, he'd played them like pros, or both. Leaning on the cops was like leaning on a broken crutch—useless and bound to land us flat.

Kelly tilted her head toward Tony, eyes sharp. As he stepped closer, she nodded toward Frank and murmured, "He's coming in. Follow him—we need to know which room he's in."

Without waiting, she looped her arm through mine, pulling me close, her scarf hiding half her face. I tugged my cap low and we headed for the door. As we stepped out, Frank's guards came in—close enough to brush shoulders. My pulse jumped, but they kept moving, parting just enough for us to pass. Frank was right behind them, eyes forward, never clocking us.

We kept walking, steady, following the curve of the sidewalk past the gray Mustang parked near the lobby doors. The cops inside didn't turn their heads. Our pace never changed as we crossed the rows of cars to my rental, waiting at the far end of the lot.

Once we made it to the car, Kelly had me shut off our main phones. She yanked a burner from her pocket, fingers flying as she tapped out a message. The screen's glow lit her face, casting sharp shadows beneath her eyes—as if the phone held secrets only she could see.

OMG! Are you ok, what's happening?

I'm fine. I'm following him through the lobby, but he's got a few tough-looking goons with him.

Be careful!

I'm in the elevator with them. They're going up to the penthouse on the 10th floor. Got off on 9. I'm heading back down to the lobby now.

Ok, we're about to come back in.

Wait—hold on! Stay put! They're coming back down!

I reached for the door handle, but Kelly's arm cut across mine, stopping me cold. We were parked in the far row of the hotel lot, line of sight across from the glass doors.

"Wait," she hissed. "Tony said they're on their way down."

A few beats later, we were in the car when, right on cue, Frank and his crew spilled out of the hotel doors. Sunlight caught their faces as they scanned the lot. I sank low, tugging Kelly down beside me, eyes on the dash, heart thudding with each crunch of their footsteps in the snow.

One of them—a slab of muscle—jerked open the SUV's back door. Another, lean and watchful, stood sentry while the driver adjusted the mirror with a smirk. Frank slid into the back, his crew folding around him like wolves. Then they rolled out, slow and smooth, toward the exit.

"We have to go after them—" I snapped.

"No. We have to wait for Tony-"

"We don't have time!" My foot hovered over the accelerator when Tony burst from the hotel's side door, lumbering toward us. His face was red and slick with sweat, eyes locked on the car.

"Hurry, get in!" I barked, watching him squeeze his bulk through the door. His foot hadn't even cleared the frame before I hit the gas. The tires spun on the snow, spitting slush as we slid out of the lot.

It was high noon when we pulled out of the hotel, but now the clock crept toward three, and our gas gauge was sinking right along with it. We couldn't afford to stop—God knew if we stopped, we might lose them, and if we lost them... I didn't want to think about it.

We were grinding up I-25 somewhere between Colorado Springs and Denver, two cities maybe an hour apart on a good day—but today wasn't a good day. The radio hummed quietly in the background, some half-familiar song that did nothing to settle my nerves. In the rearview, I caught Tony in the back seat, eyes sagging like he was about to drop off any second. I glanced at the passenger seat. Kelly was hunched over her phone like the damn thing held the secrets of the universe—maybe the only thing keeping her from coming unglued.

Me? I had one thing on my mind—bringing Natalie home. My wife was out there somewhere, and I had no way to reach her. No clue if she was alive or dead. The not knowing chewed at me, a slow, relentless grind. I bit down hard, eyes on the road, holding myself together—until a warm, steady squeeze closed around my hand. I glanced over. Kelly was looking at me, her fingers curled around mine, her grip solid as a rock.

"We're going to find her," she said, her voice steady, almost as if she believed it. "She's going to be okay." And for a split second, I wanted to believe it too.

"Then why the hell didn't we just break into his room?" Tony rasped from the back seat, his voice brittle and parched. His bloodshot eyes were tired but lit with grim determination.

"Because if he's got Natalie, he's not keeping her there!" I replied, a chill settling in my gut. "There's no way he'd make it past the hotel cameras without raising a single eyebrow. Someone would've noticed. Someone always notices."

Kelly cut in, her voice low and cold. "These days, people get away with anything. Hotel cameras? They're just smoke and mirrors. All it takes is a bit of grease, a bit of know-how… just look at that girl they found in the hotel freezer."

A silence fell, thick as fog, and the truth hung in the air, sticky and unwelcome.

"Hey, look!" Tony pointed at Frank's car, three ahead of us. "They're getting off the expressway."

My hand slid across the wheel, gripping tight as I swerved through two lanes of traffic, tailing them down the ramp. I stayed close, but not too close—didn't want them catching on. Just close enough to keep them right in my sights.

"Hey, slow the hell down! You're gonna get us all killed, goddammit—" Tony barked.

"Would you shut it?" I muttered, my hands gripping the wheel so tight I could feel my pulse hammering in my fingertips. The car ahead was taunting me, slipping away at every damn light. Green...yellow...red. Damn it!

"Are you kidding me, man?" Came the voice from behind, sharp as a razor and just as grating. "We drove an hour or two for this, and now we're sitting here? They're getting away!"

Seconds ticked by, and every nerve in my body screamed to gun it, to tear through the intersection and keep going. But that red light felt like a taunt, flashing in my face, almost daring me. Then, just as I was about to take the risk, a squad car rolled up a few cars behind us. That sealed it—I couldn't move.

I watched helplessly as Frank's car made a right turn, disappearing from view. We waited, teeth clenched, until the light finally changed. I eased forward, sticking to the speed limit, then made the turn where we'd last seen them. Of course, they were gone.

My eyes scanned the neighborhood. It was the kind of place that told you to keep your windows up and your doors locked. Even in daylight, people loitered in clusters on street corners, their eyes wary and hands restless. Drug addicts moved along the sidewalks like *The Walking Dead*, rubbing their arms and twitching, searching for their next hit. The houses, many of them were boarded up and rotting, seemed to slump under the weight of it all. The sun shone, but it was swallowed up by the shadows that covered every corner, draping the whole place in a gloom that felt permanent. Time was bleeding away, and Frank was just out of reach.

Chapter TWELVE

THE DARKEST TURN

"Where in the hell are they?" I hissed, gunning the car into backstreets glazed with ice. Corners came too fast, U-turns wrenched like a madman's hand on the wheel. Sunlight flared off shop windows. Graffiti-smeared walls blurred past.

We were only about a minute behind them—just a goddamn minute! And now I was stuck, staring down two sketchy paths: one narrow and choked with leaning brick buildings, the other vanishing into an alley of rusted metal siding and deep shadow, each one somehow looking worse than the last, as I circled the blocks.

I hadn't come this far, hadn't risked this much, just to lose them here. If that bastard had anything to do with Natalie's disappearance— God help him. Because I wouldn't. Something in me snapped, and the wheel was no longer just a wheel.

One moment, I was driving, eyes on the road. Then rage and grief slammed into me. My hands locked on the wheel, white-knuckled, the asphalt streaking past in a blur. I wasn't in the car anymore. I was somewhere deeper. Darker. A place I didn't know existed.

The pain was hollow, sharp, filling me whole. My own voice screamed inside my head: Let it out. And God, it felt good. Terrifying, but good. Fury ripped through me—the words I'd never said, the ones Natalie said I swallowed. She was in trouble. I'd failed her. The tires shuddered as my foot pressed harder. The engine growled, promising to tear through anything in my way.

"Slow down, Lorenzo! You're blowing through red lights!" Kelly gripped the dashboard, bracing as if impact was only seconds away.

"I don't give a damn anymore!" I snarled, voice raw as I slammed my foot down, the speedometer climbing like a spider on silk. "Natalie's out there somewhere. She's suffering—I can feel it in my bones—"

"Are you out of your fucking mind?" Kelly's voice was sharp and terrified.

"—Maybe I am," I snapped, my pulse hammering in my ears. "Crazy for my wife. But tell me something, Kelly… just who, in the fuck are you?"

"Wha—what?" she stammered, blinking, that pretty, innocent look cracking like a cheap mask.

"When in the hell did you become some computer science genius?"

"I–I already told you, in college—"

I cut her off. "And you were with her last night. What kind of person leaves their sister with a goddamn stranger? Start talking, Kelly. Otherwise, I'll crash this damn car, and we all die right here, right now." My voice was venom, and I meant every damn word of it.

From the backseat, Tony's shout cracked high with terror. "Dude, you're fucking psycho! Slow this goddamn car down! Now!" The wind roared through the broken window. The speedometer kept climbing—60, 70—the lines on the road blurring into one long streak. And the more he yelled, the harder my foot sank into the pedal.

"How do I know you and Tony didn't plan this whole thing?" I growled, eyes locked on the road. "Maybe you and your boyfriend cooked up something real nasty for Natalie. Or hell, maybe you faked her disappearance and figured you'd all run off with Frank and split the insurance money. Four million dollars can make people real fucking ugly." I shot her a cutting glance. Her face twisted into something fierce and dangerous—a look that scared me more than I'd ever admit.

"Are you fucking serious?" she spat, voice trembling with rage. "You're accusing me? Me? Of plotting to hurt my sister? How fucking dare you, you piece of shit—"

From the back, Tony barked, "Enough!" His hand shot forward for the wheel, but he didn't get close. My fist snapped out, catching the same swollen eye I'd given him last night. He recoiled hard, smacking into the seatback, clutching his face with a muffled grunt.

I leaned forward, voice low and razor-edged. "Don't test me," I said, each word dark and heavy.

"Lorenzo!" her voice rang out, sharp and biting, laced with something feral—so close to Natalie's it sent a chill down my spine. "Look at me! Look at me, you bastard!"

Her eyes blazed—fury, yes, but something else flickered under it. "I didn't tell the detectives, but… Natalie mentioned a foreign client at her bank. Said he was coming on to her. I think she went out with him once or twice, but that's all I know. She never told me his name. That's Natalie for you… the perfect angel she always pretends to be." A beat, then softer. "But you think I'd hurt my own sister?"

I didn't answer. My brows furrowed. Kelly wasn't the only one in her family playing dangerous games; Natalie was too. Her words lodged in my head, something inside me cracking. My grip on reality slipped. I couldn't look away from her—couldn't think past the doubt eating at me. *How had I come to this? Accusing her sister of staging her own kidnapping for an insurance payout?*

The engine's growl blurred into a low, rattling thunder. Tires hissed. Sunlight flashed—too bright, too sudden. Kelly and Tony's voices rose, but I barely heard them. I was drifting—and then I snapped my eyes back to the road. The blunt chrome grille of a semi filled the lane, sunlight flaring off steel. Massive. Closing fast.

"Oh, shit!" The words slipped out of my mouth, barely more than a whisper, as the world shattered around me.

Chapter THIRTEEN

BLOOD ON THE SNOW

Kelly's fingers clamped the wheel like she was trying to crush it, the leather creaking under her grip. She yanked hard—tires screamed. The car snapped toward the shoulder. An 18-wheeler blasted past, horn punching through my ribs, the driver's face a smear of panic behind the glass. We spun, the world tilting, hurling me sideways as we whipped toward a rotted gate in a lot filled with rusted shipyard containers—their edges jagged like teeth, waiting to tear us open.

My breath locked in my throat, frozen like it knew a scream would tear free if it moved. The car juddered to a stop—mere inches from a grave of twisted metal. I trembled, heart pounding so loud it drowned out thought. Forcing myself to look around, I saw every face twisted, eyes wide as if they'd glimpsed something that should've stayed hidden. At last, I pulled in enough air to rasp, "Is everyone..." My chest cinched tight. "...okay?"

Kelly's face twisted, feral and unhinged. She sucked in a jagged breath. "You motherfucker—I'm going to kill you," she hissed.

Before I could react, she moved—like a rabid animal. Her hands shot forward in a blur, giving me no time to defend. She was already on me, striking again and again, and I knew I was nothing more than meat to her—meat that had wronged her and could have cost her her baby and Tony's life.

"You almost killed us!" Kelly's voice was feral, her red-rimmed eyes glistening. "What the hell is wrong with you?"

116

Tony lurched forward from the backseat, one hand outstretched, as if he could hold back her fury with sheer will. "Kelly, stop. Calm down—"

She shoved his arm away, her voice sharper than thumbtacks. "Get off me, Tony! Don't you dare tell me to calm down. He almost killed us!"

"Yeah, I know," he murmured, his tone a low rumble, steady as bedrock. His bruised eye from yesterday's fight pulsed.

"But look—Kelly—we're still here. Just… breathe."

I didn't know what to say. My mouth was dry, the words jammed somewhere deep. I'd just thrown our lives into a bonfire for someone who, deep down, might be laughing with someone else. God, what a fool I'd been.

My gaze slid past Kelly's tear-streaked profile, catching the shimmer of daylight through the passenger window. There—about a hundred feet ahead—Frank's car crouched in the shadow of a rust-streaked cargo container, its dented metal flaking like old scabs.

The shipping yard stretched around it, a maze of stacked crates and narrow lanes, the air thick with salt and the slow, aching groan of cranes. The car didn't move. It just sat there, still as a corpse, like it had been waiting for us.

After all the dead ends, here it was—plain as day. Not a coincidence. More like a shove from something unseen, pushing us toward whatever waited next. They stared at me, wide-eyed, their expressions caught between confusion and anger. *A look I knew well. The one that asked: Is he crazy… or just right?*

"Shut up and look!" I snapped, my finger already stabbing toward the passenger window, twitching like it had an urgent message—a terrible secret dying to spill.

"No wayyyy…" Tony dragged out each syllable, his eyes narrowing with curiosity.

Kelly's head turned slowly, almost unnaturally, as if testing the limits of bone and tendon. "What are the odds…" she murmured, her whisper edged with something unholy.

"I don't know," I muttered, gripping the door handle as a chill ran through me. "But fate must be on our side." My gaze swept the shipyard—more graveyard than dock. Rust and salt hung in the air, massive cranes looming over stacks of containers, their shadows long and cold. In dry dock, the Meiling 15 sat scarred and weary, waiting for either repair or the scrapyard.

Near the fence, a few cars were parked at odd angles, headlights glowing, doors open—an unspoken invitation for unmarked bills to change hands. You didn't need a sixth sense to feel it; the air itself bristled. A prickle crawled up my neck, settling in my chest like cold fingers. Each dull beat was a reminder that something dark and dangerous was coming—counting down to explode.

"Wait for me," Kelly said. By the time my door slammed, she was already out, moving fast, drawn toward something I couldn't see. Every instinct screamed at me to leave, but I knew there was no turning back.

"Cmon–what are you doing?" she gestured at Tony, jerking her head toward the shipyard warehouse.

But Tony just sat there—a 6'5" plus-size frame with more rolls than a bakery. Right now, though, his skin had gone the color of sour milk, eyes wide with fear. I couldn't blame him; it wasn't his wife's life on the line, and we had no idea what we were walking into.

"Leave him," I said, eyes flicking to Kelly. "Besides, if the shit hits the fan, somebody's gotta be our getaway driver."

We left Tony in the car without another word. Ignoring the danger, we slipped past the empty vehicles, the midday sun pressing down as I darted between stacks of containers. The lot was quiet, and though the light was unforgiving, I managed to stay out of sight, ducking behind rows of empty cargo. Kelly trailed close, every movement tense and alert, her gaze sweeping over every corner.

As we neared the warehouse, unease prickled the back of my neck before I even saw the gangsters. We slipped along the wall, easing toward the open bay door, the air growing colder with each step. Inside was definitely a gang meeting. Two groups—about forty men in all—stood in tight knots, their suits out of place in the cold, their voices sharp, their eyes sharper. The sunlight caught every crack in their cool. No one trusted anyone.

We kept low, letting our eyes roam past the suits to the rest of the place. The warehouse was a sprawling maze of stacked crates and steel beams, shadows pooling in the corners. Rusted catwalks lined the second floor, overlooking the open floor where the suits held their ground.

Silence pressed up to the rafters, cold enough to catch in your breath. We weren't here to play hero—just to see if he'd lead us to Natalie. Kelly pointed to a glass-walled office perched above. I leaned in, whispering so low it barely left my throat. "I'll check upstairs. You stay here."

"Careful," she mouthed. Her eyes flicked to the phone screen, then back to me, trembling. She held it out, the message on the screen screaming: Only text. I swallowed and nodded, edging toward the ramp, forcing my breath steady as I climbed. Every creak in the structure seemed too loud. I slipped into an empty office and scanned the desk—papers scattered, nothing worth keeping. Then my phone buzzed. Kelly:

Lorenzo, what's taking so long???

> Chill out! I just made it into the dark office that looked as if it hadn't been used in years.

Find anything?

> Just a bunch of papers scattered on the desk.

Lorenzo: Look around. there's gotta be something useful.

> Hold on... wait...

> I think I found something!

It looks like they're trading guns for money

> What did you find?

> There's a blueprint of the club with some hidden rooms.

> Perfect. Grab it and get back down here.

> Ugh, you're so annoying.

> Screw you.

> I didn't mean to send what I was thinking… I'm OMW! 😜

I grabbed the blueprints, shoving them into my pocket. The warehouse office was dim, cluttered—files heaped in careless piles, the air thick with old coffee, rust, and machine oil. Shadows clung to the corners, dust dulling every surface. The place reeked of Frank—his kind of hideout, where deals were made and skeletons stayed half-buried.

Any lead, no matter how flimsy, was a chance to find Natalie. Then the image hit me—her mutilated, her delicate hand gone. It twisted in my gut, horror and rage coiling into one raw ache. *What kind of monster could do that to someone so defenseless?* The thought screamed in my head as I stepped toward the door… and froze.

Footsteps!

My breath caught. Someone was coming. No place to hide—the desk was too small, too exposed. The doorknob began to turn. With no other choice, I slid behind the door, crouching low, every muscle locked, praying he wouldn't look. Sweat beaded down my brow.

The door creaked open. A tall silhouette filled the gap, the air carrying the scent of cheap cologne and stale smoke. Russian—no doubt about it. He leaned in just far enough to scan the shadows, fingers still on the handle.

As long as he stays out there, I'll be fine, I told myself, a lie I didn't believe. My eyes locked on a mirror across the room, fifteen, maybe twenty feet away—something I hadn't even noticed before hiding.

Then I saw it. Hiding.

Something in the mirror snagged my gaze—small at first, just a pale glint. Then it sharpened into two eyes, flat and dead, glaring straight through me. My pulse kicked hard as the truth landed—he wasn't just looking into the room, the bastard was looking directly at my reflection.

He stepped past the threshold, his shoulder brushing the edge of the door that shielded me. His arm pressed into it, the muscles in his neck and shoulder tight as coiled steel. One hand stayed near his waistband, fingers twitching close to the gun. He moved with purpose, opened the door, and stepped in.

I crouched low, sliding around the door and clamping his hand to the holster. No time for subtlety—I drove my head into his face. His lip split, blood spraying warm against my cheek.

He was on me before I could blink, faster than I'd expected for his size. His hands clamped down, hauling me up and slamming me onto the table. The wood didn't give—a small blessing—but the thud echoed, and if I'd heard it, so had someone downstairs. My phone buzzed in my pocket. Had to be Kelly, asking what the hell that noise was… while a two-hundred-plus-pound Russian bear tried to squeeze the fucking life out of me.

He loomed overhead, eyes locked, a predator's grimace carved into his face. I slid one arm between his, broke his grip from my throat, and twisted—using the momentum to scrabble for the pistol at his waist-band. A muffled thud-pop split the silence, the shot swallowed between us. My heart jolted, cold shock flooding in. Our eyes locked— one of us was hit. *But who?*

He shifted his weight to pin me, and the table beneath us groaned, then gave way with a sharp crack. We crashed through, splinters biting into my back as his weight drove the air from my lungs.

Then his body slackened against mine, breath hitching in short bursts. I slipped out from under him, his blood warm and slick between my fingers. I stood up, unable to look away from the corpse.

In my hand, a black semi-automatic pistol—the unnatural weight pressing into my palm, sudden… and terrifyingly real.

I didn't know much about guns—Call of Duty had taught me just enough. And enough was all it took. A bullet dead center in his chest, his eyes dimming, his face settling into something like peace. My phone buzzed against my leg, insistent, almost accusing.

Bzzz—bzzz. Like a pissed-off wasp in my pocket. I yanked the phone out and glared at the screen:

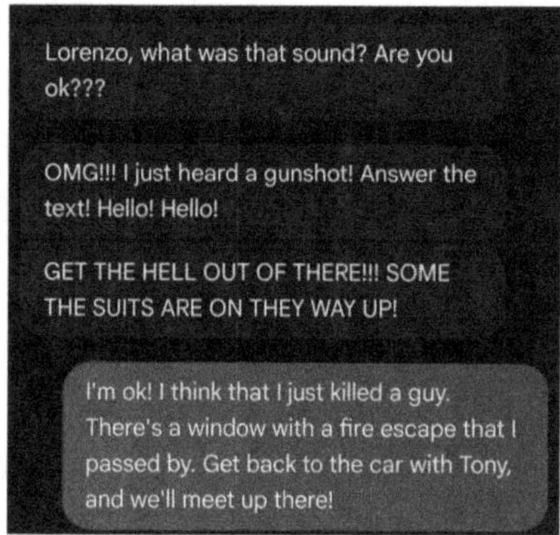

I crammed my phone into my pocket and bolted for the door, the floor thudding under my boots. Below, in the cavernous warehouse, voices barked orders. Footsteps clanged on metal—hunters sweeping the shadows.

The hall stretched ahead, ending in a cracked window pane flaring with light. Cold air leaked through, carrying the scent of rust and dust. Just beyond the glass, the fire escape clung to the outside wall, its metal steps warped and rattling in the wind.

One glance down revealed the shipping dock—wood splintered from years of brutal cold, iron railings buckled and cracked. It faded into a pale, knife-edged sunlight.

Below, Kelly tore through the cargo yard, arms flailing, feet slapping the snow in a frantic, uneven rhythm. She stumbled, lurching forward like a puppet on cut strings—straight out of an 80s horror flick, right before the monster strikes.

I pounded down the rusty fire escape. From here, I saw him—a thug in a slick suit, sliding out from the far side of the warehouse, a predator closing in on its prey. If she kept running like that, he wouldn't have to kill her—she'd do it herself. I had to reach her first. *But the odds?* Astronomical. One way or another, someone was going to die. Halfway down, Kelly froze mid-run in the yard.

Blam—blam!

The gunshots cracked through the cold air, sharp enough to rattle the steel beneath my feet. She threw her hands up, body jerking like the sound had hit her harder than any bullet. She stumbled, dropping to her knees. The scrape of skin against frozen asphalt reached me even from here.

"Next bullet goes into the back of your fucking brain, suka!" The Russian thug's voice carried up to me, rough and biting. He had closed the distance fast. Kelly stood in the open near the edge of the cargo yard, frozen. The shipyard stretched around her—crates stacked high, steel beams casting long shadows in the pale light. His pistol hovered a few feet from her head, finger tightening on the trigger. "What the hell are you doing here? Who are you?"

Kelly squeezed her eyes shut, tears slipping down her cheeks as she choked out her response. "I—I got lost. I don't know how I ended up here. I heard the shots and I… I ran…"

The man let out a low, mocking snort. "And you ended up here? You expect me to believe that? Where's your car, huh?"

Kelly's heart pounded as her mind scrambled for a lie—one that might hold. But the words stuck in her throat.

The Russian's laughter came again, cruel and sharp. "Bitch! Do you think I'm idiot, huh?" His voice echoed in her mind as the weight of the gun pressed closer, her world narrowing to the muzzle hovering just behind her.

"I swear, I don't know anything about an exchange," Kelly stammered, her voice breaking. She glanced back at the Russian, searching for something human in his eyes.

But he just grinned, teeth like a wolf's in the glaring sunlight. "Who said anything about an exchange?" he sneered. "I don't like rats." His arm stiffened, finger settling on the trigger. A heartbeat later, the shot cracked. Kelly flinched—

Blam!

Chapter FOURTEEN

DEAD IN THE DAY LIGHT

The world snapped silent. Kelly's breath hitched, her jaw slack, eyes wide. The Russian staggered a few steps behind her, sunlight glinting off the muzzle, smoke curling between them. Then came the wet thud of his body hitting the ground, a sound she knew she'd carry forever. Her ears rang. Shapes blurred. Through the fog in her head, my voice ripped through—raw, urgent.

"Kelly! Kelly! Are you okay?" she looked up at me, eyes wide, still half-dazed. "We don't have time," I muttered, my voice barely audible over the hammering of my heart. "We gotta go!"

I stepped over his dead body, snow crunching beneath my boots, and grabbed his gun from where it had fallen. It was cold in my hand before I shoved it into my waistband, keeping mine ready. I reached for Kelly's wrist—stronger than it looked—and started to pull her away.

But she didn't move. Instead, her arms came around me, sudden and fierce, clinging like she was afraid I'd vanish. The cold of her coat pressed against me, her breath hot in the frigid air, and for just a second, everything faded. Tears streaked her cheeks, wet against my neck.

"It's okay, Kelly. It's okay," I murmured, giving her one quick squeeze before pulling back. "But right now, we have to get the hell out of here."

We broke into a stumble-run, boots slipping on the slick sheet of ice. Shots cracked behind us, ricocheting off metal crates stacked like a makeshift fortress. Bullets whined past, grazing cargo and sparking slivers of ice into the air.

I fired over my shoulder, blind, with Kelly on my left. No chance in hell I was hitting anything, but it made them think twice—about ten stone-faced bastards spilling from the bay door. We sprinted across open ground, bullets sparking off the ice at our heels, and dove behind a waist-high shipping crate that expanded ten feet in width. My hands shook. This was supposed to be in and out. No one told me it'll turn into a goddamn war zone.

Then Kelly slipped a hand down my waistband, a gleam in her eye I'd never seen before. Gone was the loud-mouthed, spotlight-hungry Kelly who turned every problem into a scene. Now she held that gun with an eerie calm, fingers curling around the trigger as if she'd been born to shoot.

She took aim—blam, one shot, one kill. Blam—two more dropped. Fast, unnervingly precise, and something in her expression made my skin crawl. There was someone new standing next to me now—a person I'd never met, someone with an unsettling familiarity with this world of gunfire and blood—a natural-born killer.

"Who—who in the hell are you!?" I whispered, almost afraid to hear her answer.

"Where's Tony?" she snapped, gun smoke curling in the air as she pressed her back to the rusted crate.

I scanned past the crate, mapping our shrinking options. The bay door was thirty yards behind us, Frank's men fanning out into the open yard. Ahead, the warehouse wall ran east toward the chain-link perimeter, the rusted gate hanging crooked where it met the fence. We'd left the SUV parked just inside that gate, near the south corner of the lot. Now it was gone—only a jagged skid in the snow marked the spot. My stomach twisted. "Tony. That bastard left us!" My jaw clenched as boots crunched closer through the frost.

From the corner of my eye, I caught it—the low roar of an engine, headlights slicing through the cold glare. My rental SUV smashed through the hanging gate, the metal groaning as it gave way. It was Tony at the wheel, driving like a lunatic, one eye swollen shut, his battered face set in the same bull-headed determination I'd come to know. That sick truth churned in my gut: we weren't walking out of here. Not alive, at least. But in the past twenty-four hours—even if I'd wanted to strangle the shit out of him—he was the closest thing to an angel right now.

"Get in!" Tony shouted, rolling the window down, his belly wedged between the steering wheel and his legs.

We scrambled in—me to the back, and Kelly riding shotgun—crouching low as Tony hit the gas. Bullets punched the rental, each impact making it shudder. Wind tore through the open window as we shot toward the intersection, tires screeching.

Behind us, two hulking SUVs swerved in the glare, closing fast. Their tinted windows were black mirrors, reflecting nothing—eyes without a soul. They kept creeping up, trying to edge us into the curb.

One lunged first, grinding into our rear fender and shoving us toward the sidewalk. Tony fought the wheel, the tires spitting slush. The street was mostly dead—just two junkies leaning on a lamppost, springing back with a speed only desperation could buy.

We were still door-to-door with the bastard when Tony grinned like a lunatic, all teeth and lunacy, and jerked the wheel. The front corner of our SUV slammed into theirs. The crunch was deep, metal folding against metal. The other driver lost control—tires screamed, the whole vehicle fishtailing into a pole. The impact rattled through the street, followed by a second, sharper bang as it plowed into a bus stop.

I looked over at Tony. Sick son of a bitch had my respect—maybe not all of it, but a crack in the dam was still a crack. I was stoked. "Where the hell did you learn to drive like that?" I asked.

He just smirked, that kind of cocky smirk that made you want to either buy him a drink or punch him in the teeth. "Race car video games. I always wanted to be a driver. Just never... y'know, followed through."

It hit me then—Tony and Kelly had depths I never saw coming. Maybe I did too. I clapped a hand on his shoulder, feeling the sweat-slick leather. "Well, whatever. It paid off—"

—Boom!

A gunshot cracked and blew out our back window. Glass sprayed in, cold shards biting at our backs. We ducked low, hearts hammering. Conviction didn't even cover it. Instinct. Survival. We were rats scurrying from the shadows of the barrel, hoping the next shot wasn't our last.

The second SUV came barreling down with murder in its eyes, firing in broad daylight. It wasn't just reckless—it was pure desperation. They didn't care about witnesses or consequences. All they wanted was us, dead. We didn't think; we acted. And Kelly guns came up, barking fire. The driver jerked the wheel, the SUV veering hard as bullets thudded into the car's metal, making it jolt.

You could hear the panic in the engine's growl as they swerved. The driver wasn't just experienced—he was a pro. But up ahead, the Metra train loomed, gates down, red lights strobing. The whistle split the air, sharp and deafening. In the rearview mirror, the SUV closed in, its headlights burning. Nowhere to go—steel ahead, killers behind.

"Tony, what the hell are you doing?" Kelly clawed at the dashboard as the train bore down.

"I've got this!" Tony muttered, stomping the gas. The car lurched, tires screaming. "Shit! Shit! Shit!" His knuckles whitened on the wheel. Inside was mayhem—screams, prayers, curses. Each second rattled in my chest, in the frame, in Tony's grip. Time didn't just slow; it froze!

I could feel every second in my chest, in the rattle of the frame, in the tremor of Tony's grip. Then came the jolt—I braced for the sound of metal on metal. It never came. The car cleared the tracks, suspension groaning, and for a split second, we were weightless.

When we slammed back down, the tires skidded across the packed snow, and my heart nearly leapt out of my throat. For half a second, silence held—just the rattle of the frame, the echo of the whistle.

Tony let out a howl. "Holy shit! Did you see that? That was awesome! Hell yeah!" His grin stretched across his face, too wide, like it didn't belong there.

"You almost fucking killed us, Tony!" Kelly snapped.

I twisted in my seat, peering out of the shattered back window. The goon's car sat stranded on the other side of the tracks, their brake lights pulsing red in the snow. I leaned forward and gave Tony a firm slap to the back of the head. "Nice driving. Now, unless you want to die in the next thirty seconds, hit the gas."

"Got it!" Tony yelled, still riding the adrenaline. He clamped the wheel, knuckles pressing white against the skin, and with a growl of the engine, we tore down the road. The GPS had gone dark, leaving us in an electronic void. We drove blind through the maze of streets, every turn a gamble, until the signal sputtered back to life. We sat at a red light in the far-right lane of a three-lane street—and tossed words back and forth, trying to make sense of the map that looked like it had hidden compartments inside the club's infrastructure.

Hell, we'd just fought through it—and now I had blood on my hands. One man, two, didn't matter. I'd never killed before, not like that. But it was them or us, and I chose us. I wasn't sure I could live with it, but I had to do whatever it took to bring Natalie home. I leaned back for a second's reprieve—streetlamps waking up and sliding across the dashboard, the cold leaking in through the shattered back window. That's when the SUV slid up alongside us on the left in the middle lane.

I should've known it wasn't my day. They'd found us. All that time wasted, driving around like idiots, and the nightmare just kept getting worse.

A SUV crept closer, engine humming low beside us.

The back window slid down, and the man with a scar carved across his scalp leaned into view, shades catching the streetlight as he smirked devilishly into the car. "So you're the little cunts causing the pain in me arse, huh?" Frank drawled, one elbow hanging out the window.

I slowly reached down, careful not to give away the reach for my gun.

Kelly tried to reach for her gun, too, but Frank noticed her movements. "Don't you even think about going for a weapon, unless you wanna die, love!"

Kelly swallowed hard and raised her hands.

"You either, fat-arse! If you put your foot on that accelerator, you're not going to make it. I'll splatter your brains all over the dashboard, mate!" He looked us over, eyes narrowing on Kelly. "Now here's the deal… wait a minute. I remember you!"

"—Fuck you!" I snapped. The word was still hanging in the air when a squad car rolled up on the driver's of Frank's SUV, its paint gleaming under the fading evening light.

The two cops turned their heads, faces unreadable, eyes razor-sharp. They studied us, gaze drifting from one to the next. Fear must have been plain on our faces—they must have seen it. My stomach knotted as the question pressed in: *What happens now?*

"Everything okay over there?" the cop in the passenger seat asked, lowering his sunglasses as he chewed his gum slowly.

Frank chuckled. "Of course!" His voice carried too much enthusiasm as his gaze locked on the uniforms. "Just having a chat with a few of me mates here."

The cop's eyes traced over the three of us. "That true?" the driver asked, narrowing his gaze as if he could catch the lie before we spoke.

We smiled, but it wasn't the kind anyone would believe. "Yeah, sure—just chatting, running a little late," I said, my voice steady enough, though my gut flipped in somersaults.

Then the green arrow blinked on—our out. Tony swung the wheel right, and I tossed up a lazy peace sign. "Bye," I said, my hand steady only because I forced the tremor deep down. Frank's teeth ground as he glared, the cops at the light still chatting, oblivious—or maybe just not caring. Then Tony punched the gas, and the car leapt forward. The speedometer climbed, streetlights smeared into lines, shadows slicing across the dash. His eyes kept darting to the rearview, nerves pulled tight as wire.

The road behind us was empty, but that didn't mean Frank was gone. He wasn't the kind of threat you outran—he was the kind that burrowed in, waiting for the moment you slipped. If he had Natalie, every second we hesitated cut her chances in half. We couldn't stop. Not now.

Chapter FIFTEEN

DRESSED TO KILL

hree hours later, we were still on the highway, snow drifting across the lanes. Kelly leaned over blueprints spread across her lap in the dim light. The SUV swayed with the road, wind howling through the blown-out rear window, glass crunching underfoot at every bump. The car was full of noise, but the silence between us was worse—a noose tightening inch by inch.

My eyes burned from too many sleepless nights, each mile pulling me lower. But there was no rest, not with Natalie still out there. Sleep dragged me under anyway—a dreamless void. When I woke, I was sprawled across the back seat, jaw aching from a deep yawn. Tony's handiwork glared at me—he'd Tony-rigged a black garbage bag, duct-taped over the goddamn window, rattling in the wind. Every crinkle set my nerves on edge.

"Where are we?" I asked. My eyes snapped to the front seat, struggling to focus.

"Not far now. Hotel's just a couple of blocks ahead," Kelly said.

"What time is it?"

She looked down at her phone. "A little past seven."

"And it's this dark… already?"

"—Winter in Colorado," she answered under her breath as the early night pressed in. "Welcome to the dark." Her shrug was casual, but her eyes scanned the hotel parking lot as we rolled into view.

A few beats later, Tony pulled the SUV into a back-lot space, under a busted lamp that flickered and died as we parked. The engine ticked as it cooled, the sound too loud in the silence.

No one said it, but we all felt it—Frank was close. Maybe too close. We hadn't seen him, but staying at the same hotel was just asking for trouble. Our only advantage—he didn't know we were here. Better if he never saw us at all. His not knowing was the only edge we had, tipping the odds in our favor. Before anyone touched the door handle, Tony's vibe was off—but then he spoke.

"Do you guys find everything a little odd?"

"Like how?" curiosity piqued my interest.

"This Frank guy may or may not have Natalie, we aren't sure!"

Kelly shot him a sharp look. "We're aware of this already. Seriously, Tony?"

"Well, yeah, seriously!"

Kelly sighed.

"Let him speak," I said. "Go ahead, Tony—entertain us."

"All I'm saying is, what if Frank isn't our guy—and someone's just making it look like him?"

I swallowed hard, shame clawing its way up—my wife tangled with another man. The sting burned behind my eyes, but I shoved it down. "So far, all the roads lead to him. My wife—she had an affair with him. I saw them at the club, and his organization is tied to Natalie. Those aren't theories, those are facts."

"Yeah, but the affair thing?" he said, letting it hang. "That's not a fact. Not yet. And doesn't it all feel a little too perfect? Like someone wants you looking at Frank. Guy's a killer, knows how to cover his tracks. If he really wanted Natalie, why not take her in our city—right under your nose? I'm saying maybe it's bigger. Someone higher up, pulling strings we can't even see. Like Illuminati?"

I didn't say a word. Couldn't. Deep down, I knew he might be right. The bastard had a point, and I couldn't argue this time. Something dark was taking root in me, pulling me toward inevitability. The universe whispered down my neck: It's gonna be you. And I knew it—I'd be the one to end it. I'd have to kill whoever had Natalie.

For a moment, the world paused. We sat in the suffocating quiet, three figures in the dark staring at the windshield as if it held an answer. Finally, we exchanged a glance and turned to the inevitable—scrambling to piece together a plan before it all fell apart.

Time crawled, and then Kelly broke the silence. 'You guys—look.' She'd hacked the hotel Wi-Fi on her phone and tilted the screen toward us, her eyes gleaming in the blue glow. "Frank's got a dinner reservation tonight. Eight-thirty. Five-star joint, on the house courtesy of the manager. And check this—room cleaning scheduled for today.'"

I could almost see the gears turning in her head as the puzzle pieces snapped together. "I have a plan to get into his room!" She cracked the door and slid out quietly, moving fast but low.

"Where in the hell is she going?" I asked, eyes wide as we watched her slip into the shadows. A few cars sat in the back lot, and near a side door, a couple of staff smoked, their voices low. Kelly kept her head down, moving cat-like between the cars.

"No clue, but damn, she looks smokin' hot right now," Tony muttered, breathing heavier than I was comfortable with.

I tried to ignore it. "I know this is random, but congrats on the baby and for saving our asses back at the shipyard. That was some kick ass driving you did back there."

"No problem," Tony muttered. Then he dropped the line that totally messed me up: "None needed. It's not mine."

What the in actual fuck did he just say? *Lucky you, reader—you can scroll up. Me? I didn't get that privilege.*

My jaw hung open. Tony just shrugged, as if he were talking about the weather.

He kept going. "Yeah, after my third kid, I got a vasectomy—you know, shooting blanks. She doesn't know that, so keep it on the down low." Then he rambled on with a dozen reasons why he wasn't the father, while my brain checked out, eyes fixed on the empty hotel doors.

I always knew Kelly got around, but hell, many people did. But this was different—screwed up beyond belief. And Tony just sat there like a beaten-down mutt, too tired to bark. How did a man swallow that kind of humiliation? Letting her walk all over him while she strutted off to whoever she wanted.

I couldn't help it—I felt bad for the guy. He didn't even flinch when she let the baby slip, just sat there making peace with the truth: it wasn't his. I was watching a train wreck in slow motion, and the worst part? He didn't even try to look away. I just kept talking, and I kept tuning out. That's when I saw movement outside. I cut him off. 'Tony, shut the fuck up for a second! There! Look!" I pointed.

It was Kelly, slipping out the hotel's side utility door with her arms full of pink and gray clothes, a wild little smile on her face. For a split second, she looked unreal—something out of a dream. But after the last 48 hours, I knew better. This was still a nightmare.

The passenger door slammed shut behind her as she slid inside, lifting the clothes like a trophy.

"How'd you get these uniforms?" I blurted.

Kelly shot me a smug grin over her shoulder. "These breasts are for more than holding my bra on! I promised one of the bellboys a peek if he'd let me borrow one. Only catch? All they had was a maid's uniform. So either you or Tony's wearing it." She tossed it onto the armrest, and Tony and I stared at it like it was about to self-destruct.

"Not a chance in hell!" me and Tony blurted in unison.

"I can't fit that," Tony protested, puffing his chest. "I'm six-five, two-forty."

Kelly arched an eyebrow, giving him the once-over. I mirrored her, just to rub it in.

"Okay, three-thirty-two. But my weight fluctuates."

"—Fluctuates?" I snorted. "That's not a swing, that's a seismic event."

"Bite me," he shot back, flipping me the bird.

"Enough, you two. Dang!" she snapped, shoving the uniform at me. "Lorenzo, you're smaller—and by smaller, I mean less likely to turn this thing into sausage in a rubber band. You're putting it on, or the whole plan's shot."

Tony grinned, all teeth. I stared at the getup—pink, frilly, with a skirt that barely hit the knees, I guess commando was out. Probably the most humiliating thing I'd ever seen.

"Fantastic," I said flatly. "My dignity just left the group chat."

Kelly's voice was sharp. "Lorenzo, I don't care about your fragile little egos. Natalie's life is on the line. You get that? So what matters more—your pride, or saving her?"

I wanted to argue. But the words dried up, dead on arrival. She was right. God, I hated that she was right. But if this was what it took to find Natalie—then fine. I'd wear the damn thing: hairy legs and all.

As soon as my hand reached for the SUV door, our phones exploded with sound. It was Natalie. I answered first, fumbling with the call. "Natalie! Natalie!" And then I heard her—alive. She was screaming in the background, sobbing so hard it scraped down my spine. My anger burst out. "Let my wife go! You can have whatever you want—take me instead. Just don't hurt her!"

The voice on the other end wasn't human—mechanical, dripping malice. It laughed, low and cruel, the voice changer purring as if it enjoyed the game. "We want everything,' it hissed, smooth but cold as the grave. 'Records back to 2017. Offshore accounts. You know where the files are. You know where she's hiding them. If you—or her company—don't comply within 24 hours… she dies."

In the background, Natalie's cries tore through—sharp, desperate. 'Help me! Please!' Her voice cracked, and my heart went to dust. Rage hit me so fast I didn't think. 'I'm going to kill you, you son of a bitch! Do you hear me?' I roared, loud enough to rattle the air. My chest burned, my pulse hammering. On the other end, the bastard only laughed—a hollow, metallic sound that crawled under my skin— before the line went dead.

I kept calling back, but the encryption was flawless. Once, someone answered—a confused man with a heavy Asian accent, stammering broken English. Useless. A dead end. My breath rattled, fists clenched tight. Natalie was out there—alive, but not for long unless I moved. And the clock was already ticking.

Then Kelly's phone rang. Before she could answer, I ripped it from her hand. "Listen, you sick son of a bitch," I growled, low and raw. "If you touch her, I'll gut you and leave you bleeding." Silence. A pause long enough to feel the blood pounding in my ears. Then a voice I didn't expect—calm. Professional.

"Mr. Moretti, it's Detective Kowalski... We intercepted the call. We're close to tracing the location, but we need you and everyone to stay put."

I blinked, adrenaline still burning through me. My grip tightened on the phone. "And what about Frank? Isn't he the guy you're looking at?"

The voice on the other end hesitated. "I can't share any active investigation details right now, but—"

"Bullshit," I cut him off. "You do things your way, Detective, but let me be crystal clear: I'm doing things my way. And whoever has my wife had better pray to every god they know that you find them first. Because if I do? There won't be enough left for you to slap the cuffs on."

"—Mr. Moretti, don't do anything you'll—"

"Regret?" I cut in, a dry laugh slipping out—sharp, humorless. "I'm already there."

"Wait, Mr. Moretti. Mr. Morett—"

Click! I ended the call and shoved the phone in my pocket. Talking wasn't going to bring her back. Hearing her scream made me want to break—but I couldn't. I didn't have the luxury of falling apart. Not now. If Frank had Natalie, I had to move.

I dragged a hand down my face, trying to steady myself. The SUV felt like a coffin, air stale, silence too heavy. That's when Kelly finally spoke, voice low, almost careful.

"I almost forgot—when you were sleeping, those hotel blueprints you had… something about the club—looked off. Maybe secret rooms, sealed-off spots."

My eyes lit up. "Then I need to go there. Now."

"No!" Kelly snapped, her tone sharper than a thumb tack. "I need you watching my back if Frank's goons catch on. If things go sideways, I don't want to end up a red stain on a white wall. Got it?"

Tony nodded, slipping into his wannabe action-hero act. "Alright, I'll hit the club—check those rooms. You two take the penthouse. If it blows up, I'll roll in guns blazing." He snatched the pistol off the passenger floor, flashing it like a badge. "But you—you watch my girl. Make sure she's solid. No excuses."

I leaned in, my voice a threat. "If anything happens—anything— you call me. Immediately. Understand?" He grinned, cocky and wild, like he was already halfway to martyrdom. For a second, I almost believed him. Almost. "No," I said, dry as dust, "I should go instead. Be honest—you couldn't find a secret room even with GPS!

"Damn, I thought we were having a moment," Tony said, shaking his head, but I caught the edge of worry under the sarcasm. It was time to slip into something a little less comfortable, now.

I stepped out, clutching the ridiculous maid's uniform. The stiff fabric chafed, bare legs goosebumped, beard shadow making me look like the world's ugliest undercover agent. The absurdity wasn't lost on me, but nobody was laughing.

Tony rolled down the window, arm outstretched. For a beat, I hesitated, then clamped his hand—hard. Not a handshake, but the grip of men heading into the trenches, both knowing only one might make it back.

"You're alright, Tony. Don't forget what I said—if anything happens, you tell me. No waiting."

He nodded, lips pressed tight. I turned away, shoes crunching snow over gravel, Kelly falling in behind. The maid's dress clung to her, squeezing every breath. We were stepping into something from which we might not walk away. And I was ready.

Chapter SIXTEEN

MAID TO SUFFER

O r at least I thought I was—until Kelly dragged me into her room, a battlefield of perfume bottles and scattered makeup. That's where she went to work, turning me into some kind of macabre Barbie doll. Lip gloss thick as axle grease. Legs shaved raw. Stubble fighting back with stubborn pride.

She held up pantyhose so small they could've fit a Barbie doll—thin beige, the color of dead skin—and ordered me to squeeze in. Kelly knelt and shoved them at my feet, and before I could protest, I was wobbling on one leg while she yanked them up. The fabric clung like cobwebs, squeezing my thighs, crushing my crotch. Let's just say this outfit came with a strict 'no erections' policy.

I stood there—five-ten, toned, bushy-browed—a caricature of masculinity trussed up in drag. *The pièce de résistance?* She crammed tissue into my bra, puffing me out like a bargain-bin mannequin faking curves. I caught my reflection in the full-length mirror wedged between Kelly's messy bed and a dresser drowning in perfume bottles —and barely recognized myself.

Despicable didn't even cover it. Kelly, on the other hand, chuckled and declared that I looked *'perfectly appropriate for the occasion.'* I felt like a sideshow freak stumbling into a church social. *And the worst part? The pantyhose—God, how do women tolerate those things?* I can handle yoga pants, but this was medieval torture. Then Kelly crowned me with a maid's cap, smirking as she told me it'd make me look more official...'

Official my ass!

"Give me a sec," she said, already hunched over her phone, thumbs frantically clicking away.

I dropped into the accent chair by the window like I owned it. Spread my legs wide, then tried to cross them—bad move. A seam nearly popped right where I didn't need a hole. I straightened fast, pretending it was intentional, but the window behind me made it feel like someone was watching. "What the hell are you doing?" I muttered, just to break the silence.

Kelly didn't even look up from her phone. "I'm texting Tony. He's there at the club now." Her thumbs kept flying.

I studied her face, but it stayed blank—the kind of mask you wear when you're holding something sharp inside. Her voice dropped a notch. "Tony says the club looks closed. A couple of guys in suits outside. No, Frank."

"Then he's either headed here or straight to the restaurant. We have to hurry."

"Already moving," she barked, as we both strided for the door. "I told Tony to text me if he finds anything."

Kelly yanked the door open—catching the bellboy mid-knock. He froze: pale, rail-thin, maybe mid-twenties. That surfer-stoner glaze— half-baked and oblivious. He leaned on the doorframe, mouth twisting into a lazy smirk.

"You still need the keycard for the penthouse? Cart's ready. You puttin' out for it, right?" Then his gaze snapped to me—quick as a lizard's tongue. Narrowed, just enough to piss me off. "Who's the freak you've got hanging around?"

"Motha fuc—" The words were halfway out when Kelly's palm landed on my chest, shoving me back—not hard, just enough to park me like a misfiring shopping cart in heels.

The heat bubbled up, but Kelly's grip was iron—an unspoken don't you dare. She was right. Natalie was the bigger picture. Restraint mattered.

Then he cracked his gum, loud enough to wake a graveyard, and leaned back with that smug valley-boy smirk. I wanted to claw it off. I hadn't realized how casually cruel men could be to women—the ones they didn't find pretty—until I stepped out in this uniform.

Kelly flashed a smile, still pressing her hand against my toilet paper-stuffed breast. "Oh, this is m—my cousin, yeah, my cousin, um —umm… Lauren."

He worked the gum a little harder now, jaw moving in short, deliberate jerks. His arm hung loose against the splintered doorframe, eyes stoned but focused. "What up, baby girl? Lauren."

I wanted to crack him badly. Felt like women everywhere would've cheered, but I had to stick to the script—keep the plan, keep control. Find proof. And help Natalie. "Hey!" I grunted, eyes rolling to the ceiling.

"Don't mind her. She's fiery," Kelly said.

The clown smirked, eyes glinting like snake scales. "Fiery, huh? I spent a few years in San Francisco… I like 'em feisty." His tongue dragged slowly across his lips.

What in the actual hell was this? Five minutes as a woman and I was already sick of men as a species.

"Let's raise the stakes," he said, leaning in just far enough to make the hairs on my neck stand. "I want you and Laura. Tonight. You like owing me, don't you? Well, time to pay up."

My eyebrows slammed together, fists clenched before I even knew it. Kelly slid in front of me, arm out. I was already boiling. Six minutes in heels and I was about to be pimped out—Christ.

"Hey!" his voice cracked like a whip. "You two both have to agree, or there's no deal. You guys DTF or what?"

"What's DTF?" I whispered.

Kelly spun around, her eyes pleading. "It means Down To Fuck. Lauren, come on—"

"I'm waiting—but not all day. I get off soon, so I need an answer."

"Lauren —Lauren, please!" Kelly's voice broke at that moment, becoming shaky.

"Too late. I'm gone," he turned, turning and pushing his cart toward the elevator with the kind of calm that made me want to throw something at him, or maybe even throw him.

I threw my hands up, defeated. "Fine, okay! DTF."

He stopped midstep, and the smirk returned like it had never left. "Excellent decision," he said, rubbing his hands together as he turned back toward us. "I'm off at midnight, but I'll cruise by at, like, 11:30 to stash the cart and put the keycard back. You chicks better be good to go by then, yeah?"

"Yeah, sure. Whatever," Kelly muttered, her voice tight with barely-contained disgust. We stood there, both of us stewing, watching the little prick swagger his way onto the elevator. The doors slid shut, swallowing him whole—he left the cart parked in the hallway, penthouse keycard perched on top.

While we waited for the next elevator, Kelly leaned close, her voice low and urgent. "Look, this is in-and-out. I need to see if he has a laptop, files, or anything I can hack into. So whatever you do, act natural. We can't draw attention."

Shit… She should've thought about that before turning me into a Hulk Hogan drag queen. Kelly swiped the keycard, and the penthouse button glowed; the elevator hummed higher than felt natural.

After a few moments, the elevator slid open onto a corridor lined with plush carpet and gilded sconces. Dark wood panels gleamed, polished to catch every shard of light—money on display—quiet, deliberate, impossible to miss. My grip tightened on the cart as we stepped out. The carpet swallowed our footsteps, the hush pressing in. Lights burned behind jeweled sconces, their glow casting odd angles across the hall.

Then I noticed the vines. They crept along the panels and ceiling, impossibly green, as if the place had been grafted with a jungle. A faint mix of moss and jasmine lingered, sharp and out of place. This wasn't a hotel anymore. It felt like a temple—and I was already trespassing.

Twenty feet up the hall, one of Frank's guys planted himself square in front of the door, arms crossed, eyes sweeping slowly. No shock— Frank wouldn't leave his front line unguarded. What threw me was the silence. No cameras, no blinking lights, no mechanical eyes. Just us, the guard, and the heavy weight of Frank's idea of privacy.

"Can I help you, ladies?" he asked as we approached. I hung back, letting the cart and Kelly shield me, chin dipped just enough to avoid his eyes.

Kelly spoke. "We're to provide cleaning for Mr. Richardson's room."

"Cleaning? Cleaning isn't scheduled until later today—"

She was sharp and didn't back down. "Management's breathing down our necks. This room's on the checklist. Unless you're eager to explain to Mr. Richardson why it's not, I'd suggest letting us through."

He darted a glance our way, suspicion in his eyes. "I'll have to confirm with Mr. Richardson," he said, his Russian accent clipped and hard. He pulled out his phone, the kind of man who thought authority lived in his thumbs. "You two, wai—"

He barely got the word out before another voice carried from deeper inside the penthouse—a woman's, soft but commanding. "Ivan, why are you giving the cleaning crew such a hard time?"

I froze. That voice—I knew it. My heart hammered, rattling my ribs. Then she appeared, moving into the doorway with an unhurried grace. "Esperanza," I breathed. She stopped at the threshold, and I panicked, snapping my head away so fast my neck popped. *What in the fuck was she doing here?*

"Come in," Esperanza said, her hand lifting in a graceful flick as Ivan stepped aside. Her tone was light, almost airy, but beneath it was the weight of someone who'd never heard no. "Don't mind Ivan. He's a little overprotective. Right this way."

"Sorry, Mrs. Richardson," Ivan muttered, voice low, posture shrinking like a dog freshly kicked.

Kelly shot me a sharp look, one eyebrow cocked—the kind that said, what the hell is wrong with you?

And there we were, stepping into Frank's domain. Esperanza led the way, and the silence was expensive—engineered to keep secrets. My eyes swept the space for anything—a shadow out of place, a flicker that might point to Natalie, or prove Frank was pulling the strings. A sharp jab hit my ribs.

"Why are you acting so weird?" Kelly leaned in and whispered at my side.

"I'm not," I muttered, keeping my eyes ahead on Esperanza. "You're acting weird."

Kelly breathed out a low chuckle, barely a sound. "Right. Then why'd you turn your head when she came to the door—like you were hiding your face?'"

"I didn't—"

"You did."

Before we could continue arguing, Esperanza stopped abruptly and turned, her sharp, dark eyes boring in like needles.

My stomach dropped. I crouched low, pretending to fuss with the laces on my fur Crocs—a ridiculous invention, but one I was suddenly grateful for.

"Did you say something?" Esperanza asked.

"Just tying my shoes," I mumbled in a forceful, high-pitched woman's voice.

Kelly stepped forward, her smile too big, too bright. "I was just telling my coworker how big and beautiful this place was!" Kelly said, her voice unnaturally loud, too eager.

Esperanza held Kelly's gaze for a beat, then let a slow smile bloom before turning away. Her heels picked up their sharp rhythm again, and we followed, my pulse hammering as she led us deeper into the palace.

"Lauren can handle the living room. I'll start in the office—"

Esperanza's hand shot out, fast as a whip. She crossed the hall to the office door opposite the open kitchen and closed the door before Kelly could finish. "No!" The word cracked out of her, sharp, almost panicked. For a breath, it hung in the air. Then her gaze shifted, and she softened, smoothing the outburst away. "That's... my husband's space. His sanctuary. He's very particular about it."

Figures. She told me that everyone had secrets—hers was married to an alleged killer. But the way she rushed that excuse... polished, rehearsed.

Her hand clung to the knob like she was holding something back. Kelly caught it, too. That door wasn't technically locked. Still felt like it. Something waited on the other side. Something Esperanza didn't want out. Or worse—didn't want to look back at us.

"Ooo-kay," Kelly drawled, curiosity undercut with something sharper. "I'll start in the kitchen and work my way around. Does that work for you?"

"Perfect! I'm doing my makeup—I've got a dinner date with my husband. I'll be in the bathroom for a while; you won't even notice me." Esperanza's voice stayed sweet, but edged with dismissal. Her heels clattered on the marble as she disappeared down the hall.

The penthouse was all glass and height—open sightlines, no cover. We didn't have time to think; Frank was coming, and Esperanza's presence meant he wouldn't be late. We needed a distraction, fast, something to draw her off. Every sound felt magnified in the hush as I glanced toward the hall where she'd vanished.

I whispered to Kelly. "We need to move. Now."

"On it."

Kelly tiptoed toward the office, each step careful. Then Esperanza stormed back in, heels cracking against the floor in rapid-fire rhythm.

Kelly froze mid-step. We scattered without a word, roaches caught in the light. I grabbed a duster from the cart and slipped into the living room; Kelly ducked toward the stove. The kitchen and living room bled into one another—open space, no real cover. At least we could keep each other in sight, signal if she turned our way. I bent to the dust, watching it dance in the light.

"Hey, almost forgot. Here's some shoe covers for you guys." Esperanza said suddenly, her voice sharp enough to make me flinch. She shoved a pair into my hands, and I turned away fast, slipping them on without looking back. My heart thudded, heavy and slow. She then walked over and handed Kelly a pair too.

The shoe covers came up almost to our knees—maid thigh highs, if you squinted. Sneaking around was bad enough; doing it in those ridiculous things, trying not to skid across her polished floors, made us look less like pros and more like second-rate burglars.

After a few distracted minutes of fake work, my eyes slid to Kelly. She was propped against the kitchen island, phone in hand. The screen lit up her face, revealing all its angles and shadows. Focused. Dangerous.

"It's Tony," she murmured, eyes still on her phone. "He followed the two men inside. He's checking the club now. Says there's another section that looks sealed off, but not solid."

For a second, the world felt smaller, confined. Something was about to happen—something big.

"Tell him to let us know if he finds anything!" I said. She nodded and slipped into Frank's office. I stayed by the door, nerves twisting in my gut, scanning the dim hallway for movement. Inside, I heard her rifling through papers and drawers, hunting for anything useful. Then her voice came—sharp, but low enough not to carry.

"Lauren. Get in here."

I stiffened. "Don't call me that. And no, I can't. I'm watching the hall."

"It'll take a second," her tone had that sharp, insistent edge that I started to dislike. "The drawer's locked. Frank's hiding something in here—I know it. You need to get something to open it."

I sighed, torn between keeping watch and the gnawing curiosity of what we might find. Against my better judgment, I pulled a small knife from the kitchen drawer and slipped into the office, heading for the desk. The room smelled of expensive cologne and brandy—a place where secrets festered.

"Is there a key around?" I asked, already knowing the answer.

"Do you see one?" she gestured impatiently, her eyes flitting to the door. "I've checked everywhere. You know how to pick a lock?"

"Do I look like a professional criminal to you?"

"No—you look like some pissed-off Italian mom about to go full Godfather on this desk," she said, grinning. "Brows all knotted up like that."

"Sorry, forgot to tweeze them this morning," I shot back, my words edged, but her grin only widened. If things weren't so damned serious, I'd have given her a piece of my mind. Instead, I crouched. "Almost… almost." I fiddled with the drawer, then the lock popped. "Got it."

Kelly's fingers hovered over the drawer, but I yanked it open first. My pulse spiked as the wood scraped. Inside—an envelope. My breath caught. Pictures. Frank. And Natalie, draped in ballroom masquerade clothes.

But this wasn't a gala. The room in those photos reeked of money and sin—champagne spilled like water, faces hidden behind Domino masks, secrets traded at a price no soul could afford. Surrounding her were men in suits, the kind who crushed lives with a signature. Natalie wore a mask, but the heart tattoo on her left arm gave her away—the one with our names inked inside it.

I shook my head. She had no business being there. But it was her. I knew it. Darker than Kelly. And then I saw what they were doing. My stomach turned, sweat prickling cold. These weren't whispers or messages. Not an affair.

These were photos—evidence I couldn't unsee. Natalie had been doing things with them—things I never thought I'd see, things she'd never done with me in bed. And in that instant I wondered if I'd ever really known her at all.

People say what your woman won't do for you, she'll do for the next man. Looking at those photos, I knew it wasn't just true—it was brutal law. The thought chewed at me, bitter and raw.

Then a voice sprang from behind us—sharp and ragged, like nails dragging across a chalkboard. "What the fuck do you think you're doing in my husband's desk?" Esperanza's eyes darted between me, Kelly, and the broken drawer.

Chapter SEVENTEEN

THE DEVIL IN ARMANI

spun around just in time to see her hand dive into the mouth of her purse, emerging with a phone gripped tight as if it were a loaded gun. Her lips pulled back in a feral snarl. "I'm calling the cops!" she spat. Her eyes were wide, unblinking. And her feet were already edging her backward out of the office, step by step, toward the door.

"Wait!" I shouted, the word exploding in my throat as I lunged, only a few feet between her and the door. Her head snapped toward the hallway, and that's when she screamed for him. *Ivan.*

Damn… Ivan. You remember him, right? The meathead who guarded the front door like a watchdog?

I tackled her hard, driving her to the floor, and clamped my hand over her mouth, knees braced outside her hips, while Kelly stood frozen by the broken drawer, eyes wide, unmoving.

Esperanza didn't freeze—she thrashed, twisting under me like I'd climbed onto a bull. Then she sank her teeth into my goddamn palm, hard, and a sound I didn't recognize tore out of me. My grip slipped; my weight shifted. I couldn't let go—not with Ivan right outside the door.

Esperanza slid a leg free and whipped it up between my thighs, wiry and unhinged. Fuck! That's when it came… A flash of sharp motion, the arc of her leg, and, God help me, her high heel drove square into my groin. "My nuts!" I croaked, folding off her and sprawled on the floor, pain radiating in hot waves through my groin—a cruel reminder of just how breakable a man is.

Through the haze, I caught Kelly in the corner of my eye—she bolted out of the office into the living room and launched herself at Esperanza like a linebacker. They tumbled across the sectional near the glass coffee table, a blur of limbs and snarls. The room erupted like an MMA fight with no ref to break it up. I tried to stand, but pain flared white-hot between my legs, scattering stars across my vision. One hand clutched my crotch, the other braced against the wall as I staggered toward them. If I didn't break it up fast, someone was going to get hurt—or worse.

Esperanza's fist slammed into Kelly's chin with a sickening crack, whipping her into the glass coffee table. It exploded on impact, a deafening blast of shattering glass spraying shards across the room. The walls were thick—maybe thick enough to swallow the noise—but I couldn't count on that. If she reached the door and got Ivan involved, it was over. For Kelly. For me. For all of us.

"Esperanza! Stop!" I pleaded, desperation knotting my throat. "It's me!"

She froze mid-step, her back half-turned toward the front door. And, slowly, she pivoted to face me—eyes wide, like she'd just seen a ghost—a ghost in a maid's uniform.

"Lorenzo?" she blurted, her voice a razor-thin wire stretched between disbelief and hope. "Is that... you?"

I sagged against the wall, knees buckling like they forgot their purpose. Through gritted teeth, I forced the words out, humiliation burning on my face. "Yeah..." I muttered. "It's me."

"What the hell are you doing in my suite? And why are you dressed like a woman?"

I froze, caught in the glare. "Uh... It's a long story," I mumbled, my voice barely a whisper.

Her hand shot to her phone with purpose. It was halfway to her ear before I found my voice.

"Wait! I can explain!" I shouted, hands up fast.

Her thumb hovered over the screen, then pressed the call button anyway. "Hello, 911?"

"Okay, okay!" I stammered. "We—we think your husband, Frank, might have had something to do with my wife's disappearance."

Her lips parted, a breath catching in her throat. For a split second, I thought I'd broken through—then the operator's calm, sterile voice bled through the receiver:

"911, what is your emergency?"

"Look!" I nearly screamed, thrusting the envelope toward her. Photos spilled out—a cascade of glossy, damning evidence.

Frank wore a domino mask that hid only his eyes, but the scar carved across his head gave him away. And the setting—God, it was a den of sin. The kind of place you wouldn't even dare whisper about in confession. Her eyes widened, pupils shrinking to pinpoints as the photos took effect.

The voice on the line snapped her out of her trance. "Hello? Do you need police assistance?" The operator's voice was calm.

My heart slammed against my ribs. The lump in my throat wouldn't move. This was bad—the kind that clings. We didn't need more cops sniffing around. And we sure as hell didn't belong here. I waited, every nerve strung tight, as she weighed my fate on a breath.

"No, no, I don't need your service," she said, her voice trembling just enough to betray the lie. "Everything's fine. It was a mistake." She hung up mid-sentence, cutting off the operator. For a beat, she stood frozen, staring at the photos—faces familiar yet wrong. The penthouse, with all its space and high ceilings, suddenly pressed in. "It has to be a mistake," she whispered. But she knew better. Mistakes didn't leave shadows. She sank onto the other end of the sectional across from where I stood, hand clamped over her mouth, eyes wet and wild. The photos littering her lap felt like evidence—each one a shard of something broken.

I helped Kelly up from the shattered glass table in front of the sectional. Shallow cuts streaked her arms and legs, nothing serious. But she looked frayed, strung too tight. Across from us, Esperanza's silence pressed in, louder than any scream.

"Are you okay, Kelly?" I asked, as I eased her to her feet.

"I need a first aid kit. And your washroom," Kelly said, steady but slow, turning to Esperanza. Her voice was calm, but her face was a mask—whether of pain or something deeper, I couldn't tell.

Esperanza hesitated just long enough to be noticeable, then pointed down the dimly lit hallway. "Straight ahead. Second door on the left. The first aid kit is in there." Her tone was neutral, but a weight hung behind it—a wariness she couldn't hide.

Kelly nodded but didn't move. I reached out, offering a hand. She slapped it away—not hard, just enough to send a shiver through me. Her touch wasn't cold. It was hollow. Then she looked at me—eyes that had already seen too much. "So this is the bitch you were cheating on my sister with?" she said, each word driven like a nail. Her gaze flicked to Esperanza, then she limped down the hall.

For a moment, the walls held their breath. This wasn't awkward anymore—it was dark, coiled, waiting to strike. I glanced at Esperanza and felt a stab of pity. She hadn't deserved this, no more than I had. Both of us were fooled. Both betrayed—by the people we trusted most, and with each other's partners. Absurd enough to laugh at, if it didn't cut so deep.

The photos on her lap slid onto the couch between us, glaring up like evidence from a crime scene. I told her everything—no softening it, no hiding. Shots of him with Natalie, tucked in an envelope like a poisoned gift. She tried to defend him, her voice shaky, but her faith was already crumbling. Still, I caught it—that flicker in her eyes, desperate for any excuse to believe he was innocent. But then I noticed another man in a suit and mask, a big plus-size man, built like Tony. My eyes narrowed, a question forming—when my phone buzzed. Kelly's name lit the screen.

A shiver ran through me before I even answered. She said that the guys at the club spotted Tony, and they were in a shootout. She notified the police to dispatch to the club's location. Her text said she'd gotten us an Uber.

I glanced up and blurted. "Esperanza… someone's in danger. I have to go." The pain in my groin vanished as adrenaline took over. I turned toward the hall, shouting, "Kelly—hurry up!" Her muffled voice or movement never came back—only the drip of water behind the bathroom door.

I yanked the front door inward and slipped into the hall, moving fast. Ivan stood off to the side, but I didn't look at him—I was already angling for the elevator just a few feet away.

Then movement caught my eye. The elevator's door slid open, slow and certain. A leg stepped out first, sharp, deliberate, the crease of an Armani suit pressed tight and precise. Frank…

Everything froze. I stood there, locked in place. Frank's eyes pinned me, peeling me raw, leaving me exposed, nothing to hide behind. My hand twitched for my gun—then the truth gutted me. It was still in the car. Out of reach. Useless. Just like me.

"Oi," he said. Just that—simple, cold, casual. His eyes flicked my way, sharp enough to draw blood.

I snapped my head the other way and kept moving. His steps slowed, the silence thick around us. Then the stare hit—long, steady, invasive. It followed me to the elevator. I slipped inside, breath held, as his footsteps stopped mid-step.

"Excuse me! Excuse me!" his voice barked, sharp as a crack of lightning.

I hammered the elevator button until my fingertip throbbed. The doors clanged shut, cutting him off mid-sentence. A flash of bitter satisfaction—gone in an instant, drowned by panic. Kelly was still in there. Alone. Hurt. And now with him. I fumbled for my phone, thumbs shaking as I typed a quick text. No reply. I called. Nothing. "C'mon, Kelly. Pick up, pick the hell up!"

My stomach dropped to lead. Tony had been in a shootout. Frank was in the penthouse—with Kelly. And Natalie was still missing. Too much at once, and I didn't know who I could save, or if I could save anyone at all.

I closed my eyes, listened to the voice that wouldn't let me run, and it dragged me back to Frank's door. Ivan was still there, rigid as a guard dog. *Maybe Frank hadn't noticed her. But the shattered glass table? No one misses that.* I swallowed hard, forced my face into something steady. Then I spoke. "I think I left my phone on the couch," I said, my voice a little too tight, too high.

Ivan tilted his head, the way a dog does when it hears something strange, then shrugged. "I'll have to check with the boss."

I reached out and touched his hand—warm, solid. "It'll only take a second," I said, trying to sound calm. "My coworker's still inside. I promise it'll be quick."

He didn't move at first—just stood there, eyes raking over me, hunting for a crack in my story. In them, I read one thing: don't push your luck. Then, finally, he nodded. Too deliberate for my liking.

It could've gone either way—smooth as silk or jagged enough to leave scars. I braced myself as Ivan let me through.

Inside, the penthouse had gone dim, shadows thick across the room. "Kelly?" My voice barely rose above a whisper as I started walking through—no answer—just silence pressing in. I moved toward the open kitchen on my far left. A figure sat on a barstool at the island, lit by the faint glow from the ceiling lamp. My chest tightened. "Kelly…?" She turned, her face etched in dread as the dim ceiling light cascaded across her face. My blood froze.

And then—movement behind her, deep in the kitchen's shadow. Frank stepped out, gun raised, aimed square at my head.

"Un-un-un—not so fast," he growled, a grin curling his lips. "You again. The tough guy from the club... and earlier today. I'm just the luckiest son of a bitch on earth!"

My hands clenched so hard my knuckles cracked. Rage tore out of me in a snarl. "Let her go, you piece of shit!"

By the time I saw Ivan, it was already too late—his reflection flickered into the shattered glass coffee table crunching beneath my feet. He surged from the doorway; the butt of his gun smashed the base of my skull. My knees hit the floor. Kelly screamed. Then nothing—just black. Figures. My luck always seemed to cash out in the shittiest ways possible.

Chapter EIGHTEEN

THE LAST DAWN, THE FULL MONTY

Consciousness dragged me up by the ears first. Bells still rang in my skull when I caught her voice—trembling. Close. Natalie's? My eyelids fought me, but I forced a crack against the searing white glare. Shapes fused together, swimming, refusing to come clear.

I tried to say her name, but my throat was dry as sandpaper, and the words died before they reached my lips. Something hard pressed against my tongue. Her voice trembled on my name, each syllable torn apart. "Lor… en… zo… wa… ke… up…"

"Nnnatalie!" I forced her name past the gag in my mouth, barely more than a muffled groan. A vein throbbed at the side of my head as my vision fought to focus—two Franks swam at the dining table, then bled into one, a gun steady in his hand. I blinked past Frank's shoulder. Behind him, glass walls revealed a rooftop atrium—steam curling from the heated pool as snow flurries danced against the mountains.

I turned to the right—and there she was… Natalie—no, Kelly. Her muffled cries rattled in my ear, just a few feet beside me, tied to a chair. Duct tape everywhere. Wrists. Ankles. Even her goddamn mouth had been sealed under that gray grip! There was nothing funny in her eyes —just terror, the kind of sick shit Quentin Tarantino would've cooked up.

Suddenly, the realization hit me: I was in the same situation. Body bound. Arms taped behind the chair, tape biting into my skin. Every attempt tore at the fine hairs, raw and useless. No safe words, no games. Just cold restraint and the certainty that this wasn't ending with us alive. And something else was gnawing at me. A knife of pain twisted in my back, nerves screaming, refusing to shut the fuck up.

Frank's eyes snapped to me the second I groaned. "It's about time you woke up, Sleeping Beauty!" His voice was gravelly, soaked in nicotine and sarcasm. "You've been out for five days now." He shot a glance at Ivan, who stood at his right side. "Practically a fucking coma."

I gasped hard, my eyes felt like they might pop out and roll onto the floor.

Frank scoffed as Ivan stood there, arms folded, silently judging. 'I'm fucking with you, you moron! You've only been out'—he checked his watch—'five fucking minutes, and you're already looking like you're about to shit yourself!' He snarled, then jabbed at Ivan. 'Can you believe these fucking Yanks?' Ivan chuckled, shaking his head."

"Well," Frank's voice slid out smooth before his grin turned devilish. "Looks like your funerals are coming up sooner than you'd like—depends on how you answer my questions."

The gun stayed trained on my head, steady as his dead eyes. Fear and rage surged, colliding hard in my chest. I scanned the room fast—Esperanza was nowhere in sight—

"Eyes on me, fucker!" Frank barked. "I'm the one talking." He nodded once, satisfied, and Ivan stepped forward and ripped the gag from my mouth, then loomed at my left side.

The air was stale, metallic. Kelly's jaw was set, eyes burning. She was counting on me. And Natalie's life still hung in the balance. "Look, just let her go, I—"

Frank didn't let me finish. He cocked a brow at Ivan. A beat later, Ivan slid his gun free, the butt flashing across my head. Kelly flinched beside me, her fists clenching, but her eyes stayed locked on mine. The crack was sharp, wet. Vision burst white. Skin split above my eye. Blood ran warm into my sight, painting the world red on one side.

"You son of a bitch!" I spat, turning my focus to Frank, half-blind and furious. "I'm gonna kill you, asshole!"

Frank started making his way toward us, tossing a glance at Ivan—a silent signal passed between them. Ivan was on me again before I could brace, his fist slamming into my gut like a sledgehammer, knocking the breath clean out of me, doubling me over.

And that's when I felt it worse, once I hit the floor—a sharp, deep pain seeping a little deeper into my lower back. Something was lodged there, cold and nefarious—glass. A shard buried in my lower back, maybe a quarter inch deep, maybe less, but every breath made sure that it hurt like hell.

Low laughter circled me, jagged at the edges. "Kill me?" Frank sneered, leaning close. "Don't flatter yourself. You're a dog on a leash—my leash, and I'm holding the chain." He leaned in, bitter coffee breath hot on my face. "I give the orders. I ask the questions. You?"

His grin was all teeth, crawling under my skin. "You bleed. Then you talk." He yanked my hair, eyes glittering cold. "Or should I spell it out for you?' He cut a glance at Ivan. "Pick this piece of shit up. Nobody bleeds on my ninety-K floor.'"

Kelly's muffled cries rose as Ivan hauled the chair upright, tape still gnawing into my skin. Frank launched into his alpha-male tantrum. Kept my head down, silent, maybe I was still alive only because I hadn't answered any of his questions. His rant broke off, eyes sliding over to Kelly. The gun followed.

"Fine. You wanna play the tough guy? How about I skip the games and put a bullet in your girlfriend's pretty face right now? Ivan, grab the suitcases from my office. We'll pack 'em up nice and neat, and slip past the cameras before anyone catches on... besides, I'm a professional."

I couldn't take it anymore "—Wait!" I blurted, my voice cracking, eyes darting between them. "What do you want to know?"

"The obvious, mate!" he snarled, a nasty grin twisting his face. "Why the fuck are you in my penthouse, dressed like a *BoysTown* sissy from Chicago? And what the hell were you yanks doing snooping around my shipyard?"

Kelly shook her head, a silent plea with her eyes for me to stay quiet. But I didn't. "We—we came to see if you... had something to do with my wife's disappearance."

His grin dropped instantly, replaced by cold fury. He leaned in, leveling the gun at my head from a few feet away. "Natalie, eh?"

"—Don't you fucking say her name, you son of a bitch" I snapped, the words ripping out of me.

The grin vanished as he closed the distance and pressed the barrel to my head. I leaned into it, not giving a fuck—a guttural yell tearing from my throat. *Today I was ready—ready to risk it all by laying my life on the line for the woman I love.*

"—Oh, shut the fuck up and pipe down, wanker," Frank scoffed, flicking a glance at Ivan. "Can you believe this idiot? I'm holding the bloody weapon, and somehow, in his delusional little world, he's the hero. Breaking into my house, pulling stunts like a cowboy—what kind of lunatic thinks this ends any other way than a body bag?"

He sneered, stroking his chin. "And that trick at the red light with the cops… cute. Real cute. Think anyone's forgotten? Wait…" His eyes narrowed like a snake. "There were three of you. Where's the lardass who was driving?"

Blank stares from us. No one moved. His gaze lingered, sharp enough to peel flesh. "Okay, have it your way then. Ivan, fetch me a potato from the pantry."

Ivan shuffled off, and the weight of the room got heavier. We watched without moving, too scared to twitch. Frank tilted his Kangol just so, his voice dropping into an almost conversational tone. "I don't even know your name. You were the hardass at the club, the one who knocked my hat off because you thought you could grab a woman—"

"That's not just a woman!" I snapped, before I could stop myself. "That's my wife—"

"Yeah, yeah, your wife. Real nice piece of chocolate ass you got there. I see how it is. Pink little manhood chasing something exotic."

Rage coiled in my chest, tight as a spring. I wanted nothing more than to wipe that ugly ass smirk off his face.

"Hey!" he barked, snapping the gun toward Kelly. "Try a move, and I'll paint these walls with her brains. Go on, test the water—fuck around and find out."

Ivan came back from the kitchen that sat behind me, angled to the right, a dusty potato in hand as if it were some sacred offering. From where we sat in the living room, I could see the counters spilling into the open dining space beyond, the pantry door cutting between them. Out here, it all ran together—living room, kitchen, dining. A big place, but the openness made it feel like there was nowhere to hide.

Ivan held the potato out. "Here you go, boss."

Frank grinned, locking eyes with me as he held it up in admiration. "You like potatoes?"

"What?" I blinked, thrown off by the absurd question. His eyes stayed locked on mine, drilling into me, daring me to look away. I didn't even notice what he was doing with his other hand until—

Blam!

Frank jammed a potato over the barrel. The shot cracked—loud yet dulled. The potato burst across me, and Kelly's muffled scream followed.

"Always wondered if that'd work." Frank's tone was curious as he eyed the shredded mess in his hand, then looked at me. "Figures the potato trick's just Hollywood bullshit." His grin crept in—slow, crooked.

Pain exploded through my shoulder, toppling me backward in the chair. The world tilted. Blood ran hot and sticky down my arm. A gasp tore out—half scream, half choke—and all I could think of was my mother. *Funny, isn't it? Men face death, and the first thing they do is cry for Mom.*

Frank scoffed, standing front and center between me and Kelly, just a few feet away. "You'd think I shot you in the goddamn heart!" He sneered, stepped closer, and loomed over me. "Quit your whining. It's a fucking shoulder wound. You Americans are so goddamn soft. Ivan, pick up the pansy."

I winced through clenched teeth, letting out a whimper for effect as Ivan hauled me upright again. The pain was real, sharp enough to blur my vision. My shoulder throbbed like hell, but Frank was too busy playing The Godfather to notice what my hands were up to. A second pool of blood spread beneath me, separate from the drip down my arm. That shard of glass—the one buried in my back since this nightmare began—I'd finally worked it loose. My fingers closed around it, slick with blood, and I started sawing at the tape binding my wrists.

I looked at Kelly. She was trembling, eyes wide, but she caught the signal when I gave her *the look*—the kind you trade in Spades when you're about to cheat your ass off and need your partner to play along. Subtle. Quick. But unmistakable.

Pain roared through me, but adrenaline was louder. *I had to survive—for Natalie's sake. If I lost her, I wouldn't see the point in going on. I'd just find some shitty motel and finish the job myself. But not yet. Not today. I still had a chance to save her. It wasn't just my life on the line—it was all of ours. Because losing Natalie wouldn't just kill me—it'd erase me.*

The thought barely had time to settle before shouts erupted from the bedroom, crashing into the living room like a tidal wave. Esperanza's voice tore through it all—a raw, fierce scream that made even Frank *Capone* flinch: gangster, my ass.

High heels clicked across the floor outside the bedroom on my left. "What in the hell is going on?" Esperanza barked.

Frank snapped his head toward the doorway down the hall, already scowling. "Stay in the bloody room—"

"—No, Frank! What the fuck are you doing?" she stormed into the living room, wild hair catching the dim light, eyes flaring.

He held up a hand like a traffic cop, his tone was slick with fake calm. "We're handling a little dispute here. Nothing for you to worry about—"

"A little dispute?" she barked out a laugh, the kind with no humor. Her eyes darted to me, slumped and bleeding out like a gutted deer. "I heard a gunshot! Oh my god. Did you really shoot him!?"

He bristled, face tightening like a noose. "Now hold on—"

I seized the moment. "You shot him and then tied them up." A smug grin crept across my face. "Well, not in that order exactly."

Esperanza's voice hit a fever pitch as she stormed forward and dropped to a crouch beside me. Her hands fluttered near my wound—hovering, never touching, but close enough to sting. "Jesus Christ, Frank! You said you were just going to talk to them!"

Frank's mouth twisted into a grim parody of a smile, barely

masking the venom in his voice. "We're just talking." He threw a glance at me and Kelly. "Some of us, a little more than others—but hey." He spread his hands like he was offering a gift. "I think we're finally starting to get somewhere."

He walked over and grabbed her arm, his fingers sinking in—talons tugging her into the kitchen. "Honeyyy." He drew the word out in a whisper, too close, his breath hot against her ear. "I just want to scare them. That's all, I swear. Let me handle it. Ivan and I will clean them up afterwards and send them on their way."

She flinched at his words. "You shot a man, Frank! What the hell's gotten into you?"

For a moment, his face stayed blank, like her words hadn't landed. Then his lips twitched, curling into a smile that wasn't his. Too wide. Too sharp. His pupils shrank to black needles.

The light above them flickered with a haunted-house effect, and the whole kitchen seemed to lean in around him. Her stomach twisted. This wasn't Frank. Not the man she had known, not the man she had married, not the man who had kissed her on cold mornings or held her when the nightmares came. This was something else—dark and coiled, clawing its way out of him. Not her Frank. Not anymore. Whatever had surfaced in him made her skin crawl, the hair on the back of her neck standing in warning.

She winced as his fingers clamped down on her jaw, hard enough to make her teeth ache. His eyes bore into hers, cold and unblinking, and then he leaned in, pressing his dry, lifeless lips against her forehead. The touch lingered just long enough to leave a stain she couldn't wipe away.

"How about you make me some coffee since you're already in the kitchen, love?" he said, his voice oily and sweet—a salesman pitching poison. "Shouldn't be too much longer. I'll be done here by then."

"Don't hurt them." The words were brittle in Esperanza's mouth.

Frank paused, a grin splitting his face like a knife wound—jagged and humorless. "Hurt them?" he said, his voice dry as dust. Then he laughed—short, brittle, more cough than mirth. "Oh sure, sweetheart.

Scout's honor. Why don't you get some coffee started for me and my pals here, huh?"

Deep down, she had always known. Denial was a tricky bastard—it hadn't just whispered sweet nothings in her ear; it had built her a castle out of lies, complete with smiling portraits and walls that held back the truth. But castles crumbled, and monsters always found their way to the light, their teeth bared in a grin that said, You were a fool to think I wouldn't win.

"Sure!" she chirped, moving toward the coffee maker by the sink as if nothing were wrong. Her hands stayed steady while she poured in the water and set it to boil.

Frank turned to face us, his grin sharpening. "Now, where were we? Oh... that's right—your wife." He sank back into his chair, casual as a snake on a rock. "What do I have to do with her?"

I shifted slightly, testing the bonds at my wrists, careful not to let him see the intent flicker in my eyes as Ivan drifted back to Frank's side. "You know my wife, the woman from the other night. The woman you helped disappear."

Frank's face didn't flinch, but his smile tightened, like a noose pulling taut. "I don't know—well, didn't know—your wife before yesterday. So why would I magically make her want to disappear?" He lifted his fingers in mocking air quotes, dripping sarcasm.

Ivan's finger twitched.

A beat later, a low, bitter laugh escaped me—deeper than anger and colder than hate. "That's funny, Frank. The cat's already out of the fucking bag. We've got pictures of you meeting her—not just once, but several times. And I'm not talking about casual run-ins at the grocery store."

Frank's eyes darted after Esperanza, guilt flashing across his face before he locked it down. "You're crazy. I never cheated on my wife. Especially not at sex parties." He stopped, then bit the inside of his cheek so hard it almost drew blood.

"Go on, Frank!" Esperanza barked from the kitchen. "What sex parties?"

He hesitated, his gaze flicking to Ivan, who shifted under it, eyes dropping for a beat before hardening again.

"That's what the hell I thought!" I replied coldly. "You just told on yourself. I never said anything about sex parties, Frank. However, now that you've mentioned it… Tell us more about it!"

The color drained from his face. He scratched the back of his neck, the guilty tic of a man who's run out of lies. "I swear, I—"

Ivan's phone buzzed, still unable to break the tension in the room. He glanced at the text, his expression hardening. "Boss, we've got a problem. Someone broke into the club. They're holed up in the basement—you know, *the private room area.* Our guys are trading fire. What do you want me to do?"

Frank's composure cracked, just for a moment. His eyes darted back to me, but I wasn't about to let him off the hook.

"No-no-no, Frank," I leaned forward, voice low. "You swear you haven't cheated, but sex parties? That's some freaky shit. What's your safe word… pineapple juice?" I let it hang, then dropped the blade. "By the way—I saw the photos. You. My wife. And… "a guy." My gaze cut to Esperanza. "So tell me, how's that gonna play out with your wife here?"

—Frank's mouth opened, but no sound came out.

"Look at him, Esperanza," I growled, pointing with my chin. "This is the man you married. The one who's been lying to your face for God knows how long. You've seen the pictures, haven't you? Or are you still blind to the devil sitting behind the table?"

She moved toward Frank, slow and deliberate, her eyes locked on him.

"Shut up!" Frank snapped, glowering at me, his voice cracking as he clung to the last thread of control.

"Tell her, Frank!" I snarled, my voice sharp enough to make him flinch. "Tell her how you've been working for the Russian mob. Or are you going to keep lying? Go ahead. Spin another story."

Frank shook his head, that nervous, twitchy smile creeping back onto his face. "Don't listen to him, honey. He's just trying to—"

"—Damn… lying again," I cut him off, my tone freezing the air.

"I've seen the emails, Frank. The photos on my wife's laptop? The same night, I ran into you at the airport. You thought you could cover your tracks, didn't you? Thought you could keep playing your games, but now… It's all coming out."

Frank's sharp intake of breath told me I'd hit my mark. He was unraveling, and I wasn't about to stop. "The articles, the evidence, your so-called circle jerk—all of it ties you to murders across the country. Tell me one thing, Frank. How does it feel to stare into the mirror and see a serial killer looking back?"

The air in the room wasn't just still—it was wrong. Oxygen sucked out. Esperanza froze mid-step, eyes narrowing as if she could feel it too. Frank noticed. His jaw tightened.

"I never said my wife's name," Frank uttered, his voice low and dangerous. His ice-cold gaze snapped to her. The hot coffee pot in her hands quivered. "You've been fucking my wife!??? You son of a bitch!" His rage exploded—not through the gun, but in his voice, raw and thunderous. "You're dead!" He pointed the weapon at me. "Esperanza, I'll deal with you in a minute. First him—then that bitch of his."

"Frank, no!" Esperanza shouted, her voice trembling as Frank's finger moved to the trigger.

And then I saw it—his face, a stony mask of violence about to erupt. His eyes weren't just angry; they were hollow. I was prey now, a target marked for execution. Time didn't slow—it shattered. Death wasn't creeping toward me. It was here. It wore Frank's face, and its clock had just hit zero. My eyes shut tight as I braced for the flash, the pain, the nothingness. The gunshot came, but it didn't hit me.

A guttural scream tore through the room, raw and primal. My eyes flew open just as Frank staggered back, clutching his face. Steam rose from his hands, flesh peeling from his cheek like melting wax. Esperanza stood trembling, the empty coffee pot clutched in her grip, fear and defiance battling in her eyes. I didn't think—I lunged, driving Kelly to the floor. We hit hard, her gasp hot in my ear as I slashed through the tape at her wrists and ankles. Then the second shot cracked, merciless. The room froze. My hand stalled above the final strip of tape, the shard of glass trembling in my grip, suspended in that thin, fragile space between heartbeats.

Next came the shattering of the coffee pot—sharp and final. Esperanza hit the floor, her mouth open, a whisper that never formed. Blood spread across her blouse, dark and fast, her legs folding beneath her. She crumpled only feet from Frank.

Frank's scream tore out, raw and broken. He crawled to her, blistered face and hands reaching for her limp body. "No, no, no! Baby, it's okay. Do you hear me?" His voice cracked as he shook her. "Stay with me—I'm right here!"

Ivan stood in the same spot, his gun still smoking, his face pale. He looked bewildered, like a child who'd realized too late the consequences of his actions. "Boss!" Ivan muttered, his voice hoarse. "She… she attacked you."

Frank didn't look at him. He didn't look at anything except Esperanza's face, rocking her like a child clutching a shattered doll. Death hadn't left the room. No. It was still here, patiently, watching, waiting!

He looked over his shoulder and gave Ivan a sinister scowl.

"Boss, wait!" Ivan's plea had been half-formed, barely getting the words out.

The bullet had already drilled into his forehead, erupting in a spray of blood and brain, splattering the floor behind him in a violent, grisly arc.

For a moment, he stood frozen, eyes wide with shock. Then his legs gave out, and he crumpled, lifeless, leaving only the smear on the ninety grand tile to mark his end.

I ripped the tape from Kelly's mouth, and she gasped, desperate, like someone breaking the surface after drowning. We didn't pause, didn't look at each other—we just ran. Behind us, Frank's voice erupted in guttural shouts, words slurred with fury. His aim was slipping, thanks to Esperanza and the scalding coffee she'd thrown in his face.

The sharp cracks of gunfire chased us, bullets tearing through drywall and splintering wood. Each step sent a jolt of agony through my back, blood trickling down my spine to soak my shirt. The room reeked of gunpowder and copper. Frank staggered, one hand clutching his ruined face, the other waving the gun blindly—still terrifying. Another shot thundered past, close enough to raise the hairs on my neck as a splinter of drywall nicked my shoulder.

"Do you think you can get away from me? You fucking cunts! My wife's dead because of you! And your wife—that bitch Natalie—is gonna die next!" he yelled, his words slurred as he trailed behind us.

We made it through the door, the hallway stretching ahead, every shadow a threat. My legs burned, lungs screaming for air—but the wound in my back was worse, tearing wider with each step. Kelly hauled my arm over her shoulder as I staggered forward. I didn't dare look back. Frank's boots pounded closer, each step hammering—death closing in.

"Faster!" Kelly's voice cracked, pushing me harder. The elevator loomed ahead at the end of the hallway, close but not close enough. My fingers stretched toward the call button, every thought narrowing to one mantra: *If that door doesn't close, we die.*

Frank's bellow thundered behind us, rage and pain echoing down the corridor, his boots pounding closer. Each step tore at the wound in my back, pain flaring hot, but I clenched my teeth and drove forward. I slammed the button, blood-slicked fingers smearing the polished metal as the doors shuddered and began to slide open.

My heart surged with hope—then a shot cracked, the bullet shattering the mirror at my side. Glass rained over me, slicing my arms and face. The elevator doors slid open at last. I shoved Kelly inside without looking and staggered forward, still in the hallway, as Frank's shadow closed in, his boots pounding nearer.

"Police! Put your fucking hands up! On your knees! Interlock your fingers!"

The command blasted from behind and ahead. I spun—and that's when I saw it. The elevator wasn't empty. It was crammed with a SWAT team, rifles leveled, barrels aimed straight at us, while more officers poured from the stairwell.

"It's not us!" Kelly shouted, her voice shaky. "We don't have any weapons! A guy is shooting in the hallway! His wife is dead and killed a guy—"

A shot cracked down the hall. The bullet whipped past my head so close I felt the air shiver. I barely registered the SWAT team yanking me into the elevator—shouts, gunfire, everything a blur of chaos.

"Police! Put the gun down!"

"Send that fucking Yankee cunt out here!" Frank roared, spit flying, the words tearing out of him just before another shot cracked. Frank was unhinged, a walking hurricane of rage. He wanted blood—my blood.

The SWAT team didn't fuck around. These weren't doughnut-eating beat cops—they were hounds of war in black Kevlar, and you complied or you died. One minute Frank was center stage in his Italian gangster flick, all bravado and slick talk. The next—badda bing, badda boom—a flash grenade erupted, a sun in a box. My ears rang, thoughts slipping underwater. Shouts battered me, then gunfire—sharp, endless, overwhelming.

They shoved me down hard. My knees smacked the floor, pain exploding in my bones. That's when I saw her—Kelly—pinned against the elevator floor, eyes wide, locked on mine. Smoke rolled in, reeking of gunpowder and scorched metal. Muzzle flashes strobed through the haze, lighting up silhouettes—men in motion, phantoms with rifles. The air throbbed with gunfire, each shot a steel whip. I gasped for breath, lungs pulling in smoke and panic. I covered my ears. This was a fucking war zone! The hallway littered with shell casings, the hall floor slick with blood. And through it all, one thought cut cold and clear: This is how people die. And Frank Richardson did just that…

Chapter NINETEEN

WHAT LIES BENEATH

The ambulance driver patched me up outside in front of the hotel, his gloved hands moving fast and efficiently, like a man changing a tire in the rain. He was persistent in taking me to the hospital, but I refused to go. No way in hell was I letting them wheel me under blinding fluorescents to poke and prod at whatever was left of me. I could handle it. At least, that's what I kept telling myself.

The scene was pure chaos. Ambulances screamed, their lights strobing the night. Police cars lined the curb, news vans vying for a shot, cameras eager. A black SWAT truck loomed, turning the hotel into a warzone set. If I didn't know better, I'd have thought it was a movie—one of those thrillers where the hero takes a bullet, spits out some blood, and growls something manly before limping off into the night with the woman he saved. But this wasn't a movie. No retakes. No stunt doubles. And I wasn't the hero. I was the guy pulling glass out of his back, shoulder burning from a bullet graze—"minor wounds," sure, but it throbbed like it had its own heartbeat. Reminding me I wasn't as tough as I pretended. Worst part? The nightmare wasn't over. Natalie was still missing.

Kelly had been calling Tony since I climbed into the ambulance. Over an hour ago, maybe a little more, and still nothing—just silence on the other end. Alive? Dead? In a ditch somewhere? The not-knowing dug into me worse than the glass shard ever did. We didn't get much time to dwell on it, though. The next act had already started.

Colorado's finest—Detective Hoffpauir and his partner, Pornstache

—decided to take us for a ride, get our statements, and fire off a few questions. They came rapid fire—the how, the who, the why, the what. We kept it simple. They weren't ready for everything. Hell, I wasn't sure I was ready. Eventually, they muttered about sending a few units to the club. Maybe they'd find Tony. Maybe Natalie. Or perhaps just more pieces to a puzzle we weren't close to solving. As the lights flashed and the night stretched on, one thing was clear: we were far from done.

Detective Hoffpauir glanced into the back seat, voice smooth as a knife edge. "We went through Frank's bedroom. Found a suit— stained. Little specks of blood. Lab says it's your wife's. From her hand. The one we found at the scene."

I felt my breath glitch. "We found her phone, too," he said. "In his office. Along with pictures—him, your wife, the heart tattoo on her arm matching the photo you showed us, and a few others." He let the silence crawl between us, heavy and alive.

Kelly placed her hand on my forearm as I grunted, running a hand through my hair. 'Yeah, we saw the pictures too. Frank told me—right before your cop buddies killed him—that my wife was next.'"

"He's dead now. And that's our advantage," Kowalski said confidently.

"—How does that help if we don't know where she is? A dead man can't talk!" my voice cracked at the edges.

Detective Hoffpauir cut in from the passenger seat, steady but firm. 'We've got units tearing through every property Frank and his crew own. You said Tony was last heard from at Frank's club—that's where we're going now. I promise, Mr. Moretti, we're not stopping until we find her. Count on that."

Shortly after the words left his mouth, the radio crackled with dispatch:

"All units, be advised: reports indicate a shooting occurred at Club Flamingo approximately two hours ago. Multiple victims reported on scene. Requesting units to respond and secure the location."

Detective Hoffpauir snatched the radio. 'We're seven minutes out and en route." His voice was calm, clipped, all business. He cut us a glance in the rearview, eyes cold, then flipped on the sirens—their scream splitting the quiet city—and stomped the pedal."

Seven minutes? Ha. Not with his driving. We made it in three, tops. The scene hit like a gut punch. The Club Flamingo's neon sign hummed, bleeding pink across the sidewalk. Outside, a man leaned against the brick wall, cigarette trembling between his fingers. Manager, maybe. His face slack, eyes flicking to the doors like he expected the devil to walk out.

No crowd yet—strange. Usually, crime scenes drew a pack of lookie-loos, buzzing with morbid curiosity. But here? Just that guy and the low electric hum of the city, like everything had paused, waiting. Then it hit me: the feeling. It crawled up my spine, slow, deliberate. The club loomed, its glass doors reflecting the pulse of red and blue from the cruisers. Something was wrong. Not just the bodies I knew waited inside. The place itself felt coiled, holding its breath.

I swallowed hard, pulse drumming in my ears. Beside me, Kelly shifted, her fingers flexing at her sides. She was ready. We both were.

Hoffpauir cut in, voice sharp. "Mr. Moretti, you're not going in there. Not unless you're itching for a bullet—or worse. We don't know who's left, what they're packing, or if they'd love to give you a lobotomy with a lead slug. So sit tight while we figure it out. Capiche!"

Capiche, my ass. I wasn't going to sit in this car like some obedient dog while my wife might be in that hellhole. My fingers curled around the door handle, ready to bolt—until Kelly's hand stopped me. Her touch was barely there, her grip? Iron.

"It's okay, Lorenzo," she said, calm, deliberate, as if steadying the air itself. "Let them do their job." But her eyes told another story— burning with the same fear gnawing at my chest.

Before I could argue, the car door slammed. The detectives were already moving, boots crunching through the snow as they stormed the club with guns drawn, swallowed by the dark past its doors.

Kelly didn't wait for their footsteps to fade. She leaned closer, her voice a low hiss. 'We're not staying in this car. Tony's in there.'

We moved as one, hopped out of the car, and headed for the club. The manager stepped in front of us, arms spread.

"Stay back! You can't go in there," he barked, but his voice was nothing more than background noise. We shoved past him without a second glance.

The second we crossed the threshold, the air was metallic, sour, heavy. It stank of sweat, gunpowder, and something else—darker, dead. Inside, the place was a slaughterhouse. Walls riddled with bullet holes. Tables overturned, splintered like matchsticks. I grabbed a broken leg from a barstool, and Kelly snatched up a wine bottle lying a couple of feet away. It wasn't much against a gun, but hey—better than nothing.

Up ahead, blood speckled the floor—just a few drops at first, scattered like breadcrumbs, dragging us forward. But deeper in, the specks stretched into streaks, smeared thick across the club's tile.

Luckily, Kelly managed to ping Tony's burner phone—he was still inside. It led us off to the right, past the wreck of splintered tables, to a wall too smooth, too perfect. Kelly broke off toward it, her boots crunching over glass. A hidden panel. She pressed it, and the seam gave way.

Cold air bled out as the slab swung inward, revealing a narrow, rusted stairwell that twisted down into the dark of the basement. My gut knotted. Each step down pulled the dread tighter, wire around bone. I felt like something in the cellar was waiting for me.

Black suits lay scattered as we made our way down the stairwell into the basement. The dim light spilling from the club behind me caught their faces just enough—locked in agony, eyes staring at nothing.

The copper stench overwhelmed the air. Gunpowder burned in my lungs. Whoever had fired here hadn't been sloppy—clean shots, deliberate. If Tony took these men out, then he sure as hell knew his way around a gun. The thought twisted worse than the stench. *How much had he been hiding?* The image of him at Frank's side—arm around Natalie, grinning behind that mask—flickered in my mind. *What side of this bloody mess had he really stood on? And what the hell was I still not seeing?"*

The questions gnawed at me as we pushed deeper into the basement, still stepping past Frank's fallen goons. Kelly kept a few steps ahead. I let my eyes drag over the bodies littering the stone hall, walls slick with damp and mold. The place smelled like a sewer wearing cologne.

Farther ahead, a dying light flickered—clinging to life. The air grew colder, and shadows thickened. The silence stretched too long… until it broke.

A guttural scream ripped through the dark—jagged, unfiltered, scraping against my nerves. It wasn't meant for the living; it came from a place of grief, primal and broken. My head snapped toward it. Kelly buckled against the wall, nails dragging across the concrete like she was clawing for something solid. The bottle slipped from her grip as she sagged down, shattering at her feet. Her face twisted, tears streaking as she howled Tony's name again and again, each syllable more ragged than the last, echoing down the basement corridor.

My gaze lifted past her. And there he was—Tony. Slumped against the brick wall in the weak glow. Arms limp. Legs sprawled. A bullet in his neck, blood spilling across his black coat. Dead as a fucking doorknob.

Footsteps echoed behind me, sharp against the concrete. I turned, stick still in my hand.

"Whoa, whoa! Cowboy—put it down!" Hoffpauir barked. I let the stick drop with a clatter at my side. "What the hell are you doing in here? I told you to wait in the car." His words snapped off, but his gaze had already shifted past me—to Kelly, crumpled on the floor, sobbing.

He brushed past, boots over chipped asphalt, and crouched beside her. Fingers pressed to Tony's neck, searching for a pulse. A beat later, he shook his head, grim and certain, before thumbing his radio for dispatch. Rising again, he slid an arm under Kelly, steadying her as she struggled to her feet, blood dripping from her knees where the shattered glass had cut into her skin.

"Hey, get her out of here," Hoffpauir snapped, whipping his head over his shoulder at me. I just stood there, trying to process it all, but his stare lingered—drawn to Tony's black jacket, the fabric jutting oddly from his pocket.

Kelly fought against him, trying to throw herself back toward Tony. "I need you to grab her," he barked again, voice harder now. "Both of you—out. This is a crime scene."

I moved in to pull Kelly away, her nails scraping at my arm as she twisted against me. Behind us, Hoffpauir slid on a blue latex glove, crouched beside Tony, and reached into his left pocket—then paused. His hand came back holding something small, pale, and horrifying—a severed finger. A woman's…

The detective froze, body hardening into something grim and absolute. I didn't need words. That finger told me everything I hadn't wanted to believe: Tony was tied to Natalie's disappearance, and he wasn't coming back. His body slumped against the wall, eyes shut, mouth slack. A thin maroon thread of blood trailed from the corner of his lips.

"This can't be right," Kelly cried, trying to piece it all together. "Tony wouldn't do this—!"

I wanted to tell her about the photo—the one I suspected was him with Frank at that party—but the moment swallowed me whole. It all crashed down. Even in death, Tony was a piece of shit. Probably got himself killed just to duck out on the nearly five grand he owed me for the hotel bill. And now the secrets he and Frank shared were buried with them. It felt like the walls had leaned in, listening. We'd walked into a truth none of us were ready to face.

I hauled Kelly up, her arm draped over my shoulder, her sobs echoing off the concrete. As we headed for the stairwell, something to my left snagged the corner of my eye; a single brick set back deeper than the rest, mortar cracked and crumbling around. Something was drawing me to it. Gently lowering Kelly to the floor, I stepped toward the wall. Leaning closer, I felt a faint warmth slip through the narrow gap, brushing my cheek. Hidden in plain sight—an opening disguised as part of the wall.

I started plucking at the bricks one by one, yanking them loose, mortar cracking under my fingers. Each pull sent fire through the wound in my back, gnawing, but I pressed harder, tearing them out with desperation. Dust filled my throat, grit clung to my tongue. I was determined to see what was back there.

After clearing a few, I froze. My eyes dragged to the gap, widening. A shape. A silhouette in the glow beyond—slouched, still. A person in a chair. *A woman?* "Natalie," I uttered, the name breaking out of me before I could stop it. I knew it was her. My hand trembled as I clawed faster, bricks tumbling at my feet, my breath ragged.

I heard my name echoed—distant, hollow—but I didn't listen. Couldn't. My world narrowed to that glow, that shape. The light steadied through the hole, shadows peeling back. It was definitely her. Natalie. Tied to a chair, rope biting into her arms. Head tilted, lips parted. Her skin still held color in the glow, fragile but alive. Her eyes were open. Wide. Fixed on me.

My breath stuttered. I saw it—movement. Her body rose—shallow, uneven. But it rose. Relief tore through me like air to a drowning man. She was alive. Faint, broken, but alive. She didn't hear me when I shouted her name, but I told myself it was shock. She couldn't move. She needed me. She was waiting. At first, she was only a shadow in the corner of an empty cellar behind a hollow wall, and now she was everything. My Natalie. Alive!

I started forward, heart hammering, blood roaring in my ears. In the cellar's dimness, a dying glow seeped down the winding stairwell from the club above—just enough to catch the sweat on her skin, the strands of dark hair plastered to her face. Every detail seemed to sharpen in my mind the closer I came. Barely enough light to see, yet relief swelled in my chest.

"Natalie! Babe, I'm here—it's okay!" My voice cracked as I stumbled over broken concrete, feet crunching toward her. I was close enough now to see the fingers of her one hand curled lightly against the armrest. Close enough to catch the soft flutter of her lashes—*or was it?"*

Something was wrong. My steps faltered, the hope in my chest hitching, twisting into something colder. Her chest—it wasn't moving. My mind scrambled, trying to rationalize it. The dim light wavered, casting illusions that made it seem like she'd been breathing. She was breathing a second ago. She was.

I staggered forward, my hand reaching out before I could stop it. My fingertips brushed her arm. Cold. Her body swayed with the contact, and her head lolled further to the side, wide eyes staring past me, fixed and empty. The stub of her arm where her hand used to be—gauze wrapped around a gnarled mess of flesh—still dripped onto the floor.

"No!" I shouted, tears burning at the back of my eyes as my knees gave out, dropping me in front of her. I gripped her limp, unresponsive fingers. "No. No. No!" I clawed at the ropes binding her arms and legs. The truth hit. She wasn't breathing. She hadn't been breathing. I'd wanted to see it so badly that my mind fooled me into believing it.

The room was still, quiet, and cold. The chill of her skin seeped into mine, and the hope that had burned so bright a moment ago was gone, ripped out and replaced with hollow dread that crushed the oxygen from my lungs. Natalie was dead. Too late. I thought I might puke or pass out—or both. The room spun, but my hands kept clawing at the knots. They were rough and tight, biting into my fingers, and I couldn't get them loose fast enough

From the distance came the crash of boots. Heavy, determined. Voices barked behind me, sharp and jagged as breaking glass.

"Don't touch her! Step back!"

A hand wrenched me away, so hard I almost fell. The rope slipped from my fingers, leaving my hands empty, useless. Suddenly, I wasn't saving her anymore. I wasn't anything.

"This is my crime scene," one of the cops shouted, like those words meant something. Like they could explain why she was still tied up, and I couldn't help her.

My legs were rubber, twitching uselessly beneath me. My face was hot and wet—I couldn't tell where the tears ended and the snot began —and I sobbed so hard my chest felt like it was tearing apart.

The cops pulled me up as I kicked, fighting to stay with my wife. Till death do us part—those were the vows we made. I couldn't stop it.

Couldn't stop the crying, the shaking, the hollow collapse in my gut, swallowing everything whole. And her. I couldn't stop thinking about how I failed her.

Chapter TWENTY

DEATH AFTER THE STORM

Days blurred. The city of Chicago came back, but she didn't. Natalie's face burned into the corners of my mind, in that chair. Head slumped like a broken doll. Eyes vacant, staring past me into nothing. And that frozen moment lived inside my skull, scratching at the walls—a horror I couldn't outrun; no matter how far I went.

The motel door clanged shut behind me, the chain lock rattling as I slid it into place. A threadbare rug curled against the door, but the real joke was the lock—a barrier that couldn't stop a stiff breeze, let alone someone with intent.

My room reeked of old cigar smoke and faint bleach—too weak to erase whatever sins had seeped into the walls. Outside my window, the motel's neon sign buzzed and flickered, throwing fractured pink and blue lights into the room in uneven pulses—gnawing at my nerves, though I didn't dare flip the overhead light. Darkness had its advantages. It could hide you, even from yourself.

I sank onto the bed, the mattress groaning beneath me. My gun sat heavy in my lap, the cold steel grounding me against the half-gallon of Jameson sloshing in my veins. Thoughts were rats in a cage, gnawing at reason until nothing was left but fragments. I couldn't shake it—the prickling at the back of my neck, the certainty I'd been followed. Hell, maybe I had.

"Frank!" I blurted, the name ripping out mid-thought. Just saying it felt like a loaded gun. He didn't let people go. You might leave breathing, but you didn't leave free. And now I was probably on the gang's list—the kind where the only way out was six feet under. He was dead because of me, and I was certain his mafia friends would come collecting.

And once that thought dug in, the shadows started moving—stretching and twisting in the flickering neon glow. They weren't just shapes anymore—they were alive. Every creak of the building turned hostile. Every distant rumble of an engine felt like a predator closing in.

Should've kept driving. Should've crossed state lines. Should've disappeared entirely. But I knew it wouldn't have mattered. Frank's people didn't lose track. They didn't lose anything. And paranoia—it had claws. It turned every glance over my shoulder into something with teeth.

I crossed the cigarette-burned carpet and stopped at the window, bottle in one hand, the gun now jammed into my waistband. The curtain felt greasy under my fingers as I pulled it back, peering closely until my reflection wavered in the grimy pane. Outside, the world looked warped and unreal, already pulling away from me. It wouldn't take much—a knock at the door, a shadow slipping past the glass—and the fragile illusion of safety would shatter.

I took a hard pull from the Jameson, the burn scorching my throat. My hand shook as I set the bottle on the sill, but the fire did nothing to settle the churn in my gut. The cops said they'd "solved the case"—too easy, too neat. Their conclusion stank of half-truths and lazy thinking.

A few details from the police kept hammering in my head. Tony's phone pinged near the club just before the massacre in the penthouse. But Tony knew better than to turn it on when he had his burner. The cops waved it off as a mistake, just a glitch in the system. After all, "we were all at the hotel," or at least that's what their records claimed. But one thing never added up for me: if Tony and Frank had been playing on the same team, why the hell did Frank's goons put holes in him?

And then the envelope of pictures we found—the evidence. Frank had kept them hidden in his drawer. The cops couldn't explain it, and neither could I. They believed someone might have been blackmailing him. Maybe Frank hadn't trusted his own people, the higher-ups, or perhaps someone on his team figured they'd need a bargaining chip someday. But none of it mattered now. They were both dead, their secrets buried with them. *And Frank's mafia ties?* That trail had gone cold, lost in the shadows where people like me didn't survive long enough to look. There was no telling how far up the food chain this thing had gone.

I yanked the gun from my waistband and stared at it, its cold weight pressing into my palm like judgment. Standing at the window, I watched the quiet outskirts cast shadows across the glass as cars slipped past the parking lot on the road below. The room felt like it was watching me, every reflection flickering back my own face.

My grip tightened, fingers flexing. I needed to steady myself, claw back some shred of sanity—if that was even possible. The barrel touched my lips, bitter and unyielding, and I welcomed it. Metal spread across my tongue, copper-bright, like the pennies I used to steal from my mother's purse. Back when I thought the worst thing I could do was disappoint her. My heart hammered so hard that each beat felt like a countdown I couldn't stop. The thought festered, already decided.

I slid the barrel into my mouth, finger hovering over the trigger. Nothing felt real. My breath rasped, eyes clamped shut. Darkness pressed in. This was it. One pull and it's over. No more ghosts. No more noise. Just silence.

And just when I thought I'd pull the damn trigger, it hit—a buzz. Sharp. Electric. Not just a sound, but a reminder that the nightmare wasn't finished with me.

It was Kelly. Her text lit up the screen in the suffocating dark of the motel room:

'*Stay strong,* she'd written. Natalie wouldn't want us like this.' Then the usual about crying her eyes out—blah, blah. I didn't finish it. I tossed the phone onto the bed, where it landed face down, the glow dimming to black. Her words felt like a lie. 'Natalie wouldn't want this?' *What in the hell did she know anyway? She still had her life. Mine ended with Natalie's.*

I wedged the gun under my arm and lit a cigarette with shaky hands, the lighter clicking three times before the flame caught. The first drag burned, smoke clawing at my throat as the neon motel sign outside seeped through the narrow gaps in the curtains, bleeding streaks of pink and blue across the wallpaper, the floor, and my skin.

The bottle sat on the sill, halfway empty. I grabbed it, tipped it back, and let the burn settle in my gut as I paced in front of the window until the walls pressed close. Couldn't keep this up. The cold gun was in my hand—heavier than I remembered.

I carried it into the bathroom and sat on the edge of the toilet, the tiles held damp grit, the kind that clung no matter how long ago the last shower had been. Didn't need the mirror to know what was staring back—bloodshot eyes, sallow skin, a man already half gone. Natalie's face flashed through the dark—her smile, her cries—stuck on a loop I couldn't shut off. She was gone. And I'd failed her.

I swung a leg over the edge of the tub and dropped in, porcelain cold against my back. Pressed the barrel to the side of my head. A scream ripped out of me—raw, feral, straight from somewhere I didn't even know I had left. My finger shook on the trigger, barely kissing it. Then—the faint creak of the motel door. Too late. My finger tightened. Blam!

A white-hot crack split the air, deafening, tearing my world apart. Time slowed. Or maybe it stopped. I felt the recoil, the violent jerk of my body, as if the side of my skull had erupted. I slumped, weightless, the room tilting and turning around me. My head struck the edge of the bathtub's edge with a wet, sickening thud and for one surreal moment, I was still aware. Blood was everywhere, gleaming under the dim bathroom light—a grotesque canvas, straight out of a *Jackson Pollock's* nightmare.

Before the last light left my eyes, a figure filled the doorway—shadowed, blurry. My vision narrowed to a pinprick. His face came into focus. Familiar. Too familiar. Somehow, impossibly, I knew he'd show up.

. . .

The muffled scrape of fabric against the bathroom tile broke the silence —something bundled into a rug, scuffing across the cheap carpet. The motel room door creaked open, hesitated, then slammed shut, the noise carrying down the hallway like a warning. Moments later, the slow, rhythmic drag began: something heavy being pulled down the balcony stairs.

Doors along the walkway cracked open. Faces lingered in the shadows, half-lit by the flicker of the buzzing sign outside. Whispers slipped through the stillness, quick and nervous. But curiosity had limits. One by one, the doors clicked shut.

Outside, the night was heavy, the moon smothered behind clouds. Along the gravel path at the motel's side, a black-on-black four-door Range Rover sat idling in the lot, headlights dim—a pale wash across the pavement, waiting for its passenger. The handler dragged the rug, grit crunching underfoot. Misshapen and monstrous, it sagged in the occupant's grip as the bundle was wrestled into the yawning trunk of the SUV—each shove marked by a strained grunt. A pause, a breath, then the trunk slammed shut, the sound echoing like a coffin lid.

Without looking back, the passenger climbed in. The engine rumbled to life, and the car rolled forward into the darkness, headlights sweeping across the nearly empty lot. Over in the passenger seat, the occupant sat rigid, hand clenched on the armrest inked with the Roman god Janus. The air between them carried an unspoken pact, heavy as smoke.

The road stretched long and empty ahead of them, the hum of tires blending with the distant hiss of wind. Time seemed to blur, the lines on the highway sliding past hypnotically. For a moment, it seemed like they might disappear into the void, unnoticed and unmarked.

As the SUV sped past, a Grayslake Police cruiser lit up behind it, sirens wailing and red-white strobes flaring in the rearview.

The driver's knuckles whitened on the wheel as the Range Rover eased onto the shoulder, crunching over the gravel. The night seemed to hold its breath. A flashlight beam swept across the car as the officer approached, boots stepping closer.

The small-town cop, in uniform and trapper hat, brushed a hand along the trunk before stepping to the driver's side window. The glare cut through the glass, catching the passengers' faces until the window began to slide down.

"How can I help you officer?"

"Hello, ma'am," said the cop, leaning toward the window. "You know why I stopped you today?"

The driver squinted against the glare of the cop's flashlight, forcing a casual tone. "No idea, officer."

"Because you were doing fifty-five in a forty," the officer replied, eyes still scanning the black interior. "Can I ask where you're coming from tonight?"

"Just coming from the Silver Star Motel, right off Lincoln Highway." The woman glanced over at the passenger, interlacing her fingers with his. "I was just picking up the father of my child—and fiancé. We're getting married soon," she added with a smile.

The officer's gaze slid past the wheel, locking on the passenger—a blond-haired man, calm as stone, impossible to read. Then the light shifted to the driver—a woman. A heart inked on her arm, two names carved inside it.

"Congratulations to you. But I'm gonna need to see your license, registration, and proof of insurance, please."

The driver hesitated, then popped the armrest. Her hand trembled as she passed over the credentials.

"Thank you! Alrighty. Hang tight. I'll be back in a moment," he turned without another word, flashlight clicking off as he walked to his cruiser—leaving the passengers alone in the haze of the cruiser's lights.

Inside, silence pressed down. The driver's grip on the wheel tightened until her knuckles went bone-white. The passenger didn't move or speak, but the way the occupant stared straight ahead said a great deal.

From the trunk came a faint sound—soft, irregular. Not loud. Not obvious. But steady, like something dripping where it shouldn't.

The officer returned faster than they expected, his outline passing through the strobing lights. He paused near the trunk, head cocked, flashlight swinging downward. "Got a leak back here, coming from the trunk," he shouted, his tone sharpening as made his way back to the driver's window. "Ma'am want you go ahead and step out of the vehicle for me."

The driver froze. Her eyes flicked to the side mirror, catching the cop's silhouette, then cut toward the passenger. "Sure thing, Officer," she said finally, sliding out of the car and moving toward the trunk with her hands visible—the kind of movements that screamed: Don't shoot. You see where my hands are.

Inside the car, the passenger shifted slightly, his hand sliding under the seat, brushing steel that felt heavier than it should.

"Did you hit something? Got it in the trunk?" the cop asked, his hand easing toward his sidearm as he stepped back. The flashlight slid across the ground where a dark puddle spread—thick and sticky. "Ma'am, go ahead and pop the trunk for me," he said, his hand settling on the holstered grip of his service weapon.

The driver's breath caught. She shot a quick glance over her shoulder at her fiancé, then back at the cop. "I…I can explain—"

"—Pop it. Now," the officer demanded.

Inside the vehicle, the passenger shifted, resting the gun on his lap as a bead of sweat mixed with blood rolled down his neck.

The officer's beam swept lower, catching something dripping from the trunk latch. It was red. Each drip landed heavy in the silence. He drew his gun to his side and fixed the light on the woman at the trunk.

She pressed the button and stepped aside, giving the cop a clear line of sight as the trunk creaked open. Inside lay a heavy rug, rolled tight. A dark liquid pooled beneath it.

In the front seat, the passenger adjusted the rearview mirror toward the officer, then let his hand fall to the door handle while his other stayed fixed on the trigger.

The officer crouched, eyes tracing the soaked fabric in the trunk. He shot the passenger a wary glance, then hooked the corner of the rug with his flashlight, unraveling it inch by inch. Blood—or something like it—slicked under the beam as it traced over the fabric. The officer froze, his eyes darting to the passenger's back through the thin strip between the raised trunk and the rear window. Then his voice broke the silence.

"Paint?" the cop uttered with relief as he spotted the crimson streaks and the paint cans beneath them, glancing over the rest of the trunk's contents.

The passenger's grip eased on the gun, and he neatly placed it back under the seat before readjusting the mirror.

"I told you I could explain," the driver leaned against the car, a smirk curling at her lips, and nodded at the officer's stained hand. "I'm an artist. I did acting in college."

"Alright, I'll close it up. Go back to your car. I'll be with you in a moment."

"Great!" she said, giving the officer a quick nod before climbing back into the car. She glanced at the passenger, and they shared a quick grin.

The fiancé's hand drifted to her stomach, his fingers pressing just enough to linger. "Well, look at you, babe… the mother of my child— smooth and sexy." His voice was low, a purr sliding through the tension.

"Oh, you like that, do you?" her reply was laced with sweetness, but the undertone sliced through.

The officer strolled back to the car, ID in hand. "Here's your ID, Natalie."

"That's not my name," she interrupted, her voice quick but firm. "I'm Kelly."

The officer frowned, a flicker of doubt sharpening his gaze. "Huh. Says here the car's registered to a Natalie Moretti."

"That's my deceased sister."

The cop's mouth sagged into a line that wasn't quite a scowl. "Alright, looks like I got things mixed up. Your ID says Kelly, but the car comes back to your sister. In her DMV photo she looks a lot like you—just a shade darker. You two twins?"

"Not twins," Kelly replied, her words clipped and heavy. "She was older by a couple of years."

The officer studied her, his expression tightening as if something didn't quite add up. After a beat, he shrugged it off and handed her ID back. "Alright. I'm not gonna hold you up any longer. I'll let you off with a warning. Slow it down out there, we clear?"

"Crystal."

He leaned in closer, his gaze cutting to the passenger. "And what about you? Got a name, pal?"

The passenger's answer was lightning-fast, too sharp to be casual. "My name's Rick."

"Alright, Rick—" the officer flashed a smile. "You folks take care now. And make sure that she slows down. And congratulations."

"Will do, thanks" Rick answered, staring at the love of his life. His Kelly.

The cop got back into his cruiser without waiting for them to pull off. He whipped a U-turn, cutting across lanes and the median, headed the opposite way—like Dunkin' Donuts had just announced an all-you-can-eat buffet.

In her rearview mirror, his headlights shrank, then disappeared into the dark. Kelly's car rolled back onto the road, swallowed by the cornfields that closed in on either side. Inside, shadows stretched long and deep, clinging to the passengers.

"So…" Kelly said, her voice edged with steel. "Finally, Rick. I thought I would never see you again. Where's Lorenzo?"

He turned to her, his face a mask of unreadability. "Lorenzo?" Silence pressed in, thick between them. The tires whispered on the asphalt, and the corn outside murmured to the wind—words too faint to catch.

Kelly's fingers tightened on the wheel as the moonlight spilled through the glass. Something cold and unspoken crept into the space between them—a question too dangerous to ask, an answer she wasn't ready to hear. And the road stretched on, black and unending, as if it, too, had a secret to keep.

A dry, mocking laugh escaped him. "Oh… Lorenzo. You mean that loser? He's in the trunk now—stone dead, colder by the mile. I finally killed him this time. For good."

Kelly's lips curved, the smile breaking loose before she could stop it. She reached across, lacing her fingers with his. "I love you, Mr. Moretti—"

…THE END!!!

Stop here if you enjoy the mystery. The story is complete. Everything beyond this page is a confession—read at your own risk!

Book's done. The curtain dropped. But here you are, poking your big nose around where you don't belong. Curiosity, right? That little itch that killed the cat. Guess you couldn't help yourself—had to dig through the dirt like some half-drunk detective with nothing better to do. Fine. Be my guest. You want answers? I'll walk you through the wreckage, hand in hand. Just don't cry when the glass cuts deep. Buckle up—the road ahead isn't paved. Life's tough, put your helmet on.

THE REVEAL

Who said a bad story couldn't have a happy ending? In novels, the author weaves an illusion—impossible odds, a protagonist beaten and battered, only to rise and defy them. Society eats that shit up. But what if—what if I wasn't the protagonist of my own story? What if I were the villain?

Ask yourself: Did I follow the author's design and win? Did I beat the odds? Let's see—I'm the one who killed her. Yeah, I killed my wife. And I can't help but laugh at that, because let's face it—I'm a sick, twisted son of a bitch. Kelly, the mother of my child, planned it all with me. And Natalie? She's dead as a doorknob—missing a hand and a couple of fingers, respectively. But Kelly and I? We're sitting pretty with our $4 million. Time to invest in crypto.

<u>The Setup</u>

Let me paint the picture for you. Natalie loved attention—craved it like a drug. She was always the star of her own little show, a brat who thought the world was her stage. She loved her role-playing games, thought they kept things "exciting." And when she pretended to be kidnapped by the big bad wolf, she had no clue she was starring in my production—a tragedy with a killer finale.

Kelly, my partner-in-crime, and I were the masterminds. She's the kind of woman who could poison a drink while looking you dead in the eye, a smile playing on her lips like a dare. That night at the club, she slipped Natalie the pills—made sure she was so far gone she couldn't tell up from down.

Lorenzo—my weaker half—was the wild card. Poor, pathetic Lorenzo. He tried to warn Natalie, even begged her to listen. But she didn't. Natalie never listened. She thought she was untouchable. Dumb bitch. She never left the club. Down she went, to the hidden room, hogtied to the chair by her own sister.

<u>Collateral Damage</u>

Now, Tony. That fuckboy was just collateral damage. He wasn't supposed to die—just get burned, booked, and take the fall with Frank. Boo-fucking-hoo. He's dead. Do we really care who's innocent? Let's be honest: one in twenty U.S. prisoners is innocent. Look it up. Not that I give a damn. Tony was an asshole, and the world's better off without him.

The real misdirection? Kelly hugging Tony, sobbing like the perfect grieving sister, while slipping Natalie's finger into his jacket pocket. Pure fucking brilliance. We even sent Frank those photos—Kelly's idea, of course. Lured him right into our trap. And when it was time to wrap things up, I did what I do best.

But here's where it got tricky.

<u>The Kink in the Plan</u>

When the cops stormed my hotel room, they told me they'd found a hand. A 911 call had tipped them off. I stayed cool. Kelly, though—

she deserved an Oscar. Her performance was flawless: tears streaming, her voice cracking, clutching Tony as if her heart were breaking. (Side note: those acting classes in college? Worth every penny.)

But even masterpieces have their flaws. Remember the finger Kelly planted in Tony's left jacket pocket? The problem? Tony did everything with his right hand. Everything. Except wash it. Nasty fuck. I'll never forget him patting my shoulder in the bathroom, the smell of unwashed testicles smearing onto my sleeve like an oil slick.

Still, the cops bought it. They always do.

<u>The Puppetmaster</u>

Now, about Lorenzo—my weak, pathetic other personality. Ironic, since he didn't even have one. He thought he was in control. Can you believe that? This fool passed a lie detector test because he didn't even know I existed—even though we shared the same body. I was the one pulling the strings, texting Kelly, tying every loose end. That "room service" alibi? Genius. Me hiding under the cart while Kelly wheeled me out? A flawless move for the hotel cameras.

And Frank? Long gone. Rotting in the dirt, brain smorgasbord for maggots. Esperanza? Sure, she was hot, but Lorenzo was too much of a coward to make a move. I can't believe we both existed in his psyche. Me? I'd have clapped those cheeks without a second thought. But the show had to go on.

<u>The Finale</u>

Lorenzo thought he had it figured out. He believed the lie. That's what made it so easy to push him over the edge. The empty gun trick? Chef's kiss. He thought he was pulling the trigger on me, but he took himself out instead. A clean exit. Innocent? Maybe. Dead? Definitely.

And now? Natalie's cold, six feet under, and missing a hand. Frank's rotting. Tony's framed and gone. Lorenzo's dead and forgotten. And Kelly and I? We're sitting pretty on 4 million bucks.

So yeah, call me a villain. Call me twisted. Call me whatever the fuck you want.

Game over, bitches.

ACKNOWLEDGMENTS

Thanks to the poor souls who read draft after draft—you know who you are. Thanks for not stabbing me with a red pen. To Nick and John, for telling me when the jokes landed and when I was just being an a-hole. And to anyone who said I'd never finish a book—guess what? You were almost right. Almost…

—Hiroshi, creator of Hack: The Forbidden Journey novel (Infinite Shadows Universe — comic & manga coming soon)

To the ones who kept me alive on the page—you've got no idea how many times I almost didn't make it. To those who pushed me, tested me, and made me bleed, congratulations—you built me. And to the readers who followed me this far… thanks. You kept me from disappearing into the noise.

—Ivy Glass

SNEAK PEEK

From Hiroshi Yamamoto

Hack: The Forbidden Journey *(Infinite Shadows Universe Novel and Comic)*

MUGEN ⊕ KAI-INFINITE ∞ SHADOWS
HACK: THE FORBDIDDEN
JOURNEY
BOOK SERIES 1- STORY CYCLE
A Hybrid Soi-Fi Superhero Thriller Merging Dark Urban Fantasy, Action-Adventure, and High-Stakes Suspense
HIROSHI YAMAMOTO

<h1 style="text-align:center">Chapter ONE</h1>

NOW: CITY OF BROKEN CODES

That was me—Jin, your friendlier-than-most neighborhood hacker! Hoodie up, head low, standing in front of yet another ATM at 10 p.m., ready to rob it. Downtown New York City, heart of the chaos! Thanks to my little invention—nifty goggles with orange lenses—the camera only saw its reflection. Simple tech, but enough to keep my face off the grid.

The street was quiet, save for the occasional hum of a passing car circling the block, and the faint glow of city lights barely touched the shadows I stuck to.

Three months. That's how long it had been since my parents—and almost everyone else on that train—were slaughtered. The cops got nowhere. They never even found my dad's body. Just his blood. My blood.

The cops thought I was delusional. My friends—what was left of them—said I hit my head too hard during the crash. That's one way to erase a slaughter.

No one believed me when I told them what I saw that night. Incident? That wasn't an accident. That was a massacre, plain and simple. But the strangest part? They found me above ground, nowhere near the wreckage. Barely conscious with blood running down my face like some sick joke.

Not one of the ten survivors backed me up. No one saw what I saw. Or maybe they didn't want to admit it. Either way, I was the crazy one now. And if I wasn't careful, that was how I would stay.

Keeping a low profile was a necessity, and being careless wasn't an option. My dummy card hummed inside the ATM, bypassing its weak security while I scanned the area—just quick enough to be cautious, not suspicious.

Hey, I was a thief with a moral code: I only took what I needed and promised to pay it back once I landed a real job. Because that sucky minimum-wage gig at Nerd Squad, fixing electronics with my two best friends, Hunter and Matthew, wasn't cutting it. Bills piled up fast, especially since my dad's life insurance hadn't paid a cent. They called it "abandonment." As if my father—a man who worked himself to the bone for his family—would just disappear. And without that payout, I was stuck footing the cost alone.

Owning my parents' house wasn't easy, especially not for a seventeen-year-old Chinese American kid just trying to survive. One bill after the next, and I was already drowning in it. It's funny how the things we think we own end up owning us in the end. But hey… this was America. *Home of the brave and land of the—*

(The machine whirred to life, gears clicking, bills shuffling.)

"Cash!" I muttered. "Land of the free and easy money." I grinned, snatching up the $2,500, shoving it into my pocket like it was about to self-destruct. But just as fast as the thrill hit me, it evaporated.

Then I saw it… That black SUV. Circling the block again! I couldn't see the driver behind the dark-tinted windows. It stopped at the corner, headlights cutting through the mist.

What were the odds?

Once could've been by chance.

Twice was a coincidence. And I don't believe in coincidences.

But three times? That was an intergalactic mind fuck, and by then, I knew that car wasn't just passing by—it was watching me.

I hunched low and ducked off into the first gangway I saw. Not by chance. The moment I turned the corner—tires screeched—burning rubber. My footsteps smacked against the wet pavement, my heartbeat hammering in sync. I glanced back—the SUV barreled toward me. Full throttle. Headlights cut through the darkness like twin blades.

Up ahead—the intersection. I had two choices: Option A: houses with backyards, or Option B: buildings with locked doors. I chose Option A.

A garbage can stood in my way. I launched off it just as the SUV lunged—an enraged bull on steroids with bad intentions. My hands caught the top of a wooden gate. I pulled myself up and perched on the edge just as the SUV roared beneath me, only inches away. But my tongue had a mind of its own. Stuck out and followed by two middle fingers.

Then I flipped. Momentum carried me backward behind the gate. My feet hit the ground, then bolted through darkened backyards, keeping low, staying quiet—no need to wake the good, hard-working citizens of New York.

Car doors slammed—heavy footsteps.

Voices. I couldn't make out what they were saying. Maybe it was because of my heart pounding in my ears. Perhaps it didn't matter. They were coming for me.

I slipped across the yard and darted across the street between two parked cars, melting into the shadows.

Stay low. Stay invisible. But the shadows—they felt wrong. They stretched toward me, shifting like they knew my darkest fears. Like they remembered me. And maybe they did?

A chill crawled up my spine. My pulse hammered—that night. My parents were murdered.

And him! The man who walked through shadows like they were doors. That grotesque smile. Those jagged teeth.

Unnatural. Like it had been waiting for me.

www.ingramcontent.com/pod-product-compliance
Lightning Source LLC
Chambersburg PA
CBHW072129300726
48975CB00003B/988